Martin's War

Thomas M. Jardine

Published by Rogue Phoenix Press, LLP
Copyright © 2025

ISBN: 978-1-62420-854-6

Editor: C. L. Kraemer
Cover: Designs by Ms G

Dedication

I would like to dedicate this book in memory of both my father, Leslie M Jardine, deceased and my Godfather, Thomas H Montgomery, Q.C. also deceased.

PROLOGUE

September 30, 1944
Tivoli, Italy
Twenty miles east of Rome

IT WAS a moonless night in west-central Italy. In addition, a light cloud cover provided Martin with all the darkness he required as he followed Jacobs in a jeep he had borrowed from a fellow Canuck in the Princess Pats Regiment. Due to the nature of his off-duty venture this evening, he had also made sure to bring his service hand gun, a Walther P38. He had turned his headlights out as a precaution, and the open Tuscany landscape allowed him to maintain a safe distance of approximately a quarter of a mile from his quarry.

Martin parked the jeep on the far side of the villa after Jacobs had gone into the house and now he crept silently along the outer wall of the building under cover of the veranda roof. He moved stealthily, situating himself beneath a window which he determined to provide him a direct view into the sitting room. He was hoping to see his captain and close friend Reginald Jacobs with the Senorita in familiar surroundings.

Martin was therefore not disappointed when he edged upwards and saw them sitting together on the sofa, sharing a carafe of wine. It was oddly out of setting, however, when he noted Jacobs had spread a document on the coffee table. It appeared to be a map of some area and Martin was highly intrigued.

Suddenly, the same German individual he had seen here yesterday appeared from the kitchen carrying his own glass of wine, smiling warmly at Jacobs as he offered him a pleasant greeting. The window under which Martin was hiding was closed, and he could not hear what was being said.

This was all too strange. The German officer, friendly with Jacobs? All he could do at this point was sit and wait. There was also a hedge under the window which provided some additional cover, so he hunkered down and waited.

He remained hidden under the parlor window for what seemed an eternity. Every now and then from inside the house he could hear muted laughter and he was tempted to simply barge into the room and demand an explanation. Yet he waited.

As he crouched below the windowsill, he sensed movement beneath him. Looking down, he saw a huge, tan-colored spider had crawled beside his left boot and had slowly begun to move up his leg. If there was one thing Martin feared and despised, it was spiders. This particular species was a large Brown Recluse known in Italy as the 'violini' because of its distinct markings on its dorsal area, similar to a violin. More significant, it was venomous.

Martin could no longer stand to watch the arachnid approach his middle torso area. He jumped quickly in an effort to brush it off his groin, and unfortunately, his foot hit a rake that had been leaning against the outer wall of the building. It clattered against a metal bucket as it fell, loud enough to attract the attention of the German officer who immediately came outside to investigate. When the German approached, he was surprised to see a young infantryman with the iconic Canadian Maple Leaf insignia on his uniform, pointing a pistol at him.

Martin silently gestured toward the doorway of the parlor and motioned the German inside. As he entered the room behind the German, Jacobs stood in shock to see Martin holding the officer at gunpoint.

"Martin, what the hell are you doing?" he shouted. "This is Lieutenant Kelerring. We are
Friends, for God's sake."

"I can see that," said Martin sarcastically. "Sir, how could you?" he pleaded to his friend, almost sobbing.

"Now wait, Martin. You just don't understand," said Jacobs as he edged closer to the sofa which separated them. Unknown to Martin, Jacobs had removed his own sidearm when he had arrived, and it was now lying on the sofa within easy reach. Right at that moment the Senorita called from the kitchen, "Who wants more wine?"

Martin was distracted by the sound of Madellena's voice, and

Jacobs, taking note of this, grabbed his own weapon off the sofa in a quick motion and held it a foot from Martin's face. He now had the upper hand over his aide. One hand at a time, he carefully pulled his leather gloves from his inside jacket pocket and put them on, smiling menacingly at Martin.

"Okay Martin, place your gun down and I'll explain everything," said Jacobs. When Martin hesitated, Kelerring immediately drew his own Luger. This prompted Jacobs to walk over to Martin who was too stunned by what was happening to react, and he viciously hit his friend with the butt of his pistol on the side of Martin's head. Martin fell to the floor, toppling over behind the sofa, barely conscious. Jacobs retrieved Martin's pistol and placed it inside the webbing of his own belt.

The German suddenly shouted at Jacobs. "What is happening, Jacobs? Were you planning to double-cross me? Shoot this man immediately," he yelled.

Jacobs trained his gun against Martin who stared at the small bore of his friend's Beretta semi-automatic. He was barely conscious.

"I'm sorry it had to end this way, Martin." Martin England's world collapsed. He closed his eyes as he realized his friend and confidant was a traitor who was about to kill him.

The sound of the shot was deafening in the small sitting room.

PART 1

WAR'S AFTERMATH

Chapter One

April 20,1945
Halifax, Canada

RMS *Scythia* entered Halifax Harbor just after 4:00 pm on Friday, April 20, 1945. She was carrying some four thousand Canadian troops from the 1st Canadian Army who had finished their service to God, King, and Country following the Liberation of Holland. The Netherlands campaign had begun in the Fall of 1944. It was a hard-fought battle that took the lives of seven thousand, six hundred Canadian soldiers.

For many of the troops on board the *Scythia,* the 'real' war had started with the invasion of Sicily in the summer of 1943. After the Italian Campaign, these participants had returned to France from where they had literally marched across Europe into Holland. It was a grueling endeavor. Now looking back, it was hard for them to realize what they had accomplished. When they had first landed in England in January 1940, after sailing from Halifax, Nova Scotia, they had languished on various training bases for three and a half years. At that time, these same men actually looked forward to seeing action.

They were not disappointed.

Now to a man they were overjoyed to be returning to Canada. In particular for four of these young soldiers, it would only be a mere six or seven hours by train to their hometown of Chatham, New Brunswick. Martin England had enlisted from the local Army reserves at the same time as his two brothers, James and Gerald. James was now standing beside Martin as they anxiously awaited their arrival. According to the last word they had received, Gerald was supposedly returning on the twin troop carrier, the *RMS Samaria*. It should have left port in Liverpool last month. It was going to be quite a reunion for the three brothers when they were finally all together in Chatham. The return of The Three Amigos, as they had become known to their fellow infantrymen. They were beating most family war survivals.

In addition to his brother, two of Martin's close friends were on board beside him as the huge ship bore down on the awaiting throngs that occupied the docks. Fred Trainor and John Norman, two regular 'grunts', waved to the crowd below them. There was also a third figure with them, their captain, Reginald Jacobs. This man stood with his own thoughts, seemingly unaware of the celebration surrounding him.

From Halifax, the group of five would be traveling by rail to Martin's small New Brunswick hometown of Chatham. Jacobs would be continuing his journey alone to Montreal, where he would rejoin his law firm. Martin made a mental note to make sure he had Reggie's address. He was going to sorely miss the daily contact with his captain. For the umpteenth time he wondered who would be welcoming Jacobs home …

His thoughts were interrupted by the roars of the huge crowds hailing them from the docks below as the *Scythia* tied up at Pier 21 in the busy Nova Scotia seaport. Martin's heart swelled at the thought of seeing his wife, Margaret. He and 'Meg' had married in '39 while he was in basic training in Petawawa, Ontario. Lord, he missed her. He often wondered if he ever would have survived the past six years without knowing he had her love to welcome him home. The letters she constantly wrote to him during those awful years had kept him sane amidst the hell and chaos he had experienced across Europe. Fond memories of her flooded back to his mind as he awaited the transport truck that would take them to the train station.

~ * ~

The wedding in Petawawa was a small, private affair. His close friend Bill Hachey and Bill's wife Norma had acted as their witnesses. It felt like it was ages ago, and he couldn't wait to once again hold Meg in his arms.

Martin was also excited about the prospects of employment in his hometown. He was secretly hoping to get into the home interior decorating business, and he knew there were courses being offered in this field of work

6

in Saint John. He read somewhere there was expected to be a demand for this service because of the huge new-home construction boom presently hitting the country. Mortgages were even being granted to returning vets. Who would have thought? The country was exhibiting an optimistic outlook.

~ * ~

When the men had settled in their assigned sections on the train, the first thing they did was order a round of drinks: rum and cokes. Martin, who had just turned twenty-nine last month, was the youngest male sibling in his family. His brother Gerald, the eldest, was now thirty-three and James was thirty-one. As a result of their experience in the war, The Three Amigos had developed a strong familiarity with the beverage. This would not go well with their father George England, a strong Presbyterian abstainer.

Martin had two sisters. Marion, the oldest in the family, was married to Percy Bent, a mechanic, and they lived across the river in Douglastown. Next to Marion was Rebecca, his favorite sib, who was dating John Bradford, the brother of his wife, Meg. They were a closely knit bunch.

By the time the train reached Moncton, which was about an hour and a half from his home, the five of them were feeling no pain. Except, that is, for Captain Reg Jacobs who invariably managed to maintain a more sober presence. Martin and his friends had come to almost expect this form of leadership from their friend. Martin often thought they relied far too much on Jacobs.

For the moment, however, this was not on his mind as he and the captain finished their sixth and last cribbage match. He looked at Jacobs and admired the man's countenance: a symmetrical face with a strong, dimpled square chin, not unlike that of the actor Robert Taylor. A pair of wide-spaced twinkling, dark brown eyes; an even row of white, smiling teeth; and a mass of dark-brown, curly hair. He was a bachelor, though Martin doubted that would last much longer. Jacobs was a lawyer in a large, successful Montreal firm. He had joined the service as a commissioned officer and Martin sensed he was destined for big things. The man was a born leader.

As the train entered the outskirts of their hometown, James came

7

over to the card table. "Well Martin, you should finish your drink or better yet, just leave it and freshen up. We'll be at the station in no time and our wives and families will all be there."

"So what?" Martin groused, and immediately Reg overheard the somewhat belligerent tone his friend's voice had assumed toward his brother.

"So, nothing," James said, not wanting to get into an argument with Martin who began to strut around the confines of the railway car, gesturing towards Gerald in an exaggerated way.

"Here's my big brother, everyone. He's gonna make sure I conduct myself in a proper manner." He was getting nasty.

"Hey Martin, take it easy," said Reg. "We all want to be friendly here when we get off the train, right?" He took Martin by the arm, pulled him close, then looked directly into his eyes, smiled and repeated himself. "Right?"

A sudden change came over Martin and he pulled himself away from Jacobs. He then hooked his arm around his brother's shoulders. "You're right, Reg. Hell, we're The Three Amigos, right Jimmy?" he said, tussling his brother's hair. Then he left for the WC to clean up. James gave a look to Jacobs while he straightened his hair, and the two shook their heads. This was old stuff. The other two guys were sleeping in their booths and Jacobs woke them.

"Rise and shine, you beggars," he shouted. "You're home." Trainor and Norman slowly awoke and drunkenly made their way to the WC as well.

"Just as well those boys have no friends or family to greet them," said James, watching the two men reel down the narrow aisle of the train, trying to remain upright with the swaying coach which was now slowing as it made its way to the station. "The state they're in, it wouldn't be too pretty. I'll get a cab for them when we disembark, Captain. By the way, do you plan to ever come back this way from Montreal?"

"I sure do, James. I hear there are some great fly-fishing pools on the Little Sou'West that I'd like to try my hand at." The Miramichi River and its tributaries flowed through the communities where Chatham was located. It was renowned for the bright Atlantic salmon that came to its many pools, migrating from as far away as Scotland and Sweden to spawn here, attracting avid sports fishermen from all over the world.

"Well sir, let's try to keep in touch," said James, and as they shook hands to depart, Martin and Gerald came up to them, Martin looking much better than he did earlier. He embraced his captain in a warm hug.

"Well, *Mon Capitaine*, I guess this is it. When are we going to see you again?"

"Maybe next summer Martin. I was just saying to James that I'd like to do some fly-fishing for some of your famous salmon."

"I would really appreciate that, sir. My wife Margaret will certainly want to meet the man who was responsible for saving my life."

For a brief second, Jacobs seemed bothered by what Martin had said, however, he quickly recovered. "You know that was reciprocal. But I do want to meet the woman who captured your heart. I've certainly heard enough about her over the past six years."

"So, it's a deal. We'll see you next summer, then. And be sure to write, eh?" With a final handshake, Martin and his two brothers James, followed by their two staggering friends, stepped off the train and headed for the station platform where a large group of people awaited them.

Martin turned around as the train slowly passed behind them, just in time to catch sight of Jacobs watching them from a window. The two soldiers made eye contact and Jacobs gave Martin a formal salute as it moved west on its way to Montreal.

Martin's eyes suddenly welled with emotion, not just as he spotted Margaret standing on the platform with her own eyes filling with tears, but also as many visions suddenly passed through his mind: young boys crying in an observation tower, a raped woman lying in a back alley outside of Rome, hundreds of corpses along the back roads of Belgium. There had been so much death and misery. These same visions had been coming to him frequently as nightmares for the past six months.

Shape up! he commanded himself. It was 1945, the war was over, and he was safe at home as were his two brothers. He had a wife he hadn't held in six years, and it was time to be grateful, happy, and prosperous.

~ * ~

Meg England watched her husband running to her as she stood at the station. It had been six long years since she had last seen him. She didn't know what to expect regarding his appearance. From the letters he had written over the years, there had been no pictures. He had told her he suffered a couple of minor wounds: one to his left middle finger and another to his left inner bicep, both the result of bullet strikes while in action. These were not of consequence he had written, and at least there was nothing to indicate such as he made his way to her grinning broadly.

Her fear, however, lay in what could not be physically seen. Their romance and subsequent marriage was typically short for those uncertain times. Like so many other young people in love back then, they felt that they simply did not have the luxury of time on their side to wait for the traditional engagement period to lapse. The world was at war in 1939 and who knew what was about to happen, where or when?

So, while their time together before Martin had to depart for overseas was brief, it was precious. She knew Martin to his core. All his foibles and fears. His dislikes and fancies were opened to her as were his aspirations, beliefs, and values. In some of his recent letters, she thought she could detect a subtle change in his personality. Whereas his letters for the first four years had centered on his longing for her presence, during the last two years, and with increasing frequency, they had revealed a great deal of despondence. She felt from his recent letters that he almost harbored a resignation to the fact that he might not return. She had tried so hard to encourage him with light-hearted notes about their families, local events at home and such. But she wondered at times if her words were having any impact.

Well, he was home now, she thought, *so dammit, Meg, make the best of it!*

And now Martin was holding her in a strong embrace that had fueled his imagination over time and space for far too long. At last, Martin was home!

Chapter Two

The England home had been built just after the turn of the century. Martin had been born in this house, and he had many childhood memories of the property and the immediate surrounding area. The huge tree from which he had fallen and broken a leg when he was only six was still there, off the front veranda, as was the back shed that contained a rope-swing his father had hung from the rafters for him and his two brothers.

They had arrived home in the taxi after dropping off James at his place several blocks away. As they unloaded his baggage, Martin's father greeted him and explained that his mother had not been at the station to meet her sons since she was feeling poorly. His father further warned him that he may find her frail looking and that she might not seem to be her old self.

When they entered the large house, Mr. England first brought the two upstairs to see Martin's ailing mother and Martin recalled his father's earlier words concerning his mother's appearance. Even then, he was certainly not prepared for what he now witnessed. His mother lay in her bed, and she was *so small*. She was dwarfed by it. Her hair was totally white, and her eyes had lost their twinkle over the years. Hearing them come into the bedroom, she awoke and had managed to rise to a sitting position.

"Oh dear, Martin. Is that you? And Margaret?"

"Mom, yes. It's late, but I just wanted to see you before we retired for the night. We'll talk at length in the morning, so why don't you go back to sleep, and get your rest. We love you," he said, and he brushed his hand lightly over her cheek.

His mother did not need any further coaxing but simply lay back and closed her eyes. Martin cast a glance at his father who was holding back his tears at seeing his wife in this state. He motioned for Martin and Meg to follow him to one of the back rooms where they would be sleeping.

"The doctor is worried about her condition, Martin. She ran a fever two nights ago and her mind seemed to wander off in a different world. She was unaware of who I was or even *where* she was. In addition, she is afflicted at times with chest pains and severe headaches. I didn't want to say anything to you or your brothers until you were home, Martin. But there, you have it. He said it could be the onset of tuberculosis. He is awaiting the results of tests made yesterday. If that turns out to be the case, she will no doubt have to be moved to the Sanatorium." At this, he turned and silently stifled his weeping, his shoulders trembling. Martin walked over to his father and wrapped his arms around him.

"Dad, I'm so sorry. What can we do to make her comfortable?" A diagnosis of TB could almost be a death knell. Not many of the elderly survived.

"We'll talk about it in the morning, son. You two need your rest as well. So welcome home, son. Goodnight, and God bless us." The elderly man left them alone in their room.

As they lay in bed, Martin was silent, and Meg asked him what he was thinking about.

"Nothing," he said. "Everything, Meg! Life seems so unfair... what can we do? Did you see her? She looks so weak and frail ..."

"I'm sure things will work out Martin. In any case, there's nothing we can do about it tonight. It will have to wait until tomorrow and then we'll see, okay? Right now, I just want you to hold me. No more talk." She reached for him in the darkness and he softly moaned as their bodies meshed.

~ * ~

They awoke to the aroma of fresh coffee and frying bacon as it climbed the back stairs that led down to the kitchen. After they had washed and were downstairs, Mr. England sat them at the old wooden table in the kitchen and delighted himself in waiting upon them.

"Consider this your honeymoon home," he exclaimed. "You two didn't have much time by yourselves before the war separated you, so it's time to correct that. Eat up, Martin, we're going to put some meat on those bones of yours."

Martin dug into his breakfast, now and then stealing a sly smile at Meg as she did the same. "So, Dad, what's happening with your house-painting work? Are you busy?"

"Ah, I'm getting too old Martin. It's time to hang up the brushes and rollers, I guess. What about you, any plans?"

"Well, I've read there are courses that the government is sponsoring at a trade school in Saint John. There are a couple of these I might be interested in taking. Interior Home Decorating and maybe a sheet metal course. What do you think?"

"There will definitely be a demand for new housing in the country with the return of all you young men from overseas," he said. "And I would think any of the related trades should prove worthy of attention. Until you decide, you can always continue with my business that I've established over the years, both residential and commercial. You'll not get rich, Martin, but it's honest work."

"We'll see, Dad, Say, will there be people coming to visit today?"

"James and Audrey will be here, and I believe your sister Rebecca, and her fiancé, John plan on coming. Oh, and Gerald may be landing from Halifax but that has yet to be confirmed. His boat arrived in the wee hours this morning." Then George seemed to come up with an idea. He smacked his hands down on the worn old table.

"In fact, why don't we plan on a big dinner for this evening and have as many of the family here as we can round up? Meg, your mother will come, yes? And how about your sisters?"

Meg wasn't sure about her sisters. They were younger and they all had boyfriends. She'd have to call them to see what they were up to. "I'll check with them Mr. England, but probably they can make it. It will be fun." In the back of her mind, she was concerned about having so many people around the house, and whether or not Mrs. England would be in favor of the gathering. Just then who should appear in the kitchen, dressed in her finest and looking fit as a fiddle, but Martha England herself.

"Why Martha!" exclaimed George "You're up, dear, and looking very nice today if I may say," George added, a twinkle in his eye.

"You may George, since it is not yet Sunday, otherwise you know

I won't abide your lies on the Sabbath." Martha was not about to appear frail in front of her youngest boy and his wife, so she had taken pains to fix herself up. *They need not know about the seriousness of her illness at this point*, she told herself.

"Mom, I'm glad to see you up and around. Dad said last night you were, er, not feeling well?" Martin caught himself from saying something awkward at the last second.

"Yes, of course I'm fine dear, just a touch of the spring cold, I'm afraid. And how are you this morning, Margaret?" she said with a small smile, but to Meg it was not quite as sincere as it could have been.

"I'm feeling wonderful today, Mrs. England," replied Meg with a huge smile on her face as well, as she beamed at her husband.

"Yes, I see," said Martha. "Well, shall we have breakfast?"

The family of four sat at the kitchen table and finished their simple meal of hot coffee, bacon, eggs and toast. It was the best breakfast Martin had in quite some time, and he admonished himself to watch his intake of food, at least until he had some means of contributing to the household expenses. His thoughts were interrupted by his mother.

"Martin, you know I am anxious to hear all about your adventures overseas. But perhaps in the interests of efficiency, it might be prudent to save these tales of derring-do until the others are all here. I believe I overheard talk of a dinner party this evening."

Well! Meg thought, *Mrs. England seems to be in fine enough fettle today!* Then she immediately scolded herself for harboring such thoughts. It was going on ten o'clock, so she decided to get in touch with her family and start making arrangements for tonight. But first she decided to call her mother.

Matilda (Mattie) Bradford was a widow, sixty-five years old, though she did not look a day over fifty. Her husband had been killed in an industrial accident at the local sawmill over twenty years ago and she had never remarried.

Today Mattie was busy hanging out wash. The girls, as usual, were sleeping late since it was the weekend. When Meg had called, her mother was happy to hear her oldest daughter, the sensible one. They chatted for a while and Meg then invited her and the girls over to the England's for a dinner party this evening.

"If they come, they'll want to bring their flyboy friends," warned Mattie.

"The more, the merrier as they say. Is John there?"

"John is with Becky and they're down at the farm helping Doug with a new foal that's due." Doug was a brother of Mattie's that lived a short distance outside of town on a farm that grew mixed vegetables. He also had several dairy cows, some chickens, and a couple of horses he used to help him haul lumber from a nearby woodlot he maintained. Doug had been a savior to the family over the tough Depression years, providing them with fresh produce they so dearly needed and appreciated.

"Tell them about the party, Mom. Bring what you can, there will be lots of people, and Martin says 'Hi.'" She hung up and went to see Mrs. England to find out what tasks she could perform to get ready for the dinner. It was going to be a grand time.

At around four, Martin heard a car in their driveway, and he watched through the kitchen window as several people climbed out of a 1942 Plymouth coupe and approached the back door to the house. There were four of them. The two girls he immediately recognized as Rita and Rosalind Bradford, Meg's younger sisters. He didn't know the two guys with them, but they appeared very friendly with the girls, hand in hand as they were.

"Hey, the soldier boy is home," cried Rosalind, seeing Martin as he stepped out onto the back porch to greet them. "Well, aren't you a sight for sore eyes."

"Hi Rosie. You're looking pretty good yourself. Who's the little girl with you?" Martin loved to tease Rita, the youngest of the girls.

"Martin England, don't you dare start," yelled Rita. "I'm seventeen now, you know."

"Well, c'mere then, and give me a kiss. Both of you..." The girls jumped into Martin's open arms, and they hugged him fiercely while the two boys who had escorted them looked on, a bit askance. "And who might these two fellas be?" he asked.

Rosie said, "Martin England, meet my boyfriend Dave Jensen, and this is Bob Kenny, Rita's friend. They are both stationed here at the base, newly enrolled in the Royal Canadian Air Force."

"Well, we can't all be perfect," he said to the guys, just to see if he could get a rise out of them. Both of the young men took it well and, for the moment at least they stood in deference to the 'veteran'. Martin thought he could get to like these guys.

"Are you folks here for the dinner party?" Martin asked.

"We were invited by Meg," replied Rita.

Martin looked at the two young men. "Just so you know boys, this is a dry household." Then he leaned closer and whispered to Jensen. "I don't suppose either one of you would have access to a little nip or two of something?" He gave him a smile and a wink to accompany his request.

Jensen was quick on the up take. "Say, let's go for a short drive Marty, and we'll get to know each other a bit," replied Dave. "Rosie, maybe you can help Meg while we show off the coupe to Martin," he said to her, also with a wink.

With that the four young men took off in the Plymouth and the two girls ran into the house to find their older sister. When they told Meg that Martin and the two boys had gone off for a short drive, Meg just looked at Rosie suspiciously and let it go. She was afraid something like this might happen.

God Martin, she thought, *I hope you don't do anything foolish!*

Chapter Three

THE ROYAL Canadian Legion Branch # 3 in Chatham was in full swing when Martin and his new friends entered the premises Saturday afternoon around four-thirty. Only men were at tables which practically filled the downstairs main room, playing various card games. There were also several groups throwing darts, a sport which had been brought over to Canada from the pubs in wartime England. Of course, everybody was drinking. After all, it was a Saturday afternoon on the Miramichi River.

As Martin surveyed the room, he spotted his two war mates Fred Trainor and John Norman, sitting in a corner by themselves, so he guided Jensen and Kenny over to that table. Catching the waiter as he went by, he ordered a round of beer pointing to the table where they were headed and when they got there they settled down for a chat. Introductions were made and their drinks were delivered.

By the time they had each consumed four or five glasses of draft ale, it was close to six. Martin realized with concern they had better be getting home for the dinner party. His new friends agreed, but as they rose to leave, John Norman drunkenly got up with them and insisted they stay for one more. Martin shrugged and spoke to Dave Jensen. "This will definitely be the last drink, Davey old pal. I don't want to get you in trouble with Rosie," giving his new friend a wink as they reclaimed their seats.

"Sounds like your flyboy friend is a little hen pecked," slurred Norman.

"Are you suggesting something?" Jensen retorted, pushing his chair back and standing up. Other members around them stopped their activities and sensed something was about to happen.

"Whoa, back up," shouted Martin. "John, you should apologize to my young friend." He looked at Jensen to explain, "I was only kidding about Rosie." Then back to John Norman, "Besides, it's none of your business."

"Is that right, Marty? Well, who are you to tell me what to do?" and he took a swing that connected with the left side of Martin's face. Martin reacted swiftly, hitting his friend squarely on his nose, causing blood to spurt freely over the table. By this time, the doorman at the Legion had heard the ruckus developing in the corner and now made his way to see what was happening.

The bouncer, Vince Daley, was a large man of middle age who was accustomed to this type of thing occasionally happening and he clearly had the temperament and physical size to bring it to a quick conclusion.

"That'll be enough, lads," the bouncer yelled, and grabbed hold of Martin who appeared to have the advantage over the less sober John Norman, even though by this time the fight was probably going to be settled of its own accord. Martin again reacted quickly, and struck out violently at Daley, landing a solid right on the man's jaw. The bouncer fell amid a table full of glasses, sending broken glass and ice all over the floor on which several other men in the vicinity began to slip and fall, one blaming the other for their clumsiness.

Chaos soon erupted. It seemed everybody was bleeding, albeit they were all probably suffering only minor cuts. Yet it was still a terribly ugly scene. It would only be a matter of time before the town law officers would be making an appearance.

Martin felt an arm tugging him toward the front door away from the group of fighting men, and he was led to the outside of the building by Dave Jensen, just as a town police car arrived at the site with its siren blaring. They quickly reached Dave's vehicle where Bob Kenny was waiting and the three sped home for the dinner party.

When they arrived, there were at least six vehicles lined up on the lane in front of his home, three or four of which he didn't recognize. Martin had a wild, disheveled look about him. His hair was mussed, and the left side of his face was bruised and swollen; the arm of his sports jacket was torn where the seam met the shoulder, and his shoes were spotted with blood; and to top things off, he was still not completely sober.

His two companions, while also a tad tipsy, were at least somewhat presentable. The three of them, together however, emitted a strong smell of alcohol as they entered the kitchen where Martin's mother was alone, busying herself getting items from the refrigerator. When she saw them, she gasped loudly. This brought Meg running from the den, thinking something had happened to her.

Martin gazed stupidly at his wife and a look of dismay came over her.

"Oh Martin, look at you" she cried, clearly angry. Then she shifted her gaze to the two young airmen. "And you two. Where in God's name have you been, and what have you been up to?" She was irate, and Martin had no idea how to get out of the predicament.

Just then Meg's two sisters entered the scene. When they assessed the situation, they both quickly hauled their two friends out of the house and into Dave's vehicle. From there, Jensen unadvisedly but quickly drove off with Bob and the girls before having to face the crowd who were all sitting in the living room, apparently awaiting the arrival of Martin and the others before commencing dinner.

Martin decided to face the situation at once and get it over with. He strode into the den where at a glance he could see his father, Meg's mother Mattie, John Radford and his sister Becky, his brother James with Audrey, and be damned if his brother Gerald wasn't home as well. Finally, there was an unknown fellow who wore a formal three-piece grey suit over a white shirt and maroon tie. *Probably the minister,* thought Martin. When he entered the room, all conversation came to an abrupt halt. Everyone stared at him, some aghast, others with knowing grins; but all awaiting an explanation from him.

"Hello everyone," Martin said. He bowed in an exaggerated manner. When he rose to face the group, a stupid grin on his face, he could not avoid a small hiccup in the process. He simply slurred "Scuze me," and then looked at them, almost daring them to say something.

Gerald let out a huge laugh at seeing his young brother in this drunken state, quickly followed by roars of laughter from James and John Bradford. However, the three men immediately received a stern look from Mr. England, which was duplicated by both Mrs. England and Meg, and they were silenced.

"Martin," George England said. "You are a disgrace to the family. Please go upstairs immediately and clean yourself up." Martin glared at his father, then cast a beseeching glance at Meg before turning sharply towards the front stairs.

George ushered the group into the formal dining room and sat them around the extended table, there to await the son who had just been severely admonished as if he had been a child of eight or ten. Most of those there had mixed feelings about the situation. Certainly, Martin had exhibited bad behavior, and without knowing the details of everything, they were all too aware Martin had a reputation for acting out. An awkward, quiet conversation resumed around the table. At a nod to Gerald from Mr. England, they began eating. Meg politely excused herself and went upstairs to see to her husband.

Martin was sitting on their bed in the back room, his head in his hands. "Meg, you don't deserve this," he said, gesturing to himself. "I have embarrassed you in front of the family and I've only been home for one day." He reached for her, and she reluctantly allowed him to hold her. He was now sober, and he wanted to obliterate the past ten minutes. However, what scared him most was the fact that at that moment, his only thought was the one sure way to do that was to go back to the Legion. *What is the matter with me, anyway?* He wondered.

Meg knew Martin had a serious problem, but she was not sure how to go about helping him. In fact, at this point she was unsure if she even *wanted* to help him. She wasn't a doctor or a psychologist for God's sake. She was convinced Martin needed professional help but where or how could it be arranged?

Martin got up from the bed and started to leave the room. "I can't go back down there now," he stated. "Meg, please ask Gerald if he could meet me in the back shed. I need to talk with him, okay?" To avoid the others, he walked down the back stairs to the kitchen, then out a back door to the shed where his father kept his painting supplies and equipment.

While he waited for Gerald to show up, he gazed around the outbuilding and noted the various business signs his father had produced. There were hand-painted store signs to indicate 'Open' or 'Closed' even advertisements for local merchants. He wasn't aware his father had this talent, and he realized there was much to learn from him should he decide to continue with his business.

Gerald then came into the shed and gave Martin a huge bear hug. He looked at Martin seriously. "Well little brother, that was quite the homecoming display."

"I apologize for that," said Martin. "It was stupid of me to get involved in a ruckus at the Legion knowing this special dinner was about to take place. I don't know what came over me. I tell you, Gerry, there are times I get so angry at the least thing. It's like a red fog rolls over me and I just have to lash out at something, you know?"

Gerald again looked seriously at his younger brother. "Maybe you should think about going on the wagon for a while, Marty? Lots of guys have a similar problem with alcohol. Some people simply shouldn't drink, and I think you're one of them."

"Right, you're one to talk."

"Look, Marty, this isn't some kind of competition here. It was just a simple suggestion. You're a married man now, with a lovely wife. You don't want to screw up your marriage, do you? Sure, I like my rum as much as the next guy, but I'm single. Plus, alcohol affects me differently than it does you. I go to sleep when I've had too much. But you usually get your skivvies in a knot, and you just want to fight. Where the hell does all that come from?"

"Good question, Gerry. I'll give some thought to your suggestion. I mean, how tough can it be, eh?"

They went out through a separate door to the back yard. It was an unusually warm evening for late April. The sun had gone down but there was still warmth in the air, and it held a promise of an early summer. They walked to the top of the yard and reminisced of previous years playing as children. They recalled throwing groundballs to each other here in the summer on the more level part of the lawn, playing 'S.K.U.N.K.' The three amigos were competitive, and it was always a test on Martin's part to keep up physically with his older siblings.

"You're looking well, Gerald. I gather you made it okay through France?"

"Well, I'm here, brother. What can I say? It was hell, though … never again, eh?"

"No sir. There were some things I hope to never see again…"

Martin started to say more, then decided to let it ride. *There would be other times to talk about all that!*

They walked down the yard to the back door of the house where people were saying their good-byes, starting to leave. Martin approached each of them individually, thanked them for coming and at the same time whispered a brief apology to them for his behavior.

When he went into the house to help clean up dishes, he found that his mother had retired to her bedroom and Meg was attending to her as she made ready for bed. It was awkward being alone with his father, but it was necessary, so he returned to the kitchen to face him.

"You know, Dad, I am extremely ashamed of myself. I'm sorry for all the embarrassment I've caused you and Mom. It could have been easily avoided if I hadn't gone to the Legion for a couple of drinks. *" He was still downplaying things. It was* five *drinks he had, why couldn't he even admit that?*

"Martin, were it only myself, I would not have been so upset. The fact is your mother is in poor health. You were aware of this. I thought you would have given consideration to her condition before satisfying your need for alcohol. Hopefully the morning will bring a better day. You might want to think of something nice to do for her, okay?" He left Martin alone with his thoughts.

His father, of course, was right. He would buy his mother a nice bouquet of spring flowers first thing in the morning. And some chocolates and maybe a pair of nylons for Meg. He'd have to watch his wallet though, since he was getting close to using up his final pay from the Army. As a bombardier he was paid $1.70 per day. Most of that was sent home monthly but he had kept the last two months' pay knowing *he'd* probably be home before it reached Meg, so he had over a hundred dollars when he landed, now maybe seventy-five.

Martin slowly climbed the stairs to find Meg sleeping when he entered their bedroom. He carefully got into bed, not wanting to wake her. It was a stressful evening for her, and he vowed to himself he would rise early, do a bit of shopping, then make amends.

He thought of his father's little workshop out back, and decided he wanted to talk further with him about his business in the morning.

Chapter Four

BOTH MARTIN'S and Meg's families went to Sunday service the following day at the Presbyterian Church on King Street. Martin was not surprised to note the young man in the three-piece suit at last night's dinner party was indeed the minister at this church. The sermon he had just given was centered on man's weaknesses, the temptations of Satan, and overcoming bad habits. Martin could have sworn the minister looked directly at him during most of his homily. On the way out after service, the minister was greeting members as they left.

Martin shook the minister's hand. "Good morning, Reverend. My name is Martin England. Sorry I didn't get to say goodbye to you last night, nor did I properly introduce myself." That said, he was now at a loss for further words. Yet he haltingly continued. "Ah, the fact is, I could probably spend a whole day here saying 'I'm sorry' about many things, but you're a busy man. Hah." He said this a bit sheepishly and jokingly, but he had the impression the minister was taking every word Martin spoke very seriously.

"I'm the Reverend Don McBride, and I'm a friend of your family, Martin. Any time you feel like talking to me, I will make myself available." He looked seriously at Martin. "I mean that, okay?"

"Uh, sure thing Reverend. You have a good day," He watched the young minister leave to speak with the rest of the congregation as they came out of the church. James then walked over with Audrey to say hello. "So, how are you feeling today brother?" a small smile on his face.

"Never better, Jimmy What's going on today?"

"Not too much. Want to go fishing? Gerry and I were thinking of trying a little stream that empties into the Napan River, out past the Air Base."

"Sounds like fun, do you have any extra gear?"

"No problem, Marty. We'll see you after lunch."

So the afternoon was planned and Martin was looking forward to just The Three Amigos spending some time together. It had been a while since they did something like this and it promised to be fun.

After lunch Gerald rolled into the lane in his 1933 silver Packard with James. He had purchased it in 1937 from a friend who was in dire need of funds. It was a beauty, with long fender skirts and wide running boards. Martin climbed in the back bench seat and then he realized the promise he made to himself about getting some small gifts for his mother and Meg. "Gerald, would you mind taking a quick run to the pharmacy on the way out of town?" he asked his brother.

"Not at all, little brother," said Gerald, and they drove off. A quick stop and Martin was able to pick up what he wanted.

The community of Napan was a small farming area located only two miles south of the Chatham Air Force Training base. The Napan River ran through the community and emptied approximately ten miles further east into Miramichi Bay. Gerald parked the Packard on the right side of the highway just south of the river where a trail ran through the woods for several hundred yards before it came to a beaver pond. It was a beautiful spring day with only a few cirrus clouds in the sky and a light westerly wind to keep the black flies somewhat at bay. They caught several trout over a two-hour period and decided to return home.

On the way back to the car they heard an aircraft approaching from the southeast. As they turned and looked up behind them, they identified a Curtis Helldiver two-seater coming in low, obviously on a landing approach to the nearby runway. It was no doubt on loan from the U.S. to be used in training at the air base. Then, just before the brothers reached the highway, Martin suddenly went wild. He grabbed both Gerald and James from behind and threw them to the earth.

"Lay flat!" he screamed. "Keep down!"

Gerald and James looked at each other, then, over at Martin who was lying prone on his stomach, his arms outstretched with his hands folded over both sides of his head. His eyes betrayed a wild look of terror, eying the *Curtis* as it flew directly over the three men on its way to the runway approximately two miles to the west. When the aircraft was out of their sight, Gerald went to Martin and helped him to stand. Martin was visibly shaking and he simply stared at the horizon where the *Curtis* had disappeared.

"You okay, Marty?" asked James.

Getting no response, Gerald shouted "Marty, shape up!" and he shook him roughly. At that, Martin seemed to come around and he sheepishly walked ahead of his brothers to the car.

"I'm okay, guys. Just a little startled there for a minute. Sorry to scare you. One of you boys got any smokes?"

Gerald and James just looked at each other and got in the car with their young brother. James handed a pack of Pall Malls to Martin who lit up, his hands still shaking as they made their way home.

"Listen boys, please don't say anything about what just happened to anyone, okay? I had a close call outside of Booischot, Belgium. Our outfit was strafed by a *Messerschmitt* one day while we were marching in file on a dirt road. We lost a couple of men. The bastard almost got me, just good luck prevailed I guess. Anyway, let's keep this to yourselves, eh?"

~ * ~

His brothers knew of many cases where friends of theirs suffered from what some doctors were calling Shell-Shock. It was seldom talked about by those who experienced the problem, since it was considered by many to be a sign of weakness, even cowardice. Gerald and James promised to keep the incident they witnessed today to themselves. Gerald then decided to make a quick stop at the liquor store on the way home before it closed. A couple of quick shots of rum wouldn't hurt. Besides, Martin was quite wound up.

They had driven along the Shore Road, taking them down to Middle Island and Doug Bradford's farm. After parking the Packard, they sat on the shore facing the small island, and finished off the pint of rum Gerald had purchased, talking about earlier times. Gerald spotted an old rowboat laying close to where they were sitting. On a whim, they decided to row over to the island.

Whenever the three got together, there were always shenanigans in play, and today was no exception. Halfway across the short distance to the island, Martin stood up in the dory and started rocking the boat from side to side. Gerald rose to stop him and immediately lost his balance, spilling into the river. No doubt, the two quick drinks he had just finished were a factor. He soon ran into trouble yelling "I can't swim, help!"

James and Martin were able to pull him back into the dory and when they managed to reach the small island, they rolled in the long sea grass, regaling with laughter. "I thought you would have learned to swim by now, Gerry," said Martin.

"Well, I haven't, and you guys better not say anything about this to anyone," he said, obviously humiliated.

"Gosh," said James. "We're building up a lot of secrets today."

They spent the rest of the afternoon lying in the sun on that warm early May day until Gerald's clothes dried, then they drove back to town. Upon arriving home, Martin presented Meg and his mother with the simple purchases he had earlier made. The women were absolutely delighted to receive the gifts, and Martin was quickly back in everyone's good favor.

Before going to bed, Martin had a long talk with his father. They discussed George's business, how Martin might be able to make a go of it. Now lying in bed with Meg, he discussed the possibility of maybe taking an Interior Decorating program.

"Well Martin, if you're sure this is what you want to do, then, by all means, go for it," Meg said as they prepared for bed. "Leave your options open though, okay? Why not talk to George Barry about it once you know a bit more. Like how long these courses last, which of them may be more beneficial to you. I would prefer to stay here in Chatham, wouldn't you?"

George Barry was a well-known businessman in the town and a friend of the family.

"I'd be happy wherever you are Meg." He held her closely, gave her a goodnight kiss, and they soon went to sleep.

~ * ~

The Observation Post could be seen through Martin's binoculars in the distance as they made their way to San Fortunato in the Captain's jeep. From the graphics displayed on the glass he was able to determine the tower lay approximately four hundred yards to the northwest of them. Captain Jacobs had selected Martin to accompany him in an endeavor to help him capture the tower from where they could then establish their own OP. They could then relay accurate targets for their Company's guns.

The enemy currently held the city of San Fortunato, Northeast Italy, and it was vital that they be able to fire their weapons at the German front lines if they were to be successful in driving them out of the city and liberating the Italian civilians there.

The Captain and Martin had reached the tower which was apparently occupied by two or more Germans. Although they were under fire from the get-go, they had managed to get under the protective eaves of the building with neither of them being hit. Either they were very lucky or the Germans occupying the tower were terribly bad marksmen.

Darting from under the cover of the eaves, they both lobbed hand grenades high in the air through an open area at the top of the structure and two loud bangs resounded seconds later. They then climbed the stairs and carefully looked through the open trap door in the floor. Martin was first up, and upon reaching the top rung he could not believe what he was seeing.

The next thing Martin knew, Meg was shaking him roughly and he woke in terror, his body covered in sweat. He looked wildly at her, and it was obvious to Meg that he was in another world. Gradually he came to realize where he was. She held him close while he became calm and finally returned to sleep. Meg shivered. She sensed this was probably not the last she would see of these awful nightmares.

Chapter Five

THE NEXT morning, Martin was in an optimistic mood, having no memory of the previous night's terror-filled dream. He had just finished shaving and was pulling on his corduroy pants, tucking in his plaid, blue and white shirt, sitting on his side of the bed.

"Well, Meg, my dear, how would you like to start working on a new job?"

"Ha ha…who with?" she said, sidling over to tickle him.

"With England's House Painting Ltd., of course," he replied, pulling her off the bed and swinging her around in a wide arc. He then explained in detail how he planned to take over his father's business.

Things were looking pretty rosy for Martin and Meg as they began to make plans for their future. Summer would soon be here, and they wanted to be ready for the busy time ahead. Martin was finally beginning to feel like he was actually going to be contributing to the England household.

Earlier that morning he had taken a call from a lady who was looking for his father. She wanted George to complete a project she had started in the fall: carpenters had erected a veranda across the front of her house and now she would like to have it painted. Martin explained how his father was gradually retiring and had passed the business on to him. He would gladly have a look at the site in order to give her a quote for the work.

"Oh," the lady said, "Your father has already told me what it was going to cost," and she gave Martin the quoted amount. In Martin's opinion, it seemed to be quite low. Nevertheless, he agreed to honor the commitment. He obtained the address and the date he could begin work. His first job, and he was excited.

As it turned out, the address for the job was located at the lower end of town, close to Mattie's house. He was supposed to start on Monday after the weekend coming up, and he decided to take a walk and have a quick look at the project. When he arrived at the address, he was somewhat intimidated by the size of the new veranda. He could envision how the veranda would dramatically enhance the appearance of the property once it was finished with a coat of white paint and a dark forest green trim. He noted though, that he would need to bring a sturdy ladder with him, and he now realized he would need someone to help him get his gear from his father's shop to the site. *Maybe John Norman could help*, he thought.

Later that night, when his father returned from visiting Martha at the Sanatorium, Martin told him about the job he had agreed to complete.

"Oh, yes, Mrs. Flaherty," said George. "You'll find she's a bit meticulous, but she pays on time, and she'll give you good word-of-mouth advertising if she appreciates your work."

"How do you get your gear from place to place?" asked Martin.

"Well, sometimes, I have to rent a truck or taxi. You get to know where the places are, and whether or not the cost has to be considered when providing quotes.

Martin could see there was going to be a period of trial and error involved before he would become proficient at quoting estimates. He resigned himself to exercising patience as he took over his father's business. Later that day he got in touch with his brother-in -law John Bradford who agreed to help him bring his ladder and other gear to Mrs. Flaherty's house on Monday.

He decided to check out what was happening at the Legion, maybe have a quick drink to celebrate his new profession. He was at the bar enjoying a beer when he was joined by his friend John Norman. He hadn't heard from him since the altercation here on the day after they came home. "How are you making out, John Norman?" asked Martin.

"Not so good Martin, I can't seem to get work anywhere and I had to get Government assistance," he said. Martin felt sorry for his friend. "Maybe I can help you. I've decided to take over my father's house painting business and I believe I can use some help. The first job I have starts Monday. But look, because I told the lady who hired me that I'd honor my father's earlier quote, this first job won't pay that much. After this, though, we should do okay. Would you be interested?"

"Sure I would, Martin. That would be swell." And just like that

Martin now had an assistant and the two men shared a couple of more drinks before leaving with the agreement to meet on Monday at Mrs. Flaherty's house at eight a.m.

Martin spent the rest of the weekend pouring over his father's records to get better accustomed to the nature of the business. His father was happy with the level of interest Martin was showing and he hoped this would continue.

Meg, for her part, had earlier suggested to Mr. England that they might consider setting up a couple of rooms to take in boarders. George had agreed since Mrs. England was now in the Sanatorium, and there was no point in having the available rooms go to waste. A number of civilians were now employed in the community in professional positions such as drafting, electronics, and the like. They needed rooms.

Meg felt she would be able to keep a fresh supply of meat, vegetables, and milk on hand from her uncle Doug's farm. She would gladly pay him for his produce of course, and thereby she was also helping Doug out.

~ * ~

Monday morning arrived, and John Bradford came early at seven to help Martin get his equipment together, including two ladders that had to be strapped onto the top of John's vehicle. By the time they arrived at Mrs. Flaherty's house, it was close to eight and Martin didn't see John Norman anywhere around the property. *Oh well*, he thought. *He'd manage it on his own.* John left to get back to his own work at the Legion and Martin proceeded to get things ready.

He was about to start with the primer when John Norman landed. His friend looked to be in pretty rough shape, reeking of alcohol, and it was obvious he was suffering from a hangover. Martin was beginning to second-guess himself about asking John Norman to work for him.

"What do you think John Norman, are you ready to go to work?"

"What do you want me to do Martin? I've painted before, so just give me a brush and a can of paint and tell me where to start."

Martin handed John Norman an empty bucket and a short stick.

"How about first going onto the roof of the veranda at the far-left end to clear out the gutters for me. Just put the old wet leaves in this bucket. I'll put up the ladder for you, then I'll start painting behind you. By the time you get the gutters cleared, you can come over and start painting underneath what I'll have finished." It sounded like a pretty simple plan. John Norman climbed up the ladder with the bucket and stick, situated himself on the edge of the roof, and began clearing old leaves and twigs from the gutter, using the short pole to gather the debris into the bucket. He gradually moved his ladder toward the right end of the eave's trough in the process.

Martin, in the meantime, had grabbed his own brush and a can of primer then began climbing his ladder toward the eave of the veranda. As he neared the top of the ladder, a weird feeling came over him. His head began swimming in a kaleidoscope of bright colors, and he started to see images: a boy of fourteen or fifteen was approaching him from above. The boy was crying, he carried a rifle, pointing it at him. Martin panicked and struck out at the figure.

The 'boy' fell off the roof and landed on his back, no longer moving. Martin quickly came to his senses, and he carefully lowered himself down the ladder to the ground. There, lying on the lawn was his friend John Norman. Martin was puzzled. *How did this happen?* He bent over John and gently shook him. John Norman's eyes opened slowly, he looked questioningly at Martin, and shrank away from him, obviously afraid of being struck again by his friend. With great difficulty, John Norman was able to rise and he slowly moved away from Martin and began to leave the site. Turning around as he was leaving, he yelled back to his friend.

"I don't know what your problem is Martin, but I didn't do anything to you. So forget about the job, I'm through here."

Mrs. Flaherty then appeared on the veranda. "Is everything okay here?" she asked.

Martin looked at her closely. He was not sure what she had witnessed so he decided to hold back trying to explain things.

"Everything's fine Mrs. Flaherty. John Norman was going to be working with me today, but I guess he's not feeling too well, and he has decided to go home and get some rest."

The older lady gave Martin a suspicious look and returned to her house. Martin, who was very shaken up by the whole incident, slowly approached the ladder to resume his work. He proceeded to climb toward the eave of the roof once again, mindful of what had occurred only minutes before. Everything now seemed fine. He was perplexed but thought it best to continue with his work.

The rest of the day passed without incident, and he was able to complete the whole veranda with a coat of primer and the first top coat. He told Mrs. Flaherty he would be back to finish the job tomorrow and he left his ladder and paint on the veranda floor out of the way. He then went home, taking his brushes with him where he would later clean them.

It was near suppertime when he arrived home. Meg was in the kitchen busy preparing supper, and she greeted him with a big smile. "Hungry, dear?" she asked. "Did you enjoy the sandwiches today that I prepared for your lunch?"

"Yes, and yes," Martin gave her a hug and his father came into the kitchen from the den to join them.

"So how was the first day on the job, Martin?" asked his father.

"Well sir, I have the primer and first coats done. I should finish tomorrow, I expect."

"Excellent, Mrs. Flaherty will appreciate your fast work."

Now was the perfect time to tell both of them that something wrong was happening to him. Something he had simply no control over. But he couldn't begin to explain what it was. They would think he was going crazy once he told them he was having hallucinations of seeing things and people from the war.

The accompanying fear and terror today were similar to what he had experienced at the Legion, just before the big fight broke out; the same as the incident with the plane, when he and his brothers went fishing the other day. *And what about the recurring dreams he was having?* He had to talk to somebody who could help him understand what was happening,

But the moment passed and soon it was time to retire for the evening.

Martin was bothered by the fact that he had just lied to both his father and Meg through omission. *Was this thing going to control him?* More importantly, he had been very fortunate to at least not have seriously injured his friend today. John Norman could easily have been killed or paralyzed by the fall he sustained. Who could he talk with about this problem that he could trust, and also offer him some solutions?

The answer came to him immediately. He recalled his talk last Sunday with the young minister at church. Martin specifically remembered how the man sounded serious when he encouraged him to call him whenever he felt the need to do so. He decided he would do this at the first opportunity. He would finish the job at Mrs. Flaherty's tomorrow, then see Reverend MacBride on Wednesday.

He would have to be up front with the minister. Right now, he knew he really wanted a drink before he went to bed. It was becoming the one sure way of helping him attain sleep. But even then he was afraid he would again be faced with the recurring nightmare of the observation post near San Fortunato, Italy. He vividly recalled the content of the recurring nightmare:

Martin and Captain Jacobs had successfully made their way to the tower and were preparing to take control of the post. They had each thrown grenades into the top of the structure and Martin was the first to climb up the stairs to the top room.

There, huddled in each of three corners of the confined room, was a small figure. They were only kids, maybe thirteen or fourteen years old. One of them was clearly dead as the result of the flying shrapnel from the grenades. The boy's right arm had been severed, probably in a futile effort to protect his head, which also had suffered traumatic damage.

The other two German youths kept their rifles by their sides and sat in shock, staring at the two Canadian soldiers as they climbed from the ladder toward them. The young boys began crying and stayed in the corners, too afraid to move. Puddles of urine had formed beneath each of them.

This was Martin's initial up-close experience with violent death in combat and he was sickened by what he witnessed. Captain Jacobs then approached the young boys and removed their rifles from them and emptied them of ammunition. He actually comforted the boys and told them they were going to be okay. Then he went over to Martin and told him to quickly establish the coordinates needed by their unit some four hundred yards behind them.

After sneaking downstairs and making a visit to the back shed where he had hidden his pint of rum, he found the bottle and took two quick drinks from it. He then went upstairs to bed and was pretending to be asleep when Meg came out of the bathroom and climbed into bed beside him.

Meg knew her husband well and she was aware he was not sleeping. However, now did not seem to be the right time to begin a discussion for which she had no answers. Maybe she could drop in to see the doctor tomorrow. She knew Martin was drinking more than he normally did and at first, she had thought this would pass once he got settled. That did not seem to be happening, and the alcoholic fumes coming from him as he lay next to her confirmed this. She had read that many veterans experienced awkwardness upon returning home from the war to a civilian lifestyle. This was different. Something far more sinister was creating the rift between them and she would do whatever it took to bring him back to normalcy.

Chapter Six

ON THURSDAY morning while Meg visited her doctor, Martin walked quickly with a purpose toward the Presbyterian Church manse. He had finished the job at Mrs. Flaherty's yesterday, and she told him she would be telling people how pleased she was with the quality of his work. That was good to hear, and he made a mental note to himself to start keeping track of people he might be able to use for testimonials on his behalf.

It was now nine o'clock. Yesterday, he had called the minister, and he was told that he was free to talk with him this morning any time he could make it over. As he walked up the steps to the residence, he realized the minister was a single man, and not that old. He began to have doubts concerning how Reverend McBride could help him. Really, what experience would the minister have to use as a basis of reference?

"Welcome to the manse, Martin," said McBride as he opened the big door for Martin and ushered him into his living room. "Can I get you something to drink?"

A tall rum and coke would be nice, Martin mused to himself.

"Coffee would be great, if you're having one," Martin replied.

When the minister returned, he carried a plate of freshly made donuts and a pot of hot coffee which he placed on a table in front of Martin. "Help yourself, courtesy of my house lady, Mrs. Donaher."

After picking up a donut and placing it beside his coffee, Martin began. "Sir, ah, Reverend MacBride, thank you for seeing me." Martin began, but he was interrupted by the minister.

"Listen Martin, if we're going to have a chat, the first thing you've gotta do is drop the formalities. Call me Don, okay? Now, to start off, I could tell from your call earlier that you might have some reservations about seeing me. I don't know exactly what it is that you want to talk about, but I want you to know this: I'm probably around the same age as yourself, and while I haven't served in armed combat, I *have* studied many aspects of the human condition surrounding this war. Maybe I can help you with something?"

There, he left the door open, thought Martin.

"Well sir, uh, Don," he began. "I don't know how to explain this, but I've been having some disturbing thoughts lately. They seem to be related to specific experiences I had overseas. I get so afraid that all I want to do is drink and get away from everything, everyone! I see things during the day, then again at night I frequently have similar nightmares."

"You're explaining it very well Martin. You should know that you're not the only person to have this problem. And I mean right here in Miramichi. Oh, don't worry. I would never tell you or anyone who the other people are. In the same way, everything we discuss here today goes no further without your consent.

"From what I've read, some senior people in the forces refer to this problem as 'shell shock'. He used air quotes for the term and his tone was sarcastic. He more or less indicated some professionals had even gone so far as to downplay the seriousness of the phenomenon by referring to it as a simple problem as opposed to a chronic illness. Others even called it 'battle fatigue'.

"These are the same professionals who refuse to call alcoholism a disease. That said, there *are* many doctors who now believe that what you may have is the result of experiencing one or more traumatic events... things you would see or be a part of that would never occur in your normal lifetime at home, away from the horrors of war. Then, after returning to a form of normality such as to your work at home, your married life or family, some things may happen that serve as 'triggers', which prompt you to relive these past events. You understand?"

Already Martin was becoming more at ease with the young minister. It was obvious he had a gift of being able to converse with people. And it was also evident he had studied about some of the phenomena Martin was experiencing.

At this point he made the decision to describe to Don in detail the observation post incident near San Fortino that he felt was behind one of the dreams he was having. He went on to relate the hallucinations surrounding other events including the strafing by the German *Messerschmitt* fighter plane and the raped woman in Italy. He spared no details to the minister.

When Reverend McBride had heard everything, it was almost lunch time. He told Martin he had a prior engagement to attend, but he wanted him to do something. "Part of the answer, at least as far as the literature that I've read seems to indicate, is to face it head on," he said. "Some people have found it helps if they write about their experiences. Committing notes to paper about the events seems to serve as a defense for the mind. You know that *you* are in control of the past events, *they* are history, *they* can no longer harm you. Okay?

"Another thing: alcohol only helps your mind to lapse, your defense retreats, and your mind is then able to relive the events. I would strongly recommend that you try to abstain from drinking, at least for a while. Maybe see how things go. There are many other things you can do with your time, Martin. Your work, for example. I hear you're thinking of taking over your father's business. That would be a great place on which to focus your attention. Maybe take up a hobby, like writing or etching? Whatever you decide, I think you'll find it makes a big difference in your life. And remember, I'm here whenever you want to talk again, right?" Martin was grateful for the approach being taken by the minister.

"Look Don, I really appreciate the way you handled this today," Martin said. "Frankly, our talk was not at all what I expected, and I *will* give everything you said a lot of thought. So, thanks for your time. Tell Mrs. Donaher she makes great donuts."

Martin left the manse a much happier, and confident person. He was resolved to put into practice what the young minister had advised, and he went back to his wife and father to discuss the visit he just experienced.

When he arrived home, John Bradford was sitting on the back steps of Martin's house. He was looking very serious, and immediately Martin knew something had happened and that it was probably not good.

"Hi John, where is everybody?" Martin could not hide the worry in the tone of his voice.

"Martin, your father, Meg, and Becky are all at the Sanatorium. George received a call from Dr Blake earlier telling him he should come to see Martha as soon as possible. The news is not good, Martin. Apparently, she has suffered a relapse of her disease, and I'm afraid it has progressed at a much faster rate than they anticipated. I drove them there and I just returned, waiting for you. We should go now."

They sped to the Sanatorium and when they went into Martha's room, Martin could see his mother's health had failed rapidly in the past two days. His father was by her side, holding her frail hand. Doctor Blake excused himself from the group, telling them he would be right outside if they needed him. Martin went over to his parents while Meg and John stood near the entrance door. It was truly a sad scene. This woman, who only a short time ago was fit as a fiddle, thought Meg, was now passing before their eyes. It was unfortunate James and Gerald were not here, but of course they were both at work some twenty miles away. She stole a glance at Martin and saw he was looking keenly at the bouquet of flowers he had given his mother almost a week ago.

They too were wilted.

Martha passed away peacefully later that afternoon. Just before her last breath, she became fully conscious of everybody in the room and looked at each one of them, smiling as she made eye contact. She then told George she loved him, basically mouthing the words, and her eyes closed.

~ * ~

When the funeral was over George asked everyone to come to his home. He said it was important to be with family at this time. Initially, Dave Jensen and his colleague Bob Kenny had elected to stay at their PMQ's on the base, but Rita and Rosalind would have none of that, insisting they were both definitely part of this family and they had better be there as well.

When everyone was gathered in the England family living room and Meg had made tea and coffee for all with Mattie's help, George said he was glad they were all here. He decided to tell them he was officially having Martin take over his business and that they should all wish him well in his future endeavors.

"Maybe you should give some thought to having your houses painted," he said this jokingly, and Martin was surprised he could maintain some sense of humor under the circumstances.

Then John Bradford took the floor. "Well, everyone," he said. "Now is as good a time as any, eh Becky?" He stood up from the sofa and held Becky close. "We have decided to get married, and we'll be living in the apartment above the Legion. And yes, Martin, we're going to need to have some renovations completed, just as soon as you finish your next job."

Everybody clapped and congratulated John and Rebecca. Mr. England then surprised everyone by saying they should have a drink to celebrate the announcement. He went to his pantry in the den to bring out a bottle of brandy which he had been saving for 'special' occasions. Martin, unexpectedly, politely declined the brandy but poured himself a glass of cold cider from the fridge and joined in the toast. Nobody commented on this, but it certainly did not go unnoticed.

Later that night when they went to bed, Meg brought up the subject. "I notice you passed on that drink of brandy this afternoon." She raised her eyebrows and smiled at him.

"I'll not make any vows or promises of quitting drinking," he said. "But I will try. That talk I had with Reverend Don McBride the other day got me thinking, I guess. Anyway, we'll see. There are a few things I want to do, things Don suggested. So, if at times I seem preoccupied, stick with me Meg, okay? I'll explain as we go along."

He got through a job his father had arranged just before his mother's passing. A new doctor in town, Dr. Ramsay, was renovating a beautiful old home and the inside work was enough to take him through August. The word spread.

At the same time, Meg's new role as a boarding house operator was keeping her busy. There were three men now living with Martin, Meg, and Mr. England. They were all young, hard-working men who took their jobs seriously and did not engage in anything of a derogatory nature, such as heavy drinking or gambling, to distract them from achieving their goals. As such, they were well liked by the England family.

Martin was finally able to begin saving money and plans were made to undertake their own home renovations. The large house was placed on a proper foundation, a new furnace was installed, and new roofs were completed. Meg was pleased with the way their lives had turned for the better. Martin's behavior had changed dramatically. No longer did he experience day-time flashbacks like he had been having that spring, and his nightmares were few and far between.

Meg was certain this was all due to the fact that for the past six months he had quit drinking.

So, it was on a cold night in early December that she announced with a big smile to Martin that she was expecting their first child. Martin was ecstatic! The first thing he did was write a letter to his friend and former Captain, Reg Jacobs. He informed him of his good fortune and insisted that Reg come to Chatham for the coming birth in August. There was no question that he would be the child's Godfather and namesake, be that Jacob or Regina.

That Christmas, Martin and Meg received a letter from Jacobs in Montreal telling them he would be proud to accept the invitation Martin had offered.

He would see them in the coming summer.

Chapter Seven

CHRISTMAS, 1945, was also a happy time for other members of the Bradford family. John and Becky had gotten married earlier in the month; both Rosalind and Rita received engagement rings from their boyfriends, Bob Kenny and Dave Jensen; Rachel, the youngest of the girls was busy working in Fredericton as a hairdresser, and she had aspirations of opening her own shop in that city; and Meg's mother, Mattie remained in good health since she was content to have two of her daughters at home where she could dote on them to her heart's content.

To usher in 1946, Meg and Martin decided to attend the annual New Year's Eve dinner and dance being held at the Legion Hall in Chatham. They had been invited to meet with John and Rebecca at their apartment first for cocktails. Martin, sticking to his own commitment regarding alcohol, drank ginger ale while the other three had vodka martinis. They went downstairs where a large crowd was gathered for dinner prior to the dance. Martin saw his old friend John Norman hanging out at the bar, so he went over to ask him how he was doing. At the bar, he ordered himself a Ginger Ale soda.

"Oh, I'm okay Martin," said John Norman. "You know, I never did apologize for quitting on you that day at Mrs. Flaherty's. I was thinkin' about it afterwards and I realized there must have been somethin' serious behind it, 'cause you're not normally like that, Marty."

Martin was not quite sure where their conversation was going but decided to continue with it for a little longer.

"John, it had nothing to do with you." He gestured at the bar in front of them. "It was this stuff. I was starting to revisit a lot of bad things that happened overseas. So, it was my fault, and I should have reached out to you before now. Why don't I buy you a drink?"

"Sure Martin, I could never resist a free drink!" He eagerly grabbed the double rum that was placed in front of him and wished Martin well as he downed the glass in one drink.

"Better go easy on that, John Norman," Martin cautioned him. "I'll see you upstairs at the dance after dinner.

As the evening progressed, and after an excellent roast beef dinner was consumed, many of the patrons had left for the dance area upstairs, and the majority of partygoers up here were beginning to get tipsy. Martin was glad he was not one of them. It was different seeing how people acted from this side of the fence. As he watched the crowd, he noticed a group of men in the corner by the bar area were having a heated conversation. Not surprisingly, John Norman was right in the middle of the argument. While he watched the men, he could see it was getting more serious, and threats could be heard coming from two younger men whom he did not recognize. The larger of the two men shoved John Norman, and a fight soon developed.

Within minutes, a large man came running across the floor to break up the fight. It was the same character that Martin had the run-in with during his first week back from overseas. Both John Bradford and Martin were now out of their seats, watching the incident closely. "That's Vince Daley," said John, pointing at the large man. "He was the Legion bouncer when I started working here, and I've been wondering when his brutish way of settling issues might result in something serious."

"I know what you mean," said Martin. "He was involved in the fight here when I first came back from overseas."

"I heard about that. Maybe we should see if we can help straighten this out."

They both rose from their table and Martin spoke to Meg. "Meg, please wait here with Becky. John and I will be right back." The two sauntered toward the bar area when they noticed the fight had actually stopped, although there was still an argument in process.

"Hey, John Norman, what's going on?" Martin shouted to his friend. When John Norman turned to see who was speaking, the bouncer Vince Daley grabbed the smaller Norman in a choke hold and began to drag him toward the head of the stairs. Martin then ran after them in an attempt to help his friend. He was afraid the big bouncer was going to throw Norman down the stairs. Just as he reached them, the doorman turned and saw

Martin.

"England!" he exclaimed. "I thought I had seen the last of you back in April."

He released Norman and made his move toward Martin. Martin was ready for him and threw a full right-hander at the big man first. The bouncer was clearly not expecting this and fell backwards into the smaller figure of John Norman. Norman, who was already teetering from the effects of alcohol, also fell backwards, but at this point he had been standing on the threshold of the stairs.

Martin watched helplessly as his friend toppled backwards down the full flight and landed with a sickening thud on the lower floor. He lay motionless as a large pool of blood spread from underneath his head while his lifeless eyes gazed up at the group of men staring down at him from the top of the stairs.

Martin and John could not believe what had just happened. They both ran down to their fallen friend, but it was obvious there was nothing that could be done to help him. The huge crowd was suddenly quite, dumb-struck by the scene at the bottom of the stairs. In a matter of minutes, a couple of policemen and an ambulance arrived. Soon after that, John and Martin were speaking with the cops and gave them full statements. The bouncer Vince Daley, meanwhile, could be seen huddled in a corner with his two cronies, the two who had actually started the fight with the hapless John Norman.

~ * ~

A formal Court Inquest was ordered to look into the death of John Norman, scheduled for February 5, 1946. A coroner presided over the discretionary hearing which was adjudicated by a panel of five community members. They unanimously declared John Norman's death an accident. Martin was required to testify at the inquest and fortunately, he was truthfully able to say he had been completely sober at the time of the incident. Yes, he had struck Mr. Daley, but it was in self-defense. The blow had caused Daley to fall back against Mr. Norman, thus creating the deadly accident that took Mr. Norman's life. The panel did state, however, that if

Mr. Daley had exercised more prudence in the way he handled the situation in the first place, there would have been no need for Martin's interference.

Other factors were considered: perhaps the door to the downstairs should have been kept closed? Mr. Norman had been drinking...was it to excess? If so, was there not an obligation on the part of the bartender to recognize this? Tests from the autopsy had revealed a high blood alcohol content but there was nothing to indicate that was sufficient in and of itself to account for the incident happening. Finally, if Martin had not intervened, would Mr. Norman not have simply left the building peacefully?

This last question was the one that created the most guilt in Martin's mind. Unfortunately, guilt was the main thing that led either directly or indirectly back to his old bad habit of excessive drinking. As a result, the pride and interest in his work that had previously changed his values was now gone.

He lazed around the house for most of the remaining winter months, wasting what little money he had saved. His health suffered and he began finding fault with Meg and his father over the smallest things. When they tried talking to him about his problem, he told them they were nagging him. He refused to acknowledge that he even *had* a problem. Inevitably, the dreams started returning. Not only nightmares, but Martin also found himself suffering from flashbacks to the war which would hit him hard at any time during the day or night.

~ * ~

One evening after Martin had arrived home from work and Meg had prepared supper, he had started drinking. An argument soon developed over the way Meg had prepared the meal. One thing led to another and soon he was yelling at her in a demeaning way. She could not take any more of the abuse and started to turn away from him to go to their bedroom. Martin then grabbed her arm and spun her around toward him. She struck out in anger, perhaps more in frustration, and slapped the side of his face. Martin then reached behind her to the table and picked up a steak knife. She looked at him in horror as he brandished the knife in a threatening manner!

Suddenly, Martin seemed to realize what was happening and he dropped the knife, held his head in his hands and started weeping. He begged her forgiveness and told her how sorry he was and that he would never do anything to harm her. One thing was certain: they were both aware this was a new level of abuse and that unless something was soon done to help him, their marriage was certain to fail. And now she was expecting their first child in five months…

Unknown to both of them, Martin's father had witnessed the incident in the kitchen. He called his son James and asked him to discreetly speak with Martin about his problem with alcohol. James himself had enrolled in Alcoholics Anonymous two months ago and had not mentioned it to anyone except his father.

The next evening, James made a visit to Martin's house, and they went for a walk downtown. It was now spring, and the evening held a promise of warmer weather to come. People were outside raking last year's fallen leaves into piles in their backyards. Kids were playing ball, the younger ones skipping rope on the sidewalks. It was a lovely evening.

"Well brother, how are you doing?" asked James as they made their way through the park in the Town Square. They passed a large cenotaph which had been erected there in honor of local men who had given their lives in World War 1. For a moment Martin was caught up in the memories of his own war and wondered how soon it would be before the town officials began putting up similar structures for his friends who had died more recently. They stopped to sit on one of the many park benches.

"I'm not doing well, James. Last night I came close to killing my wife." This statement was made as if he were telling his brother that he had a headache, and it stopped James in his tracks.

"Good Lord, Martin! What do you mean?"

"I was drinking. We argued about something, I don't even know what it was about, come to think of it." At this point he let out a chuckle, but it was in a hysterical way. "I need help, James."

Chapter Eight

"MY NAME is George, and I am an alcoholic!"

The man was not known to Martin. He was about 45 or so, a meek-looking individual, clean-shaven, and very presentable. He made this declaration in front of a dozen or so other men who sat around several tables in the hall. The man went on to talk about how he had lost his only source of income several years ago due to alcohol. He was now sober for three years and his life had dramatically changed for the better. He had returned to the workforce, and now he was able to provide for his family. He humbly gave thanks to the help he received from the AA organization and returned to his seat.

It was Friday night, and as agreed, Martin was attending the AA meeting with his brother James. He was surprised to see a couple of people here from town whom he never would have suspected were alcoholics. Not all, but some of the men took turns in telling the group stories about themselves which usually depicted the abuse they caused others, especially those they loved. They told of their shame and self-destruction, and of their struggles to attain and retain sobriety. After each man's turn, the group politely applauded them for their honesty, and mainly, Martin sensed, as a form of self-encouragement in their continuing battles against alcoholism.

These men were not professional public speakers. In fact, the majority of them usually had trouble telling their stories in front of the group. In turn though, they received the respect of the others for their honesty and commitment to the program. Martin was impressed with the solemnity of the meeting and the obvious seriousness displayed by the attendees regarding their common problem, and the help they promised to provide each other.

When the meeting came to an end and Martin and his brother were leaving the hall, they were approached by a familiar figure. It was Reverend

Don McBride.

"Good evening, gentlemen. James, nice to see you again and I'm glad you brought your brother with you. How are you, Martin? Welcome to our group," said the Reverend, smiling broadly.

"Oh, hi Reverend. Good to see you as well," said Martin. He was suddenly embarrassed to be seen here by the minister. McBride could sense his discomfort and quickly changed the subject.

"So how about the ball team this year? Do you think you might be able to play for us? You know we need your arm on third base Martin. ..."

"Well, I hadn't given it much thought Reverend," he began, but was interrupted by McBride.

"Here, everyone calls me Don, Martin. Say, there's practice tomorrow after supper. Can we see you there?"

"Uh, I guess so Rever…. uh, Don. See you tomorrow."

Before enlisting to go overseas in the Second World War, Martin England was an accomplished baseball player. He played third base for the town's entry in the Miramichi Valley Senior Baseball League, and he played it well. The 'hot corner' required a player with a strong throwing arm to first base and above average agility to field ground balls and execute the double play at second. Martin had both of these prerequisites. As for hitting, he was capable of getting on base more often than not by spraying the ball in all directions of the field. He would say "I try to hit it where they ain't."

That Friday evening, he walked with purpose to the Ironmen playing field which was located in the center of a horse racetrack on the south side of town. He knew most of the players there and he was warmly greeted by several as he entered the gates of the diamond. He was immediately quite surprised to see Don McBride standing at home plate hitting grounders to a group of players, leading them through an infield practice.

He was looking specifically at the third baseman, and he was wondering why he had been requested to come to the practice. The guy there certainly seemed capable of handling the position. When they were finished with the infield drill, the Reverend noticed Martin watching them and he ambled over to him.

"Hey Martin, glad you could make it."

"Well Don, I'd say that's a pretty tight infield those boys have out there. I don't see where I can be of any help as you had suggested earlier this week."

"Nope, you're wrong there. The guy you see on third is good, but he's our star pitcher. Hey, Josh!" McBride yelled over to the young man on third. Martin didn't know him. "Come over a minute and meet somebody." The tall black man trotted over to the side of the dugout where Martin and McBride were standing.

"Josh, meet Martin England. Martin played with the team regularly on third before the War. Martin this is Josh Freeman. He just moved here from Boston with his family. His father is one of several US Airmen stationed at the base."

Josh greeted Martin warmly, shaking hands and smiling broadly. "I've heard some of the guys talk about you, Martin. All good of course. I was hoping you'd take over third. The hot corner is a little too much for me."

"Well, I wouldn't say that," said Martin. The two men stood awkwardly kicking the dirt in front of themselves. McBride came to their rescue by handing his glove to Martin.

"Say, why don't you boys throw a few," and he gestured toward the sidelines.

Before long Martin was back into the game he dearly loved. McBride watched the two from the dugout. He was glad Martin had decided to come to practice. Not so much for the welfare of the team but more for Martin's own mental and spiritual health. He'd make sure to keep an eye on him and help him where and when he could.

Before it turned dark, McBride had a quick team meeting to introduce their new third baseman and go over the starting line-up for their next game. It was scheduled for six pm Sunday evening in Newcastle. After the meeting, Martin approached McBride.

"So, Don, seeing you at the AA meeting the other night was a surprise. Do you often go to them?"

"I do, Martin. I like to make myself available if anyone so desires. It's not my intention, though, to bring religion with me. In fact, we make a point of letting members know that all people, regardless of religion, are welcome to join the club.

"Well, thanks for the info, Don. Meg's waiting at home, so I better run. We'll talk again, though, and soon. Okay?"

"Any time Martin, and we'll see you Sunday evening for the game, if not before," he said with a wink, maybe as a reference that he'd expect him at church.

On his way home, Martin decided to drop into a local convenience store and purchase some cigarettes. As he was paying for his purchase, two men came into the store and Martin immediately recognized the larger of the two as Vince Daley, the doorman at the Legion.

True to form, Daley sneered at Martin as soon as he saw him and commented "Well, our local war hero. What's going on, hero? Not drinking with your war buddies and causing shit at the Legion tonight?"

"Look, Daley, I thought we could forget about what happened with John Norman at New Year's. It was an accident, so let it go at that, okay?"

"Bullshit! I don't care what the inquest ruled. You and I both know if you had minded your own business he wouldn't have died. And now I've lost my job as a result of your interference. You owe me, England!"

"I owe you nothing." He reached into his pocket for his wallet to pay the store owner, George MacDiarmid, for his purchase.

"Don't turn your back on me, hero. You sucker-punched me the last time, and it won't happen again." Just as Martin turned around, the big man swung at him. The next thing Martin knew he was lying on the floor of the shop trying to come to his senses. In the meantime, Daley and his friend were leaving the store laughing to themselves. A *red* feeling came over Martin as he struggled to his feet. MacDiarmid came around from behind the counter and helped him up. Martin started to go after Daley, but he was held back by the owner.

"Never mind the guy, Martin. It's not worth it," George said. "Besides, there are two of them and you're bound to take a bad beating. I'll call the police if you want?"

"Nah, never mind, George. I'm okay," he said, rubbing his mouth. I'll just go home and take it easy."

"Say, I've got a pint out back. Care for a small nip?"

Martin hesitated for only a fraction of a second. "Well, that's not a horrible idea," he said.

George MacDiarmid's store was only a couple of blocks from Martin's house, but it was nine-thirty by the time he arrived home. And he was not sober. Nor was he looking very good. His upper lip was badly swollen where Daley had hit him, and his clothes were disheveled. When Meg saw him coming into their kitchen, she immediately ran to him. But when she smelled the alcohol, she started crying, not in sympathy but in anger and frustration.

"Oh Martin, look at you. How could you? I thought you had quit drinking?"

"Meg, I can explain everyth___."

"No Martin," Meg interrupted, "no more excuses. I just don't want to hear any more," and she ran upstairs.

Now what? Martin thought to himself. God, he really needed a drink. He went out to the back shed where he soon found the pint of rum he had carefully hidden away. And he drank all of what was left in the bottle.

~ * ~

Later that night he fell asleep on the couch in the den. It was Saturday evening, May 26, 1946, and Martin was in bad shape. His nightmares had returned, and he was not anywhere close to quitting his habit. His wife was now over six months pregnant with their first child and she was despondent.

Chapter Nine

SUNDAY MORNING arrived with a vengeance. Martin awoke on their couch with a hangover, and after splashing water on his face from the kitchen sink, he went outside to face the day. It was a beautiful morning. The sun was just rising, and birds were singing in the backyard trees. He recalled the previous night's activities all too clearly, and he berated himself for letting Vincent Daley goad him into the mess in which he now found himself. He decided to go for a walk by himself before Meg and his father came downstairs. He was not in the mood to hear a lecture from either of them, nor did he feel like going to church today or playing ball, for that matter. He simply wanted to be alone.

He walked along the train tracks leading to 'the Hollow' where Meg's family lived, thinking it would probably be good to go for a walk along the Shore Road and maybe even row over to Middle Island.

Nobody would know where he had gone, and maybe that would be a good thing. The thought simply made itself known in his mind. Although it was a warm morning, Martin shivered involuntarily.

~ * ~

John and Becky Bradford were looking forward to their first child. Their baby was due in September and John was extra careful about every little step Becky took. They were presently walking along the Shore Road themselves, on their way to spend some time with John's uncle Doug. It was still early in the morning and the road was basically empty of any traffic.

Movement in the water to John's left caught his attention. At first, he thought it might be a large dog swimming over to the opposite side of the river, but when he looked more closely he realized it was much larger. It was definitely a person, and as he watched the man, his arms flailing, and it became apparent the swimmer was in trouble.

John wasted no time in racing over the bank to the river's edge, discarding his outer clothing and his shoes as he ran, then he dove into the water. John Bradford was a strong swimmer, and he set out toward the struggling target using long, forward strokes. Halfway to the drowning man he passed a dory which had taken on water and was partially submerged. It was the same old boat in which Martin had upset the other week. No doubt the man had been in the rowboat and was forced to abandon it when it began to sink.

John had almost reached the faltering swimmer when he realized with shock it was his brother-in-law. His efforts were strengthened, and he was able to get his arm around him. Slowly but surely, he brought him to the safety of the north side of Middle Island. They lay gasping on the beach, until finally they were able to talk. John asked,—"What in the world happened, Martin?"

"John, you saved my life brother. I'm just glad you didn't have to perform mouth-to-mouth resuscitation," he sputtered. As they lay on the island's sandy beach, Martin explained how he had tried in vain to scoop water out of the leaking dory with only his cupped hands until he became exhausted and desperately tried to swim to the island. They walked south through the trees toward the side of the island facing the shore, and his uncle's farm. Again, they rested.

Twenty minutes later, his sister Becky arrived with John's uncle Doug who brought with him two sets of dry clothes and a newer dory in the back of his half-ton truck. He quickly rowed over to the small island to get them.

Nothing was said as Doug rowed back to shore and they drove up the lane to his farmhouse. When the men were settled in the front room, Doug offered them a drink while Becky busied herself in the kitchen making coffee. Martin was quick to politely decline his, and this drew a questionable look from both Doug and John.

"The reason I was in the river in the first place lies in that bottle," he said. "Gentlemen, I've got a problem, and I need to quit. I hope you'll understand. John, I'm sorry to have put you and Doug to all this trouble. Again, thanks for saving me. I surely was not going to make it."

Martin then got up and said "Doug, you've been more than kind. I'll get these clothes back to you in due course. And thanks for the lift." He was long gone before Becky returned with coffees, leaving them with a number of unanswered questions.

By the time Martin returned home, the house was vacant, and he assumed Meg and his father had gone to church. Martin went up to his room, changed into his own clothes, and lay on his bed. With competing thoughts swirling around in his mind, he finally fell asleep. It was not until he heard Meg and Mr. England coming in and he awoke. He went downstairs and asked his father if he could have a private word with Meg. He added he would explain it all to him later.

They went for a walk and Martin tried to explain how yesterday, just after his talk with Reverend Don McBride at the ball diamond, he was feeling so good about himself; and how determined he was to make things right again. He also described the brush-up with Vincent Daley at MacDiarmid's store, and how easy it was to accept George's offer of a drink to help him get over the incident.

"I had to get away by myself this morning, Meg, and go for a walk. I had to think about things." He did not mention the near-drowning episode and hoped Becky and John would not say anything about it until he had another chance to talk with them. He needed to speak again with McBride. And then he remembered the game that he was supposed to be playing this evening.

He explained to Meg about tonight's game and asked her if it would be okay if he went to play. He stressed it was important to him, and she reluctantly agreed. At first, she was tempted to think this was just a way of avoiding having to talk with her about his actions yesterday, but the more she listened to him she realized this was something he needed to do. *As a matter of fact,* she thought *she would go with Martin to the game!*

Meg could understand why Martin loved the game. Not that his fondness for the overall atmosphere of the venue was foremost on Martin's mind, but she was sure it was part of why he was drawn to the sport. She heard the crack of the bat hitting a pitch, and the loud thud of the ball when it was thrown by the pitcher into the catcher's mitt. The yells of camaraderie from the players to each other and the heckling from the crowd to the umpire and certain players. It was special and enjoyable.

The game edged through eight innings with each team scoring two runs… going into the last inning, the score was still tied at 3-3.

Josh Freeman faced the bottom of the Tigers' line-up, and he was able to strike out the first two batters. The third hit a soft grounder to Martin who handled it easily and that ended the top half of the last inning.

When the Ironmen came to bat, Martin led off. Although he hit from the right-hand side of the plate, he smacked the third pitch sharply to left field, and this time he was able to make it around to second for an extra base. The Ironmen now had a man in scoring position.

The next two batters struck out and it was looking like they would be going into extra innings, especially with Josh now coming to bat. To this point, the star pitcher had not done much at the plate, and that was more or less expected. That meant nothing to the partisan crowd however, and they shouted loud cheers of encouragement to the new recruit from Boston as he worked the pitcher to a three and two count.

When the pitcher was halfway through his windup, Martin left second, and Josh swung his bat at the oncoming ball. The crowd heard a solid *crack!* and watched as the ball was hit soundly between shortstop and second base into midfield. The centerfielder took it on the first hop and threw the ball with great force and accuracy toward home in an effort to throw out the speeding Martin as he rounded third base!

By the time Martin reached the home plate area he knew it was going to be close! He slid toward the plate as Dutcher, the Newcastle catcher, caught the throw. In a cloud of dust, the plate umpire hesitated only a moment, then spread his arms horizontally and yelled "Safe!" as the winning run was scored! Their first win of the season! Josh Freeman and Martin England instantly became the town's baseball favorites!

As the fans were leaving the ballpark and the two teams had finished congratulating each other, Martin saw Meg approach him from behind the backstop. She looked lovely these days with the glow that accompanies expecting mothers. He asked her to wait for one moment while he had a quick word with Reverend McBride who was thanking the umpire and collecting bats.

"That was a good game tonight Don," he said. "I hope you didn't mind me going early on that pitch?"

"Not at all!! It was a good move! Without that two-second jump, you would've been out at home! Of course, if he had thrown a ball and Dutcher had in turn thrown you out at third, you'd have been riding the pines next game!" returned McBride as he laughed. In fact, Martin had caught Josh's eye prior to the pitch and both hitter and runner knew the "hit and run" was on!

"Could've/would've," said Martin with that big grin. "Say Don, do you think I could have some of your time tomorrow evening? Nothing to do with baseball, but it's about my problem," he said, lowering his voice as he looked around the crowd, then back at the minister.

"That would be fine Martin. When I didn't see you in church this morning, I thought something might have happened? So, say, seven tomorrow night then?"

"Sounds good Don, have a good night!" and Martin met Meg behind their dugout and they walked back home. Again, he felt he was heading in the right direction as far as his problems were concerned and thus, his hopes were fortified.

Chapter Ten

IT WAS close to seven p.m. when Martin walked up the steps of Reverend McBride's manse that evening. McBride promptly came to the door and welcomed Martin into his office. After coffees were poured and Mrs. Flaherty's donuts were served, Martin got down to business.

He repeated the same words to Don as he had to his father, and the minister listened carefully to him. After Martin finished, McBride went over to his desk and pulled a book from the drawer. He dropped it in front of Martin on the coffee table between them and Martin saw it was actually an original manuscript someone had apparently given or loaned to McBride. The title simply read *"Shell Shock: What the Doctors Did Not See."*

"Take this with you Martin. It's a document from a friend of mine in Nova Scotia. He just mailed it to me, and I think you'll find it interesting. It is written by him, and it details the plight of his uncle who suffers from this problem they call *shellshock*. My friend studied psychology at Acadia with me and he wrote his thesis on this topic. It's his intention to have it published, so I'll need it back as soon as you're finished with it.

"You will note a number of symptoms described by the writer that are very similar to your own. Over the years, the same thing occurred with many soldiers and participants. Sometimes they called it 'Battle Fatigue', but it's the same thing. We could talk further on this now if you'd like, but it would probably be more meaningful if you were to read the manuscript first. What do you think? I don't mean to postpone our talk, so it's up to you."

"Well, Don. What you say makes sense. Leave this with me then, and we can get together as soon as I read it, probably this week, okay?"

Martin left and went straight home. He was anxious to read the manuscript, and he could feel that things were gradually becoming clearer.

~ * ~

It was Thursday evening, May 30th, and Martin had finished reading the manuscript on loan to him by the Reverend. He took the book back to McBride and this time they had a lengthy talk about Martin's problems.

"So where do I go for help Don?" asked Martin.

"I think you should try some self-therapy to start with, Martin. There are a number of things you can do, but probably the most important is to look after yourself. Take up a new hobby, like martial arts, or writing. Keep your mind occupied as well as your body. And hey, the ball team is another good form of therapy. You're always thinking when you're on the field, and it keeps your mind busy."

"I get it Don, and I've been trying that. But it seems just when I think things are improving, something bad happens and I take a dozen or more steps backwards."

"I hear you," said McBride. "Unfortunately, there doesn't seem to be any quick answer for this thing. From what I can gather, I'm afraid you should be prepared for a long struggle Martin. But always know that there are a lot of people behind you, so stick with it."

Spring came and went, and Martin completed several jobs. He met a number of new people in the process and his friendship with Josh Freeman grew stronger as the ball team continued with a healthy winning streak into the summer.

In the meantime, Meg was kept busy tending to meals for her boarders. The extra income was a big help, and they were able to complete the renovations to the house that they had planned for some time. Her pregnancy was going well, and she was looking forward to her due date which was fast approaching.

Then they had a pleasant surprise. During the last week of July, they received a letter from Captain Jacobs asking them if they might be able to receive him for a visit the following week. It worked out perfectly, since two of the roomers had planned on taking vacation at that time and now there would be plenty of room in the house for Martin's long-time war companion.

Jacobs arrived in Chatham on Friday afternoon, August 14th. It was late in the day and Martin had left his job early, knowing his friend might land at any time. As Martin was listening to a ball game on the radio, he heard a car enter their driveway, and looking out the den window, he saw a figure getting out of a new Mercedes Benz. Sure enough, it was Jacobs. Martin called out to Meg, "Meg, Reg is here, come on down." They both ran out to greet his friend and Martin gave Reg a huge hug.

"Captain, sir, you are a sight for sore eyes. Welcome to the Miramichi, and say hi to my wonderful wife, Meg. And Meg, meet my longtime friend, Captain Reginald Jacobs."

Meg took Reg's hand warmly, "I'm so glad to finally get to meet you, Captain. Martin has been talking about you ever since he returned, and of course, he had mentioned you in many letters over the past number of years."

"Meg, and Marty, the first thing we've gotta do is get rid of this 'Captain' stuff! From now on it's Reg. Those days are over, thank God. Meg, it's great to finally meet the woman who captured the heart of my close friend here. And congratulations on the upcoming big day," Reg exclaimed as he gestured toward Meg's obvious condition.

"Well, let's all go inside and get comfortable," said Martin." We've got a great deal of catching up to do and I hope you're hungry, Reg. Meg has been cooking up a treat for you."

They all went into the den, while Meg put on some coffee and then they began supper, which, for the occasion, she had purchased a fresh ten pound 'bright' salmon. Not just an Atlantic salmon, but a Miramichi salmon. She decided to oven-bake the fish and now made preparations for it.

Reg, in the meantime, had run out to his vehicle and returned with a bottle of Canadian Club rye whisky. "Here we go Martin. Meg, come join us in a toast to our health." Then he saw the look that passed between Meg and her husband after she saw Reg holding the whiskey.

"Right," said Martin. "Let me get my drink," and he went to the fridge for a bottle of Ginger Ale soda that he kept on hand for the occasion. He grabbed three glasses, put ice in two of them and looked questioningly at Reg who shook his head and simply said "Neat please. Then he poured the whiskey for Reg and filled two glasses with the Ginger Ale for himself and Meg, who was not drinking alcohol while she was pregnant.

"To our health," he acclaimed.

They touched glasses and took drinks. Reg then looked at Martin in a meaningful way and held up his glass.

"Congratulations my friend. I was wondering if you might have taken steps of some kind. If this bothers you, I have no problems sticking to *your* preference?"

"I've got to get used to this, Reg. May as well start now, right?" And so the evening began with the two army pals recalling incidents from the years. They both knew some of their memories were best left unspoken, but for the most part, they were filled with chuckles and good thoughts of friends now gone, and places and events they would always cherish.

It was nearing 11:00 pm and Reg decided he better get some rest. They made plans to meet up tomorrow with John, James, and Gerald. Martin elected to refrain from getting into the business of his nightmares and strange day-visions or flashbacks as Reverend McBride called them. Maybe tomorrow he would bring up this subject with his friend.

Chapter Eleven

AFTER BREAKFAST the following day, Martin suggested they should all go to the beach for a picnic. It was another beautiful day, and the weatherman had promised it would be a scorcher. He reminded Meg he had a ball game tonight at 7:00 pm against Douglastown, and he invited Reg to the game.

After returning home from the beach and changing, the three of them went to the ball diamond in Douglastown. The quickest way there was directly across the river on the local ferry boat named *The Frances Ullock,* which could carry a dozen cars along with foot passengers.

When they made shore, they disembarked and drove west toward Newcastle. The ball diamond was only a short drive from the ferry slip and Meg and Reg were soon settled into their seats as the game got underway. He could see she was really proud of Martin. This held true when he came to bat and started off the inning with a base hit to right field.

"Martin's not a long ball hitter," Meg told him. "But he usually gets on base."

The Chatham Ironmen went on to win the game rather handily in a route of ten to three over the home team. A perfect way to end the day.

~ * ~

In the morning, Reg accompanied Martin, Meg, and George to church and on the way home, Meg said she had a sore back and was going upstairs to lie down for a while. It was only fifteen minutes later that she called out to Martin and asked him to come and see her.

"What is it, dear?" asked Martin as he entered their bedroom. He watched as she began to pack her things, very meticulously folding items of clothing and placing them in her suitcase.

"The baby is coming," Meg matter-of-factly stated. "My water just broke, so we'd best be on our way."

"My God!" exclaimed Martin. "Are you sure?"

Meg simply stopped what she was doing, turned to look at Martin, her eyebrows raised, hands on her hips.

"Yes, Martin. Ask Captain Jacobs if he wouldn't mind giving us a ride to the hospital. I'll be right down."

Martin was flabbergasted. He ran from the bedroom, down the stairs, and yelled at Reg, "Let's get moving, Reg, we're having a baby!"

~ * ~

Two hours later, Martin and Reg were anxiously pacing in the maternity waiting room of the Hotel Dieu Hospital in town. From one of the windows, Martin could see the racetrack with the ballpark in the center of it. He remembered he had a game tomorrow night, then immediately he wondered how the arrival of their new baby was going to impact their lives. *Holy shit!* he thought, *I'm going to be a father*! He ran across the waiting room to his friend and grabbed him by both of his shoulders.

"I'm going to be a father!" he shouted at Jacobs, a huge grin spreading across his face. Just then, Dr Blake came into the room. Martin introduced the doctor to Reg and the doctor gave them a big smile and extended his hand to Martin.

"Congratulations, Martin. Meg is doing fine, and you are now the father of a healthy baby boy. If you'd like to see them, come this way." When they entered Meg's room, she was holding the baby and smiled warmly at the men when she saw them. Martin came over to her, kissed her as she passed the infant to him. He was amazed at how perfect the baby looked. He studied every little finger and toe, the full head of hair, the bright eyes which seemed to look directly at him …

Martin carefully carried the baby in his arms over to his waiting friend and proudly extended the child in full view to Jacobs. "May we present *Jacob* George England! What do you think of this guy, Reg?" and he held Jacob closer to Reg so he could get a good look at his newborn namesake. Reg was suddenly overcome by the beauty of it all, and a tear came to his eye.

"He's beautiful, folks! Just beautiful!" said Reg, gently passing the child back to Meg.

Meg and Jacob were in the hospital for another five days before they were allowed home. By that time, Martin had built a crib for the infant and Reg had purchased several toys which included a baseball glove, a bat, and a ball. Meg could hardly move without one of the men getting in her way. Even Mr. England was getting into the act of wanting to hold Jacob, rock him to sleep, take him for short walks in their stroller, and clumsily try to feed him.

By the end of the third week of Reg's vacation, Martin realized he had not said a single word to Reg about any of his 'problems'. For whatever reason, the nightmares never returned, nor did the flashbacks. Rather than bring up the matter with him, he let it ride.

Before leaving, Reg wanted to fit a day of salmon fishing into his time here, so he arranged a trip with John Bradford to the Little Sou'West Miramichi River. And all too soon it was time for Reg to leave and return to the drudgery of corporate law as he described it to Martin. He promised to keep in touch with them and write as often as time allowed. Upon leaving, he gave a small present to Meg along with a card.

After his Mercedes left the lane, Meg showed the card to Martin. Inscribed on the inside of it were simply the words "Thank you for all the generosity provided during my visit. Please accept this gift as a token of my appreciation. Sincerely, Reg." Inside the card was a personal cheque for one thousand dollars.

"Good Lord, Martin, how can we accept this?" she exclaimed.

"Don't worry, Meg. Reg would never have us *not accept* this. I know he really enjoyed his stay with us. Besides, he's doing very well for himself in Montreal. I'll write him a note of thanks tonight. We can put this to good use." That night Martin penned a letter of thanks to his friend in Montreal and mailed it the next day. That summer they had the house placed on a foundation, a new furnace was installed, and Martin painted the exterior of the house.

~ * ~

The late summer fair was in full swing and as usual, Meg's uncle Doug had several entries in the livestock section, including two calves and a boar. In addition to displays of home-baked goods, there were crafts of all designs, rides for all ages, and games of chance. Each night there were the sulky horse races, or harness racing as it was known, a crowd favorite which drew competitors from all across the Atlantic Provinces. A dance with live music ended each night.

On the Friday toward the end of the fair, Martin and Josh had taken Meg and Marion Johnson, Josh's friend, to the dance in the main building. It was an exceptionally warm evening for late August, and they were sitting outside at a picnic table getting a breath of fresh air, enjoying their usual Ginger Ale sodas, minding their own business.

As they began to return into the building, an older model car rolled into the parking lot next to where they had been sitting, and three unsavory men jumped out of the vehicle. As they made their way toward the entrance they were staggering, cursing, and being generally obnoxious. Martin then realized one of the men coming his way was Vince Daley, and he had spotted Martin as soon as he reached the steps to the dance hall.

"Well, look it here boys, if it ain't our local war hero and his black playmate," sneered Daley.

Martin grimaced to himself and softly spoke to Josh, "Pay no mind to him Josh, he's not worth it. Meg, why don't we just go get a coffee down at Ben's," and the four of them turned to leave the area.

"Yeah, that's right hero, run away and hide with the women," said Daley sarcastically.

Martin was starting to experience that familiar *red mist* encompassing his vision and thought process. The same rage came back to him that had happened the last time he was confronted by Daley in MacDiarmid's store. The same thing also happened with poor John Norman on Mrs. Ramsay's veranda roof. He simply wanted to strike out at this monster who was in front of him, baiting him on, and now leering at Meg.

"Hey there girl, how about comin' in and havin' a dance with a *real* man," Daley slurred at Meg, giving her a wink. She returned an angry look at Daley and moved to step around him. Daley raised his arm to stop her and Martin was suddenly in his face.

Over the summer months, Martin had taken Reverend McBride's advice and he had abstained from drinking. He had also taken on a 'side' hobby by enrolling locally in a *Tae Kwon Do* class as a form of therapy for his illness. He was a natural athlete and in good physical condition, not only from his war time experience, but also from his outdoor work and his busy baseball schedule. As a result, he adapted easily to the martial arts sport and was considering becoming an instructor in his spare time. Daley was not aware of this.

"Daley, you had better leave before I have to hurt you," he said to the drunk.

"Don't make me laugh, hero. You know what happened the last time we met. Want some more of the same?" He started his move at Martin, but before he knew what was happening, Martin had thrown him over his back and Daley now lay prone on the ground looking around himself, clearly befuddled. Martin glanced warily at Daley's two cohorts, but there was no need for any concern there. They were both too drunk to offer any resistance, plus they had just seen their friend, a man of considerable size being easily tossed by the smaller man now daring them to challenge him.

The two drunks staggered over to Daley, lifted him off the ground, and slowly returned to their vehicle.

Josh looked with admiration at Martin. "Man, where or when did you learn how to do that?" he said, referring to the move on Daley.

"I've been taking lessons in *Tae Kwon Do* over the summer, Josh. This kind of sport can come in handy, like just now. So, if you're interested, I can teach you some of the moves."

"That'd be swell, Martin, whenever you're free," said Josh and they agreed to get together every so often at the TKD center to practice.

Both Meg and Marion were happy to have the three drunk men put in their place without injuries to their partners. Martin, however, was thinking deeply about the situation and he was concerned. He would wait until they got home and then discuss it further with his wife in private. All the way home, Martin kept replaying the incident with Daley and his two cronies. He was baffled by his own reaction to the harassment by the drunks and also surprised by the swift way in which he had managed to put Daley down.

When they were home, Martin expressed his concerns with Meg. "You know Meg, I wasn't drinking tonight, yet I was overcome with the same rage against Daley as I was in previous incidents. On those occasions, either at the time, or just before they happened, I had been drinking. So why now, after I've quit? I just think there may be more involved here than only alcohol."

Meg was also concerned about his behavior, but she was careful not to give him the wrong impression. "Any girl would be forever grateful for having her partner stand up for her the way you did with that animal tonight, Martin, and I love you for that," she said. "But I agree with you. There is something happening and we need to look into it as soon as we can." Martin made a point of getting together again with McBride. Also, maybe he'd write Reg and seek his advice. He strongly felt that somehow there was a connection between his violent reaction to Daley tonight and his experiences in the War.

A cold feeling came over him and he shivered against Meg's body as he lay beside her, unable to find sleep.

PART II

HYPNOSIS

Chapter Twelve

THE FALL in Chatham had ended and winter, at least officially, was raising its ugly head. The winter solstice was two weeks away and while it was still early December, those who had lived for any amount of time on the river knew that snow could arrive any day now. And the physical presence of the white stuff defined the season, according to Miramichi folk, not some damn solstice.

Little Jacob, now three months old, was growing like a weed, and Meg and Martin were looking forward to their first Christmas with him. There had been no untoward episodes of Martin's illness since the last confrontation with Vince Daley. Martin had written Reg regarding the concerns he had but had not yet received any word back from his friend. Nor had he had an opportunity to speak with Reverend McBride.

If, in fact, alcohol was not the main driver behind the nightmares and day visions, flashbacks, etc., then that posed a whole different problem. *Was this a stage of insanity,* he wondered?

~ * ~

It was early in the morning on December 5th, and he was just about to call Reverend McBride when he heard a loud thump coming from the upstairs, like something heavy seemed to hit the floor. Then Meg called in a panic, "Martin, come quickly!"

He raced upstairs to find his father lying on the floor of his bedroom and he was deathly pale. Martin bent over his father and confirmed he was still breathing, then said to his wife," Call Doctor Blake, Meg. I'll get him on the bed."

As Martin picked him up, his father seemed to come around, but it was obvious something had happened. He was trying to talk to Martin, but his speech was incoherent, and the left side of his face was sagging, causing him to drool. When Meg came into the room, she immediately sensed that

Mr. England had just suffered a stroke. "Dr Blake is on his way," she said. "Martin, I think he has had or is still having a stroke. You tend to your father, and I'll take Jacob downstairs with me. I'll bring Dr Blake up here when he arrives." Martin stayed with his father and watched helplessly as the elderly man stared wordlessly back at his son.

Dr Blake was there within the hour, and it did not take him long to determine that this was, indeed, a stroke. He had lost the use of his left arm, and he would now walk with a pronounced limp from the effect of the stroke on his left leg.

When Dr Blake took his leave, it was still only 3:30 pm so Martin placed a call to Reverend McBride and explained the situation with his father. Don said he was available to come over, but Martin declined the offer, wanting to simply get some rest himself and see how things worked out. He would stay home for the remainder of the week since the only work he had going at the moment was a small job for a customer who was presently vacationing in Florida. He would not be returning until the spring; the job could wait.

Martin busied himself helping Meg. To that end he cleaned the floors and prepared supper for the roomers. As he was putting a chicken in the oven he heard a knock at the door, and when he opened it he was overcome with joy to see Captain Reginald Jacobs standing there, hat in one hand and a suitcase in the other.

"Hello Martin, I hope I'm not too late for supper?" said Reg playfully, and the two old friends strongly embraced each other.

"God, Reg, this is wonderful. Meg, come here quick, we've a visitor."

Meg came downstairs with little Jacob, and she was also extremely pleased to see Reg standing in her kitchen. After long hugs, they all went into the den where Reg held the child who was a little shy at first, then gradually wouldn't stay away from his Godfather. Reg couldn't get over Jacob, how happy and healthy he looked. He kept holding him, tickling his chin, and making baby noises with him. The mood suddenly changed, however, when Martin had to relate the bad news about his father to Reg.

"Reg, you would have no way of knowing of course, but Dad just suffered a stroke earlier today. In fact, Dr Blake was here and left about an hour ago. Around eight this morning I heard a thud from the bedroom upstairs, raced up there, and found him on the floor. Dr Blake has just left."

"God Martin, how awful. Obviously, you have your priorities happening. I'll get a room at the Touraine Hotel. Is there anything I can do?" said Jacobs.

"No Reg, he's on some medication and a new diet, but that's about all we can do. Hopefully he will regain control of his speech and his left arm in the near future," Martin said. "And you can forget about the Touraine. We've plenty of room here and you are absolutely welcome. The truth be known Reg, your calm and professional attitude is required here, now more than ever," he added.

Reg held Jacob and listened carefully while Martin was telling him about his father, all while little Jacob was busy pulling at his hair.

"Reg, I guess the little guy has taken a liking to you. But you can't have him… we kinda like him too," he said jokingly. "You've never said, but what's with your own situation, not to be prying? Anybody special in your life at this time?"

"Well Martin, I guess I can tell you now. Since coming back from overseas, I've met a lady. Her name is Peggy, and she's wonderful. We're thinking of getting married, but neither of us has committed to an actual date for the event just yet. I did give her an engagement ring for Christmas last year and we're waiting for the right time to make it official, I guess. Seeing this guy makes me want to get married tomorrow. So, what's happening with yourself, Martin? Are you okay? After reading your letter I came here as soon as I could. How can I help?"

"Reg, I didn't expect you to pack up everything and show up at our door just like that!" he said, snapping his fingers. "Now don't take me wrong. We love you and it's great to have you here, but you have a partner now. You should be at home with your Peggy."

"Peggy is a very understanding woman, Martin. Plus, she is well aware of the unusual bond between us and she knows I had to make this trip."

Feeling relief that he was not being an albatross on his friend's shoulders, Martin then related all the incidents again to Reg ending with the fact that he was still experiencing them despite having quit drinking. He was able to say that, although the summer was uneventful, he did manage to get into another fight with his old-time foe Vince Daley in the early Fall.

Reg looked at Martin seriously and explained to his friend. "I've kept in touch with some of the brass from our regiment over the past couple of years Martin, and believe it or not, this business of your flashbacks to the war, feelings of rage, and all that you described is not unusual. Typically though, the majority of problems experienced by the others got written off to alcohol addiction. I'd like to take this further. I know a gentleman who is a medical doctor in Montreal, and he is very interested in this phenomenon. He has been studying cases and providing various forms of treatment over the past year. Indeed, he's had some remarkable success in several difficult situations. Would you be prepared to make a visit to see him?"

"Well yes, I guess so. But the fact is Reg, work for me has slowed down coming into winter and we may have to wait until spring when I expect things should improve financially. Would that be okay?"

"Don't worry about that aspect of it, Martin. You can stay at my place while seeing the doctor. Plus, my law practice can certainly afford another air ticket. It shouldn't take too long. I expect my friend will want to get a history of these episodes from you. He mentioned different forms of treatment that he uses. Like deep hypnosis, cognitive association, and assigning various types of creative hobbies, things of interest to keep the mind occupied. Probably he'll be able to give you a form of therapy that you will be able to do yourself at home. What do you think?"

Martin deferred to his wife. "Meg, what do *you* think of Reg's offer?"

"I think you should go to Montreal Martin, as soon as possible. I'll stay here and look after the baby and your father. I'm sure James or Gerald can give me a hand if I need it. And the sooner you go, that is if this doctor is able and willing to see you, then the better the chances will be that you can be back for Christmas."

With their decision made, Reg then made a call to Montreal and spoke with his doctor friend who agreed to meet with Martin at the first opportunity.

And so it was decided that Martin and Reg would return to Montreal the following week. "After all," Reg said, "I've got to have a bit more time with Jake here, right Jake?" The baby all this time was simply resting in his mother's arms, listening to the grownups talking, and taking everything in. He now looked at Reg and gave him a big toothless grin, holding his arms out as a clear invitation to be held. And just like that, Reg had unwittingly initiated the baby's nickname. He held his arms out to the tyke and said to Meg, "Hey Mom, let Reg hold Jake for a while." Martin smiled at his friend holding his son.

"You know Reg, it's too bad life wasn't always this good. It seems the only time I experience problems with this thing is when I run into problems with people. You know, like confrontations, anything of a threatening nature, or maybe something traumatic like a death in the family."

"Life will always have its bad turns, Martin. So, we better be able to figure out how to deal with them when they come up. By the way, the doctor's name is Michel LeBlanc, and he's supposed to be very good at what he does." Martin somehow sensed his friend was picking his words carefully as he spoke with him.

"I'm not sure if you are aware of this Martin, but Michel was also in Italy during our time there. I don't think you had a chance to ever see him since he was in a different outfit from ours. I'm looking forward to having him see you." Jacobs looked curiously at his friend as he said this.

"Roger that, Captain," said Martin. "Say, are you up for a roast chicken dinner?"

"Ah, is the Pope Catholic?" Jacobs retorted.

Then Martin called out to tell the roomers who had just come home from work that supper would be ready in about a half hour. Shortly they were downstairs, and Martin introduced them to the Captain. In a matter of minutes, they were playing partners in a card game of *Auction 45* while dinner was cooking.

Chapter Thirteen

MARTIN HAD been to a number of major European centers in his time overseas. Places such as London, Paris, Rome, and Amsterdam. Plus, he had seen many other smaller cities across the continent during the war. The cosmopolitan aura of Montreal, the Quebec metropolis, brought him back to that time. He was aware that Jacobs was able to speak French and again he was impressed with the man's abilities as they sped along St Catherine Street and headed for Decarie Boulevard. It was the second week of December and snow had arrived in Montreal. All of the stores in the city were decorated for Christmas and the holidays were in full swing.

Jacobs's Mercedes sports car was not the best vehicle for traveling in winter conditions and Martin was grateful that Jacobs had flown to Moncton from Montreal on this trip rather than attempting the fourteen-hour drive as he had done on his previous visit to Chatham in the summer.

After landing at Dorval Airport, they had gone to get his vehicle in long-term parking, then they were on their way into the city. They were only a few blocks now from Dr LeBlanc's office, and Martin was excited to meet this man who might be able to rid him of whatever was causing his mental problems.

They took Queen Mary Rd off Decarie, then Cote-des-Neige Rd where they soon stopped at a newly built health clinic. It appeared to contain a dozen or so individual practices such as psychiatric offices, psychologists, and several family physicians.

"Ah," said Jacobs, looking at his watch as they entered the building. "Just about fifteen hundred hours. We're right on time." They walked up to the receptionist's desk and Jacobs introduced themselves, asking to see Dr LeBlanc. They had only been sitting for five minutes when they were greeted by a man no more than forty-five. He was tall with an angular, clean-shaven face that contained an engaging smile. Lines at the corners of his eyes, however, betrayed the years he had spent overseas and gave him an added sense of maturity. His light brown hair was cut short, lending him a military look.

"Reg, good to see you again," the doctor said to Jacobs, extending his hand in greeting. "And this, I presume, is your good friend Martin England?" again the proffer of a cordial handshake to Martin.

"Doctor, I am very pleased to meet you," said Martin. "Captain Jacobs and I go back a few years. He tells me you may be able to help me with a problem I've had since the War?"

"I hope so, Martin. Let's go into my office and get comfortable where we can discuss it fully. Is it okay if Reg joins us? I know that both of you are very close and that you have shared a number of traumatic experiences overseas together. Perhaps, as an introductory session, Reg, you can be of assistance in providing details that Martin may not recall. Does that sound okay with you Martin?"

"Sure, no problem, Doctor." Martin failed to see the facial exchanges between Jacobs and LeBlanc as he was led ahead of them into the doctor's office.

When they had all settled into comfortable high-backed leather chairs, Dr LeBlanc started off the discussion.

"Martin, what Reg has described to me about your illness sounds a lot like a certain mental condition that has afflicted many veterans over the years," then LeBlanc held a hand in a 'stop' position and added, "No, let me correct that. Not only war veterans, but many *other* people who complain about similar symptoms. You know, regular citizens. Even people who have never gone to war. And they cover the demographic spectrum as to age, gender, race and nationality. The one thing they all have in common is being subjected to, or witnessing, horrible events that they would not normally ever experience in their otherwise day-to-day lives: things like violent deaths, extreme car accidents, severe child abuse, these sorts of events, you see?"

"Yes, I understand, Doctor. Captain Jacobs and I have certainly experienced some nasty situations over there, correct Reg?"

"Roger that Martin. Maybe you can talk a bit to the doctor about the ones you feel were the worst. I'll add or modify where you think you might need help. Okay, Doctor?" Again, Jacobs and LeBlanc shared a look that was missed by Martin.

"Good idea. Let's proceed."

~ * ~

The first incident Martin discussed was the event in Italy when the two of them had captured the Observation Post. Unfortunately, Martin and Jacobs had necessarily killed one of the soldiers who was in the OP at the time.

As Martin recalled, there were three enemy soldiers in the structure when Martin and his Captain had thrown their grenades. Martin described to the doctor how he had climbed the ladder leading to the top of the OP and had seen the boy lying in the corner, his body savagely torn apart by shrapnel, clearly dead.

"Anything else you recall about the event?" asked Dr LeBlanc.

"Not really, Doc. Captain and I then relayed info to our Company, and we watched with our binocs as our boys four hundred yards behind us trained their guns on the enemy with accuracy. We then rejoined our troops."

Reginald then walked over to stand face on with Martin. He held him by his shoulders and spoke softly to him. "Martin, I'm so sorry, but all this time I wasn't aware you have been carrying a different version of this horrific event in your memory.

"You see, there were actually *four* young men in that building, one in each corner of the room. Yes, one of them had been lethally injured by shrapnel from our grenades. And it is also true that two of the boys were clearly in shock, sitting as they were in their urine. But as you ascended the ladder ahead of me, a fourth young man crept over to confront you as you entered through the trap door at the top level. He had just raised his rifle and was about to shoot you when I fired before he did. He died instantly, and yes, he was only a boy. I'll never forget the look in the young man's eyes when he realized he had been hit."

"God Reg! Doctor, is it possible that I can just block something like that out of my mind as if it never happened?"

"I'll try to explain to you what happens, Martin. The mind is a very fragile thing, yet it is also extremely adept at protecting itself by doing what it did for you that day in Italy. It can tuck some awful event away in a sort of drawer that you can keep closed if you want. You probably have a number of these special drawers for different traumatic happenings.

"With your permission, I'd like to explore these drawers with you through the process of hypnosis. It's quite possible that by facing the events head on, you can receive some relief. Reg here can help us recall certain things throughout the process as he did just now. What do you think?"

"Is it safe? I mean, I won't go insane, will I?"

"The procedure is done all the time Martin. It's completely safe under professional supervision."

"Then let's do it," Martin said.

"Let me check my workload," Jacobs said, and he consulted a small book from his jacket pocket. "It's best to schedule enough time to do this right, so I may have to clear my desk up first. Let's see, today's Monday, December 9th. Doctor, can you be available to start a series of sessions with Martin this Thursday, the 12th? It would be great if we could get him home for next Friday, the 20th. I'm sure he has plenty to do around the house with Meg at this time of year."

"That shouldn't be a problem, Reg. When you called me earlier about this, I figured it was important, so I had my secretary clear my appointments from now until after Christmas," said the doctor.

"So, Martin, I'll see you Thursday morning, say, 0900 hours?" he addressed Martin as he showed them out the door. On the way out, he took Reg aside. "Reg, including the OP incident we just discussed, if you wouldn't mind, perhaps you could sketch out several of the more traumatic incidents you can recall that Martin experienced over there. And the more detail, the better. This could get scary for him, so your presence here with us will be important."

Reg had thought this might be required, and while he was ready to help Martin where he could, the exercise was also going to be a difficult process for him as well. *Some things may be just as well left unsaid,* he thought. *He'd play it by ear for now and see how it all played out. Who knew, maybe he could benefit from this at the same time…*

Reg and Martin arrived at Reg's downtown apartment just off St

Catherine's Street on Stanley. It was a beautiful place, featuring three large bedrooms, a modern kitchen that led into a formal dining area, followed by a den/office.

"So Martin, what are some of the incidents that you want to explore under hypnosis with Dr LeBlanc?" Reg asked as they took a break from one of their cribbage games.

"Well, for one, we can revisit the OP event. Also, that time we were attacked by a *Messerschmitt* fighter plane in Belgium bothers me quite frequently, so I think we should talk about that. There are others, Reg. Sometimes I receive images of a woman that has been raped. It comes to me now and then in a very disturbing way. Also, there is a specific scene I recall where there are many corpses involved. Too many to count. God, it's awful...," his voice trailing off.

Interesting, thought Reg. *The one main event he was certain Martin would want to get into was not on his agenda?* Jacobs decided to keep this information under his hat for the moment. They spent the rest of the evening in small talk surrounding the weather, Reg's current case files, and what Martin planned to pick up for Meg and Jake as Christmas presents.

~ * ~

Tuesday morning Reg called his secretary, and they reviewed his current case files, instructing her to arrange postponements on them for the following week. The rest of the day and on Wednesday they took time to visit Old Montreal and several shopping areas; Martin picked up a nice winter coat for Meg, and a snow suit for Jake.

After coffees on Thursday morning, they were both anxious to meet again with Dr LeBlanc and begin the hypnosis sessions.

Chapter Fourteen

THE LIGHTING in Dr. LeBlanc's office was dim. Curtains on the only two windows had been drawn and only a single table lamp was left on to service the room. Martin was lying comfortably on a tilted easy chair and Dr LeBlanc was sitting beside him. A soft recording of a trickling brook could be heard from a speaker somewhere across the room and Captain Jacobs was seated in a corner apart from Michel and Martin. A tape recorder had been set up by the doctor to allow future referencing, and when Michel nodded to Reg, the captain activated the machine.

Dr LeBlanc began the session by assuring Martin he was in a safe place, always speaking softly to him, providing him with verbal images of tranquility. Michel began counting down from twenty, suggesting Martin would be sleeping by the time he reached zero. Martin was fully under at the count of six.

With notes that Jacobs had compiled close at hand, the first incident Dr LeBlanc tackled was the capture of the Observation Post in Northern Italy. He made a point of stressing that if it had not been for his captain's quick actions, they both might not be alive today. He also pointed out the importance of the work they had both accomplished that day, and how they had contributed toward the success of that particular battle in Italy, enabling the Allies to recapture the city of San Fortunato and the Rimini Ridge. He ended the session by providing a post hypnotic suggestion that Martin would hereafter not be bothered by the memory of the event. He would, however, feel compassion for the death of the young German boys, and they would no longer be able to haunt him.

All told, the session lasted approximately two hours. After the trance was terminated by LeBlanc, Martin awoke in a completely refreshed and relaxed state. He told Martin it would take several weeks to see what, if any, direct benefit had been gained from today's session. Ultimately the only true measure of success would simply be the absence of the terrors he had been having to date.

With that, the two headed back to Reg's apartment to get ready for the next session scheduled for tomorrow at 10: a.m.

~ * ~

When Reg and Martin arrived at Dr LeBlanc's office on Friday morning, they again went through the process of making Martin comfortable in his easy chair. Once the doctor was satisfied Martin was in the proper state of mind, he began talking with him, again giving him suggestions and guiding him toward the incident that involved the attack on their troop by a German plane.

Armed with information given to him by Jacobs, Dr LeBlanc spoke to his patient. "Martin, it is now two pm and you are marching outside Antwerp on a cold day in November as your Company makes its way to the Netherlands. Literally out of the blue, a rogue German *Messerschmitt* fighter plane appears ahead of you on the horizon, only a mile away. The road on which you are traveling is located on plain topography without any trees, ditches, nor buildings of any kind from which to seek cover. What happens Martin?"

Immediately Martin is immersed in the event as if it were in real time. His face became distorted, and he jumped from his chair and laid prone on the floor, his arms extended, bent at the elbows so as to protect his head. He cried out in alarm and after only ten or fifteen seconds he jumped to his feet.

"You bastard!" he screamed. "Come back here, you no good bastard! I'll kill you! I'll kill you!"

At that point LeBlanc interceded and brought him out of his trance. Amazingly, Martin immediately became totally calm and wondered why the two with him seemed so concerned.

"What did I just do?" he asked, smiling sheepishly.

"Martin, you were just exhibiting one of the most violent reactions to a dangerous situation that I've ever seen from you before," said Reg. "I know that German plane was responsible for the deaths of two of our chaps and several were wounded. In fact, as I recall, you suffered a minor wound yourself, didn't you?"

"As it happened, I was grazed by a round from the aircraft's machine guns." He unbuttoned his shirt and showed Reg and the doctor his left arm. The inside of his left bicep had a white strip of skin approximately a half inch wide and three inches long running horizontally across the surface. Because his hands had been clasped together over the back of his head as he lay on his stomach, it could easily be visualized where the bullet had narrowly missed striking Martin's head that day.

"Martin, you were a very lucky man that day," said Dr LeBlanc.

"Well, yes. I suppose in a way I was lucky," he agreed. "But in another sense, I wasn't, considering I was shot at and almost killed," he concluded, clearly still upset at the memory.

Then Jacobs interceded. "But you were in a war Martin. What would you expect? People get shot when they go to war. If they're lucky, they don't. It's as simple as that," said Reg. Martin could see Reg was somewhat upset. "Maybe you should have been giving thanks that day to some higher power, rather than cursing someone who was only doing his job."

Now, feeling contrite and seeing the situation a little differently, Martin agreed with his captain. "Yes sir, of course you're right," he said.

LeBlanc then came back into the conversation. "Feelings of contrition will always be more helpful to a healing mind as opposed to anger," offered Michel. "So perhaps today's meeting has provided you with some benefit, Martin. I think we're making some progress. Can we try another session tomorrow?"

"I'm willing if you are, Doctor," agreed Martin. Again, the two went back to Reg's apartment to spend the remainder of the day going over the past two sessions with LeBlanc. Reg had been hoping they would have been able to complete the therapy by now, but it appeared an extension of a couple of days minimum would be required.

Martin and Reg sat in the cozy den that was now familiar to Martin. A fire blazed warmly in the hearth and coffee was brewing as they relaxed. "So, Martin," began Reg. "What other events do you think may be causing you problems? You know, there may even be one or more incidents that were traumatic enough to be completely blocked from your memory.

"Really, Reg, there are only two other situations that come to mind. One has something to do with a woman who had been raped. The memory is very vague, and I can only partially recall being somewhere near Rome. I forget who was with me, nor do I remember where or when it occurred.

"The other, is a horrible scene of many corpses surrounding me. Again, I'm not aware of where or when this happened, if at all. Perhaps hypnosis will reveal these missing segments."

It was ten o'clock Saturday morning, and LeBlanc had just finished the pre-scene suggestive portion of the session with Martin.

"Martin," Dr LeBlanc started. "You are somewhere near Rome, and you witness a woman in distress. Can you describe the situation?"

Inexplicably, Martin began crying. His body racked with his sobs, his hands covering his face, and he began telling the story.

~ * ~

In early December 1944 The Princess Patricia Light Infantry still had Martin and Jacobs on loan from the 3rd Field Regiment when they made camp outside Tivoli, only 20 miles from Rome. One afternoon, a number of the men decided to visit the nearby famous Eternal City.

Their first stop was a pub in Tivoli on Via Rasella, a small side street on which a very nasty ambush had been conducted by the Italian partisans against the Nazis earlier in March of that year. A bomb had been exploded by the underground resistance fighters, successfully killing ten of the Germans. Unfortunately, the next day the Nazis had retaliated by publicly executing one hundred civilians the following day.

With morbid thoughts on their minds, from here Martin and Carrigan made their way on foot to seek out other bars in the neighborhood. Before long they came across three American G.I.'s who had just come out of an alleyway. They were loud and drunk, and they literally bumped into the two Canadians as they exited onto the street.

Martin immediately sensed these guys were not fit to wear their uniforms. He had run across men like this from all of the Allies. The Brits, Aussies, even his own country. There was just something about the look he received from the larger one of the trio. It was, like, *Yeah, I'm a badass, Canuck. Wanna do something about it?'*

The guy winked at his buddies and the three left, laughing and punching each other in a macho way, as they reeled down the cobbled street.

"C'mon Carrigan, let's get out of here," said Martin, but the young man had already started his way down the alley. Suddenly Martin heard a loud gasp as Carrigan shouted for him to come quickly.

Martin could not believe what he saw:

A young girl, perhaps sixteen or seventeen, was laying on the dirty stones of the back alley. She had been severely beaten and raped. Her simple peasant-style blouse had been ripped from her upper body, exposing her bruised breasts, and her skirt lay beside her, enabling Martin to clearly see a number of wounds to her torso where she had apparently been struck with a weapon of some sort, probably a pistol.

The face of the young girl was the worst though. It too had probably been pistol-whipped, leaving her left eye hanging from its socket, her nose broken, and her lips in shreds exposing several broken teeth. Blood had coagulated beneath her head from a large open wound.

Martin bent down to the broken figure and tried to find a pulse from her neck. He felt nothing, and her body was lifeless. She was clearly dead.

"Martin, there's nothing we can do for her. We've got to go," Carrigan pleaded.

"But we can tell the authorities, those assholes killed that young girl, Carrigan. They can't be allowed to get away with this!" He jumped up from the body and ran out to the entrance. There was no sign of the GIs. Carrigan walked up to him, clearly upset.

"This kind of shit happens in war Martin. Get used to it. There's no way any Italian official is going to bring any of their conquering allies to court over this. They'll simply deny it. They might even turn the tables around to incriminate us, for Christ's sake," cried Carrigan as he looked around cautiously for anybody that might have overheard them. He tugged at Martin's shirt and hauled him away from the alley. Martin had never mentioned the incident to another soul.

It had been buried in the depths of his mind.

~ * ~

When Martin awoke, he saw Dr LeBlanc and Reg, sadly staring into his eyes. He started to cry, aware of the reason. Only this time, he knew his tears were not only for the young unknown Italian girl who had been brutally raped and murdered in Tivoli one Saturday night in early December 1944. They were also shed in revulsion and hatred of himself, the young man from Chatham, New Brunswick who had elected to ignore the event for the past five years.

Reg quietly approached Martin and wrapped his arms around the younger man who was continuing to weep uncontrollably. "You can't blame yourself for this Martin," he said. "Yes, in retrospect, you should have gone to the authorities. Your friend from Princess *Pats* though, was probably correct in his assumption that not much would have been done to the offenders, even if they could have been found. However, you would have absolved yourselves from any further responsibilities regarding this horrible event had you done so. I'm sorry Martin."

There was nothing else to say. It was something Martin would have to live with.

Rather than returning home, they decided to stay at the doctor's office and conduct another session. It was not even noon and Martin was aware there was still an event that involved something about the image of many corpses that he had yet to face. Reluctant as he was, he preferred to get it done today, and the sooner, the better.

So the second session of the day commenced and in a matter of minutes, Martin was under another deep trance. Guided by LeBlanc, he found himself along with Captain Jacobs and a group of a dozen or more American infantrymen driving among a convoy of Bren gun carriers outside Malmedy, Belgium.

~ * ~

It was a bitterly cold day in early January. The U.S. troops to whom Martin and Jacobs, while still on loan to a platoon from the Pats, had been assigned to a troop of U.S. Marines who were exhausted. During the prior month, they had faced heavy casualties at the Battle of the Bulge in the forests of the Ardennes region of Belgium. As the outfit sped along in a column of Bren Gun carriers, one of the GIs shouted to the driver to stop the vehicle. He pointed toward a snow-covered field where they saw what appeared at first glance to be numerous dark shapes, maybe cattle laying in the snow, other smaller dark shadows moving in the air above them and on the ground around them. *How could that be?* Beef was at a premium and there was no way cattle would be left unattended to scavengers.

The convoy pulled to a halt as the men got out of their carriers and began a slow trudge through the snow into the field, apprehensive of what they were about to discover. Their worst fears were soon realized: standing over the first of the shapes, Martin saw the corpse a young man. It was obvious he had been shot in the head at close range. The others witnessed many other similar deaths. There were eighty corpses, and they all appeared to be American POWs. Their hands had been shackled and the majority of them had been systematically shot at close range, once behind the ear. Some had been shot while they were attempting to escape, others had been bludgeoned with blunt instruments, probably rifle butts. Due to the extreme cold temperatures, their bodies had not yet decomposed, so it was hard to say when the atrocities had occurred.

Afterwards, it was confirmed the bodies were all indeed American prisoners of war who had been captured on December 17th during the recent battle by the 6th Panzer Troop under Captain Joachim Peiper. During the counterattack by the Americans, the Germans were forced to flee westward and they simply did not wish to be burdened with the transportation of their prisoners.

~ * ~

The grisly sight of the numerous American corpses would remain locked in Martin's memory for the years to follow. Neither Doctor LeBlanc nor Reg Jacobs had anything to say about the incident that could bring ease to Martin's mind. It was hoped there might be some lessening of his feelings of dread, simply by reliving the experience together with the post-hypnotic suggestions made by LeBlanc. As to the results of Dr LeBlanc's work, it was similar to today's earlier session.

There was nothing more to be said.

The doctor did explain that there were things he could do to *manage* these recurrences if and when they presented themselves. They would discuss these steps at another session if he preferred.

Martin agreed to postpone any further talks on the matter.

He was looking forward to returning to normalcy…returning home to Meg and Jake.

PART III

RETURN TO CHAOS

Chapter Fifteen

MARTIN HAD just finished wrapping his Christmas present for Meg: the formal brown sable winter coat that he caught her peeking at appreciatively last week in their Sears Christmas 'Wish Book'. He was lucky to find the exact item in one of their stores while in Montreal.

Upon his return, he had given consideration to what the doctor had said about getting in touch with him concerning actions he could take to help prevent the nightmares and flashbacks from continuing. Frankly, he felt really great since the sessions, and he had no recurrences at all of any incidents since his visit there. So, with all the activities happening in the house surrounding Christmas, he decided to wait until the New Year and maybe contact LeBlanc at a later date.

Their tree was up and decorated in the living room, and Martin had even erected a small replica of it on their front veranda. A light snow was falling, lending a perfect Yuletide setting to their property.

His father entered the room just as Martin was pouring himself a coffee.

"Hi Dad. Meg and I are taking Jake over to see James and Audrey later tonight. John and Becky are going along with Helen so it should be a nice family gathering. Want to join us?" John and Becky Bradford had a new addition to their family in late September, a baby girl named Helen, so Jake now had a 'double' first cousin to play with. James and Audrey had started their family earlier. Three boys and one girl and they were all born before the War. No doubt they'd be around later tonight as well.

His father continued to struggle with the effects of the stroke he had suffered. While his speech had returned to normal, he still had a limp in his left leg and his left hand was curled in a permanent claw-like grip. Most of his time these days was spent listening to the radio and reading.

"No thanks, Martin. I think I'll have an early night. You folks enjoy yourselves. Say hello to everyone for me."

An hour later John was in the driveway with Becky and Helen. Meg bundled Jake up for the quick ride to James's house and they were soon on their way. The snow was now coming down harder and one occasion John had trouble negotiating a corner.

"Are they calling for much snow, Meg?" asked Martin. "If this keeps up, we'll have a tough time getting home."

"Hey guys, no need to worry," said John. "We'll keep an eye on the weather and if it looks like it's getting worse you can stay at our place." The Legion, where John worked as the custodian and lived upstairs with Becky and Helen, was only a stone's throw from James's house, so at least they could get that far going home. They could even walk from there if necessary. Meg thought it might be fun to stay at John's place, just to get away for a night.

They were at James's house in a couple of minutes and soon the close-knit family was enjoying a lovely evening simply listening to Christmas carols on the radio and singing along to their favorites. While the adults sang, Jake and Helen played together in a playpen that James had purchased some time ago when their own kids were younger.

After an hour, the toddlers were sound asleep, and the grownups played several rounds of cards. John checked outside at eleven, and he was concerned to see the snow was still falling in earnest, with close to eight inches down. Martin thought they should get on their way, so he and John bundled up the kids who were still half asleep, and they left for home before it became too risky to drive.

As they were returning to Martin's, and now about a block from James's home, the vehicle went into a sharp skid at one point. With that, the decision was made to go directly to John's at the Legion, thereby avoiding the need to navigate any of the hills necessary to reach Martin's home.

When they reached the Legion, it was nearing midnight and still snowing. They quickly carried their two little ones up the front steps of the lower hall, but they were immediately taken aback to find their front door ajar.

"Well, this is strange, Beck," said John as he stepped through the unlocked door. "I'm certain I locked this after we left. Why don't you girls stay here with the kids while Martin and I check around."

The two men began to search the downstairs, planning to start with the bar area. As they stealthily made their way down a hallway, they could hear laughter and muted conversation. Later, thinking back, Martin realized they should have simply called the police right then and there. But they didn't.

John and Martin walked into the bar area and saw three men drinking beers while rummaging through the counter for cigarettes and whatever else they could find. Two cases of hard liquor stood on the bar countertop in front of them, representing John's inventory for the next two months.

Strangely enough, Martin was not surprised to find that the largest of the men was Vince Daley. When he saw Martin, he sneered at him. "I don't believe it. You just keep getting in my way, England. Maybe it's time we settled this for good." he said menacingly, and he pulled a switchblade from his inside coat pocket. He snapped a small button on the handle of the weapon and a seven-inch lethal blade suddenly appeared in his hand.

Daley looked toward his two fellow thieves and smiled. They were apparently not expecting this kind of trouble, and they decided that flight was the best option for them at this point. They immediately took off down the hallway where the girls were waiting. Martin approached Daley.

"John, you go check the women and kids, make sure they're okay, then call the police," he said. "I'll have a talk here with Vince."

As John left the bar area, Daley smiled at Martin. "Do you think your Jap moves will help you now, England?"

He tossed the knife from his right hand to his left, then back again.

Martin crept around his foe in a circle, his arms extended as he walked on the balls of his feet. The different *Tae Kwon Doh* techniques came back to him like a forgotten dream. When Daley made his first thrust, the blade stung as it made a small cut across Martin's outstretched right hand. But it only lasted a second as adrenalin poured through Martin's veins and the familiar red rage filled his mind.

He easily side-stepped Daley's onward second rush and then he surprised the big man by running toward him, closing the gap and not giving his opponent room nor time to maneuver. When he was up close to Daley, he hit him hard in the kidney area with his right fist and then quickly moved behind him. He kicked Daley's right leg out from under him. As Daley fell, Martin leapt on top of him and attempted to grab Daley's arms. In the process, the knife Daley was holding had been turned inward and it slid noiselessly into the right side of Daley's neck.

When John came back into the bar, he looked with horror at Martin who was pulling the knife from Daley's neck. Blood was spurting everywhere, and in a matter of what seemed to be only seconds, Daley was dead.

"Oh God, Martin, what have you done?" John cried.

"John, it's not the way it seems!" exclaimed Martin. "He was trying to kill me. It was self-defense, John! In fact, I was trying to save him just now as you came in, I fell on him John, I, the knife, he ...." Martin's scrambled words fell away, and he dropped to his knees beside the body of Vince Daley, holding his own head in his bloody hands.

In a matter of minutes, the police were at the scene.

~ * ~

Christmas, 1946 was a calamity for Martin and his family. The cause of death to Vince Daley seemed obvious to all of the forensic people involved, which was exsanguination, or bleeding to death. They also immediately knew what led Daley's bleeding to death: a traumatic knife wound to his neck. His right carotid artery had been severed, and his trachea had been punctured. Unconsciousness had occurred in ten to fifteen seconds and death followed within a minute.

What remained unclear to the authorities, however, was the fashion in which the knife wound occurred. Reluctant as he was to do so, John had to provide his sworn statement saying that he saw Martin removing the knife from the victim's neck when he had returned to the bar. Martin did not dispute this salient fact.

Bradford also provided information in his statement that a fight had erupted between Martin England and the victim when he and Martin came upon Daley and two others during the commission of a robbery at the Legion. But that was all John could say in defense of his brother-in-law. He was not present when Martin and Daley were actually fighting.

After Martin and John gave their statements to the Town Police, Meg and Becky were also required to provide their own accounts, simply confirming where they had been prior to arriving at the Legion, what they had been doing, and the fact that the door was ajar and unlocked when they had arrived. They had stayed downstairs with the children as requested by their husbands who went upstairs to check things out. Martin was told there would be further investigation, and he was not to leave the province without first notifying the authorities.

Ironically, neither Martin, John, Becky, nor Meg noticed the small knife cut on Martin's right palm.

By the time the police had received statements from the Bradfords and the Englands, it was almost one-thirty on Christmas Eve morning. While the snow continued unabated, John poured stiff drinks for himself and Becky. Martin, however, declined as did Meg, and they made coffee.

Martin was beside himself with a number of conflicting emotions. Yes, he felt remorse at the death of this man who had for some reason been a thorn in his side since his return home; but rage was also present in his mind that Daley had brought such violence to his family, especially at this time of year. He also felt sorry for himself. Why was all this shit happening to him? Despite his best efforts, he couldn't seem to get his house in order. And what was going to happen to him now?

After some time, they all decided to go to bed. Before long, Martin was fast asleep, and he began to dream. It was something entirely new...

He dreamed of a place somewhere in Italy. Maybe it was Tuscany wine country. There was a German officer in the dream and a beautiful lady. Captain Reginald Jacobs was also a participant. Martin somehow knew there was something terrible about to take place in the dream, yet he was powerless to prevent it from happening. Thankfully, he awoke from the dream and saw on the bedside clock that it was five-thirty am.

At one point in the morning the snowstorm had stopped but it was not until after dinner that the town roads had been cleared enough to allow John to drive them home. Christmas Eve was spent at home, sitting close to the radio, listening to seasonal music. Martin, Meg, little Jake and George England considered themselves fortunate in many ways. They were in good health, they had a lovely home in which to live, plenty of food on the table, and more than enough love to go around. Yet Martin was aware these blessings were so very tenuous. He lived in constant fear that at any day it might all be taken away from him.

Things were not looking good. The police had begun their investigation into last night's affair and he was afraid of what was about to come as a result of their findings.

The warm lights from the Christmas tree and surrounding decorations in the England house did little to dispel the awful feelings of helplessness that now invaded the lives of Martin and his entire family.

Chapter Sixteen

HARRISON B Miller, QC placed the telephone back on its cradle and a large smile crept across his pale, angular face. He crossed his lengthy legs and laid them on top of his desk, folded his thin arms in a satisfied manner and leaned his frame against his high-backed chair. Miller was the Chief Crown Attorney for Northumberland County, and he was in a happy mood. It was late Friday, January 3rd, and he had just finished speaking with the Attorney General of New Brunswick, the honorable John McNair.

McNair had developed an ongoing friendship with Miller since the younger lawyer graduated from Law School at the University of New Brunswick some six years ago. At that time, Miller's father, Joseph Harrison Miller, was a well-known magistrate in the Provincial capital of Fredericton. Miller Sr. was also a friend of McNair's and a Conservative leaning adjudicator. He was responsible for many miscreants presently serving lengthy terms as guests at the Renous Federal Penitentiary.

Like his father, Harrison held similar political values. When possible, he sought maximum prison sentences regardless of the type of crime committed. For the past five minutes, AG McNair had been briefing the young Crown Prosecutor on the recent untimely death of a local man, one Vincent Daley. Miller was familiar with the case, and while he knew the facts surrounding the event were certainly not cut and dried, from what he had read it was certainly of interest. If it could be proven that a homicide had occurred, Miller could envision very favorable press coming his way should he be successful in trying such a case. Harrison B Miller was nothing if not politically ambitious, and his short talk with McNair had implied such a favor. McNair, of course, had his own political agenda in mind, given he was considering making a run for the nomination to lead the Conservative Party in this year's provincial elections later in November.

Even as late in the day as it was, Miller had no misgivings calling

Police Chief Theodore Reynolds. He brushed back the lock of thin hair that had an annoying habit of falling into his eyes as he picked up the phone.

"Ted, can you come over and see me right away? It's important."

Ten minutes later, the Chief sat at Miller's desk, and they began discussing the particulars of the England crime. Even at this early-stage Miller was convinced a crime had occurred. Daley's death was not the result of an accident.

"So Chief, as I see it, this Martin England chap has had a number of encounters with the victim since his return from the War in April 1945. He is known to be an abuser of alcohol, and he has been off and on regular employment, save for his modest attempts at taking over his father's fledgling house painting business.

"Certainly, his record in the infantry during the War is not outstanding. On the contrary, quite mundane, wouldn't you say? And I see since his return home he has gone out of his way to take up martial arts. Whatever for, one wonders?"

"But sir, as you know, there are witnesses to testify that this Daley fellow and two of his cronies were in the process of committing a theft of liquor at the time Martin and his brother-in-law arrived on the scene. It also would seem Daley started the altercation and produced a lethal weapon …"

"Well Chief, I believe I could argue England had the upper hand, having already brought Daley to submission through his knowledge and application of the martial arts in which he was a trained professional. No Chief, I submit England knew exactly at the outset how their fight was going to end. Plus, according to their statements, England and his brother-in-law supposedly snuck into the bar, unheard by Daley and the other two. One can assume they knew a theft was in process. Why then did they not immediately call the police and avoid the awful scene that followed?

"I'll tell you why Chief: because it was in England's nature to want to see this man injured, if not dead. He could thereby create the opportunity to free himself from any further aggravation from the victim."

Harrison was clearly enjoying his view of how he saw the whole affair being the perfect opportunity to further his career. He continued to address his Police Chief. "So, Chief, you have your work cut out for you. We shall need your detective to obtain whatever he can in the way of background checks against this England fellow. Perhaps his war records, a chat with his immediate supervisor, that sort of thing. Talk with the officers involved in the other skirmishes he had with the victim, see what their files reveal. And I'd like a word with the coroner along with the forensics people involved here."

Miller was quickly becoming enthralled with the case. He could almost hear the judge awarding his decision of 'Guilty' in front of an appreciative crowd. He couldn't wait.

The man that Chief Reynolds assigned to the case was Detective Frank Comeau, a senior officer who had been on the job fifteen years now, the last five of which were as Detective 1st Class. Comeau was approaching 45, a large man with an overhanging beer gut. His nose was bent, the result of having been broken in a couple fist fights earlier in his career. Detective Comeau was a local man, and up until 1944 he had been one of the best hockey players on the River. Now his knees were shot and his hockey days were over. He knew most people in the town and the Chief felt if anybody could get information surrounding the death of Daley, it was this man.

On Monday, January 6th, Comeau was sitting with John and Everett Wilks, two brothers who were with Daley the night of the alleged murder, as the police were now calling it. Comeau knew these boys had been good friends of Daley, and many a night they had shared drinks and ill-gotten gains with the man. He was reading their statements while they sat across from him at the Chatham jail.

"You say here in your statement, Everett, that you ran out of the bar area once you saw Vincent pull a knife from his coat?" asked Comeau.

"Yeah, that's right, Frankie," said the elder Wilks brother. "We didn't want to be involved in what we figured was about to happen. Ol' Vince wasn't gonna screw around with Martin this time. Ya know what happened earlier last Fall, eh?" Comeau was not pleased with the familiar way in which he was being addressed by Wilks, but he let it pass.

"I heard he got himself tossed over Martin's back."

"That's right, and all 'cause he was too drunk to put up a fight. Plus, England knew all about Karate. I swear the guy was just like one a them Ninjas. You know, like ya see in the movies. But Vince got him good down at MacDiarmid's Convenience Store earlier last summer," he added.

"Oh?"

"Yes sir," the other brother John Wilks now chimed in. "He gave Marty a bloody nose fer sure. England was real het up, wanted to fight more but George, the owner there, held him back. It was a fair fight, Frankie." Comeau noted the last comment was added without his asking for it. He made notes of his discussion and bade the two goodnight. *Well*, he thought. *The Chief will no doubt be interested in pursuing this.*

It was obvious to the veteran cop that both John Wilks and his brother were biased in their opinions regarding the guilt of Martin England. However, Comeau wasn't about to take sides one way or the other. *Hell, let the political hacks do that.*

The following day, Comeau decided to talk with George MacDiarmid. He met with him at George's store and was able to basically corroborate the information about the ruckus that day as reported by the Wilks brothers. Whether it was a fair fight or not, MacDiarmid didn't bother to elaborate.

Also, Comeau searched his files and went back to the event at the Town Exhibition last fall. The police had been called by Roland Walsh, the manager of the Exhibition Building. A disturbance outside the dance hall had been reported. He read where young England had been able to subdue the much larger man in some kind of *Tae Kwon Doh* maneuver. Amazing. He made a note to call Walsh tomorrow and discuss this further.

Finally, he also took the time on Tuesday to check older files in the office about the coroner's inquest which had been held regarding the death of John Norman, a local drunk. England was slowly becoming a viable suspect. *A force to be reckoned with*, thought Comeau. He called the Chief Medical Examiner for the County, Wilbert Hennigar, and told him Crown Attorney Miller wanted to see him regarding the Daley autopsy.

Tuesday afternoon, Harrison Miller sat at his desk with Coroner Hennigar, a tall, thin man in his mid-60s, completely bald with a thin moustache that had turned yellow from nicotine smoke over the years. During his three decades as the Chief Medical Examiner for the County of Northumberland, Wilbert had seen many forms of death, but there were very few homicides on the river during his career thus far. That was not to say that he was ignorant in the science of his work. He was an avid reader of the frequent articles he received from the masters of the craft in the larger centers of the country like Montreal, Toronto, and Vancouver. Secretly, he was hoping one day to be able to apply some of the techniques shared by his colleagues from these busier centers.

In this particular case, he was certainly interested in the wound to Vincent Daley's neck, and he was now discussing this in earnest with the Crown Prosecutor. He had spread color photos of the deceased on Harrison Miller's desktop in all their gore and horrid violence.

"The way I see it sir, the entry of the wound is compatible with this knife blade. You can see how it entered the victim's neck from a vertical position with the thin portion of the blade in a downward slant," he said, pointing to the close-up shot of the switchblade stiletto. "In my opinion I don't see how the wound could have been caused as the result of an accident, that is by England falling on top of him. More than likely, it was either because England wrested the knife from the victim and plunged it into him directly; or, he may have been able to twist it around thusly," and here he demonstrated to the attorney by taking Miller's wrist with both hands and turning it inward against the prosecutor's neck.

"Hmmm," muttered Miller, more to himself. "I can see where you are coming from, Wilbert. Interesting…"

Meanwhile, Detective Frank Comeau had been speaking by telephone with a Sergeant Lyle Herman of the Canadian Military Archives in Ottawa who was responsible for the disclosure to authorized groups of personnel records. After providing proper identification, Comeau was soon reading material which he had just received from Ottawa off one of their new-fangled Telex machines. *This England boy was a bit of a problem to somebody*, he quickly surmised. He noted in the report there were four separate arrests for public intoxication while stationed in Britain, which included fights with fellow soldiers. Finally, it seems England was promoted to Sergeant on a couple of occasions but was quickly demoted each time back to the rank of Corporal.

With this new information in hand, he strolled across Water Street to the office of the Crown Prosecutor. He was confident Harrison would be very interested in what he had discovered about young Mr. England so far.

When he arrived at Harrison's office, he could see Miller was speaking excitedly with someone on the telephone. Miller gestured to Comeau to take a seat in front of him while he pushed the stray lock of hair back off his forehead and continued the animated discussion.

"Yes sir, I totally agree," Miller said. "Yes sir, I shall be *very* comprehensive in all of our background checks regarding the suspect. In fact, sir, I am just about to receive an updated report from Detective Comeau in this regard," he said looking over at Comeau, giving the detective a 'thumbs up' signal, smiling broadly.

"That was the Attorney General McNair," boasted Miller as he hung up the phone. Comeau could see the Crown Attorney could hardly contain himself. He placed the file on Miller's desk with authority and said, "Well, here you are sir. I believe you will find some interesting tidbits here concerning young Martin England."

"Good job, Detective. Leave this with me and if I have any questions I'll call you right away." Like Miller, Detective Comeau was easily flattered by praise. Comeau left to return to the jail across the street and Miller began perusing the file. The attorney noted with interest the reference in Comeau's report to England's obvious abuse of alcohol. He saw where Comeau had spoken with a friend who would confirm England was a member in the local chapter of Alcoholics Anonymous.

He also picked up on the fact that the suspect had developed a clear relationship of hatred with the victim in a relatively short period of time. And the young man had even gone at lengths to learn a Martial Arts program. Indeed, he was considered to be at the top level of his peer group in the Miramichi Valley.

Wonderful. In Miller's opinion, he now had plenty of evidence to support a request to Judge Cripps for a subpoena to have England arrested for murder. In his opinion, there was motivation, opportunity, and enough circumstantial evidence to convict this man. With a bit more information, he thought he could get to intent.

Chapter Seventeen

IF MARTIN thought things were going bad for him thus far, he had no idea of just how awful it was about to get. On Wednesday morning, January 8th, Martin opened his front door to Police Constable Harold Dennings, a casual acquaintance of his from school days. "Good morning, Harold. How can I help you?" asked Martin politely.

The policeman sneered at Martin and promptly served him with a subpoena. The writ had been authorized and signed by Judge Robert Cripps. Martin read it in horror. The legal document outlined Martin was being charged and arrested for the willful homicide of Vincent Daley.

While he read the document, Meg came downstairs with Jake in hand and was surprised when she saw Martin being handcuffed by the policeman. As he was being led out the door, he shouted to his wife "Call Reg right away, Meg! And don't worry, we'll get this straightened out!" and he passed the subpoena to her.

Only last week, Martin and Meg had received a Christmas card from their friend in Montreal, wishing them a "Merry Christmas and All the Best for 1947, Love, Reg." Inside the card was a personal cheque for $1000. Both Meg and Martin were overcome with gratitude for the generosity displayed by Reg. And now, here she was having to make a call to ask for yet more of his time and assistance. She was afraid they were pushing his friendship beyond all bounds. But what else could they do? This was indeed an emergency…

Reg answered the phone on the second ring in his Montreal law office.

"This is Reg Jacobs; how may I help you?"

"Oh, Reg, thank God, I reached you," Meg cried.

~ * ~

Over the next ten minutes Meg brought Reg fully up to date on what had just happened to Martin. She was clearly distraught.

"Okay Meg, here's what I am going to do. First, I will call the Chief Prosecutor and obtain his permission to speak with Martin, since I will need Martin's instructions to act on his behalf. Then, there is some paperwork to be completed, enabling me to temporarily practice law in the Province of New Brunswick. Once I have these things in place we can request a summary of what the Crown has in the way of evidence against Martin. Then we can go to work preparing a defense for him. Don't worry Meg, we'll get this straightened out."

"That's what Martin said, Reg. But I'm so worried. Oh Reg, you've been so good to us, I was reluctant to call you after everything you have done for us, yet we didn't know who else to call…"

"You've done the right thing, Meg. I'll catch a flight East as soon as possible, probably tomorrow. In the meantime, don't talk with anyone about this, especially the Press. I'll see you soon!"

~ * ~

Harrison Miller was basking in glory when he got off the phone after speaking with Reginald Jacobs, Q.C. from Montreal. *This was working out perfectly,* he mused. *Big City Lawyer to Defend Local Killer in Miramichi Murder Trial!* He pictured the headlines in his mind. *We'll see, Jacobs.* He expected to meet the lawyer within the next couple of days and he was anxious to take his measure. No doubt this Jacobs will be screaming to obtain bail for England. Frankly, for Miller to argue against that would be legal suicide, in his estimation. Miller decided then and there. He would take the high road and not argue against any application for bail.

Jacobs caught the nine-a.m. flight to Moncton from Montreal on Thursday January 9th, then he was on a bus ride for the one hundred-mile drive north to Chatham. At eleven am his taxi pulled into the lane where Martin lived, and he was met by Meg at the door. She was in tears, and he held her close to him. They packed up Jake, called a cab, and the three were at the town jail within minutes.

When they entered the jail, Martin was so relieved to see his friend he struggled to keep from weeping with joy, then got himself under control. Reg quickly had Martin sign a typical boiler-plate contract and he left in a hurry across Water Street for the Courthouse. Meg and Jake stayed with Martin beside his cell at the jail, while Constable Dennings sat sheepishly behind the front counter, giving the prisoner some modicum of privacy.

Jacobs had only been gone approximately twenty minutes when he returned with a formal release document signed by Chief Prosecutor Miller. This he presented to Constable Dennings and Martin was immediately set free. Bail had been granted for a nominal bond posting which Jacobs had personally paid. The lawyer and his client then left the-jail with Meg and Jake, and they arranged for a taxi-drive home to familiar surroundings.

It was not until nine that evening that Martin had finished telling his story in detail to Jacobs. Earlier in the afternoon, John Bradford had landed along with Becky and their young daughter. Both John and Becky were able to go over their similar accounts of the awful affair with Jacobs and he now had a complete outline of the event from the defense team's perspective.

He intended to meet with other people in the town over the next few days. He would need all the support from Martin's family and associates he could gather.

Later that same day a package was delivered from the Crown Prosecutor's office. As requested by Jacobs, it was essentially a copy of the Crown's case against Martin which included the autopsy report, the forensics of the case, full color photographs of the crime scene, and a list of individuals the Crown had spoken with up to this point. Going forward, he would receive the names of any other individuals the prosecution team might be using in their case against Martin.

Jacobs excused himself while he went to his room to study the contents of the package he had received. Again, he was mindful of his responsibilities in his personal practice, and he was able to hand off most of his regular work to a capable assistant he had recently hired. Several of his more important files were exceptionally gracious in granting him extensions.

But he was also going to be under pressure regarding Martin's needs. He had insisted on a speedy trial. Indeed, under the Interjurisdictional Practice of Law Act, Jacobs was required to have his work in New Brunswick completed within one hundred days. Checking his calendar, he made note of the termination date: April 19, 1947.

Rather than upset the order of things at the England household, Jacobs decided to rent a small office somewhere in town where he could interview potential witnesses, and simply "let it all out" as he frequently did when posed with difficult cases.

There were a number of issues that led to motivation, maybe even intent, although that would have been a long shot. There was Martin's involvement with Daley on several previous occasions, the Martial Arts thing and his unwillingness to immediately call the police at the time of entering the Legion. He was confident he could easily handle these factors.

But the one thing that was mainly puzzling Jacobs was the nature of the fatal knife wound. How did it occur? Did Martin actually take the weapon out of Daley's hand and commit the deed on his own? Or did he somehow fall on Daley's hand and force it inward and downward at the same time? He decided he would go with the latter assumption.

He called Martin into the den and outlined his plan of defense along with his suggestion of moving the work area to another locale downtown. With his knowledge of the neighborhood Martin was able to suggest a place on King Street, the former office of James Barry, Liberal MP for Northumberland County whose seat had been replaced after his death last year. The office had been vacant since that time.

As they discussed Jacobs's defense strategy, Martin asked Reg when he would be requested to give his version of events.

"Actually Martin, I'm giving thought to not having you appear in that capacity. It's a dangerous step to take. I know most defendants want to voice their own declaration of innocence, a natural desire. But in doing so, you place yourself at the hands of the prosecution.

"I understand Reg, but this is my chance to tell the jury what actually happened. Surely you want the truth to come out, don't you?"

There it was, thought Reg. Should he now simply ask Martin what he recalled about the fatal wound to Daley's neck? He decided to take the chance and use this opportunity to do a small role play as a learning experience for his friend.

"You tell me, Martin," he said. "Did you take that knife from Daley and then plunge it deliberately into his neck? Hadn't you been waiting for just this type of opportunity to occur since he beat you badly the previous summer at MacDiarmid's Convenience Store? And isn't that why you took those classes of *Tae Kwon Do?* So, you could take on this guy who is quite a bit bigger than you are? And by the way, why didn't you simply call the police upon discovering the Legion bar was being robbed when you arrived there?"

When all of these questions hit Martin at once, they were like some kind of verbal assault. He jumped off his chair and raised his fists in a threatening way and shouted at Jacobs, "What the hell! I thought you were my friend. Don't you believe me? Why are you asking me these things?" And he almost started sobbing, totally out of control.

Jacobs looked seriously at Martin. "You see, this is what I am afraid can happen, Martin. These are exactly the types of questions the prosecutor will be directing at you. You do have the right to appear on the stand, but I have a duty to advise you of the pitfalls in doing so. If you still want to appear and give testimony, then we obviously have a lot of preparatory work ahead of us. Do you agree?"

Martin slowly calmed down as he realized his friend was once again the captain he knew from his war years. The man in control, the guy who was able to keep everyone else calm.

In one way Reg was grateful for Martin's outburst. He now knew one thing, which was that Martin was convinced of his own innocence. Even if he did perform the act, he was probably not even aware of it.

Now he had to figure out how to use this knowledge.

Chapter Eighteen

THEY CALLED their new workplace on King Street the 'War Room'. It was here on Monday, January 13th, that Jacobs met with George MacDiarmid, Josh Freeman, and Reverend McBride. He had made appointments with each of them and he started with MacDiarmid. Going through each of their statements with them individually, he made notes here and there and was satisfied with each of the witnesses and how they would handle themselves at trial.

Jacobs spoke with Martin after reviewing the Crown's file and asked him about the witnesses that were listed in the document.

The first individual was Fred Trainor, a friend of Martin's who went overseas with him. Martin knew no reason why the police would want to talk with Fred. As for the two Wilks brothers, Martin knew nothing about them other than they were cronies of Daley's... his local drinking buddies who would probably like to see Martin convicted if for no other reason than the satisfaction of getting even for what they perceived was a wrong that had been done to their friend.

Mrs. Flaherty was a different story. She was no doubt an upright, honest citizen, but Martin recalled the first day he was working for her and he had that flashback of the Observation Post event and nearly killed poor John Norman. Mrs. Flaherty, he was quite sure, had been witness to his actions. But there had been no bad words spoken between them; in fact, they had hardly spoken. Apparently, she was satisfied with his work performance.

The owner of the *Tae Kwon Doh* club was scheduled to appear, and this was a bit of a setback to Jacobs as he was hoping to have the man as a witness for the Defense. Maybe he could use him on cross?

Finally, with Roland Marsh, the Manager of the Chatham Exhibition Building, Martin wasn't even aware there was anybody else at the scene of the fight that night with Daley. Martin described again the lead-up to the skirmish, how Daley had been drinking and basically goaded him into the fight. Indeed, now that he recalled the incident, Daley had made an inappropriate move toward Meg with a crude suggestion and had even blocked her way with his arm when she attempted to walk around him.

Jacobs was glad to get all this extra information.

"They will have Sergeant Herman give testimony. He is attached to the National Military Archives in Ottawa and no doubt has been asked to disclose your personnel file. I believe I have all of those old bases covered, Martin, so we won't bother going over all that crap, right?" Jacobs said with a smile.

"Sure thing, Captain," said Martin.

Again, he referred to the Crown's document, in particular the forensics segment of the report. "What's this?" he asked rhetorically. "Here we have a report from their Fingerprint Analyst, Mr. Delbert Wrigley. Hmmmm,," he pondered. "What's Miller got up his sleeve with this, I wonder?"

And finally, there was the Coroner's Autopsy Report. *The elephant in the room* thought Jacobs. For a number of reasons, he did not wish to broach this subject with Martin just yet. All in due course...

~ * ~

That night Martin went to bed early and fell into a deep sleep. Some time after 3:00 am he was awakened in terror by the same dream he had the night of the fight with Daley. The Senorita, a German Officer, Captain Jacobs, an Italian villa, and a long, sharp stiletto.

When he came down for breakfast, Reg was sitting at the table holding Jake while Meg poured a coffee and sat it by his plate which held a bowl of porridge and two slices of buttered toast. His father had already eaten and was refilling wood into their kitchen stove. Martin took a quick sip of the hot coffee. "Good morning everyone, sorry I overslept."

The breakfast scene in all of its simplicity and innocence suddenly hit Martin. It was surreal. Everyone was behaving as if this was just a normal day of the week and that all of the events last week leading up to this had been a dream. *Speaking of which,* he thought...

"Reg, I had a dream last night, actually a nightmare. I had the same dream on the night the fight with Daley happened and I can't see that as a coincidence," he said.

Jacobs listened carefully to his friend as Martin described the few sketchy details he could recall of himself, Reg, an Italian villa, a lady vintner, and a German officer. It made no sense to Martin. Reg, though, knew exactly what was causing Martin to have such a recurring nightmare. Still, Jacobs held back. He suggested things would improve once they got into the trial. "Try not to think about it,' he said. *If only it were that simple*, thought Jacobs. But he knew he was only kidding himself. It was just a matter of time before the truth had to be given to his friend.

Chapter Nineteen

JACOBS STUDIED the photograph of the neck wound carefully. He laid Martin's statement beside the photo, and from time to time his eyes moved back and forth between the two objects. He was still puzzled about the position of the knife as it entered Daley's neck. According to the wound, the weapon went into the victim on a downward slant, with the narrow portion of the blade facing down, as viewed sideways.

But if Martin had driven the knife into Daley's neck as the Prosecution had proposed, how was Martin able to accomplish that angle? He was much shorter than Daley. The latent prints taken from the knife showed Martin's fingertips on the underside of the hilt, which would be consistent with him pulling the weapon from Daley's throat, not driving it in on a downward slant. Conversely, partial prints of Daley's fingers were on both the topside and underside of the hilt.

It now made sense. He could envision Daley standing before Martin, teasing him, threatening him, as he moved stealthily around the room seeking an advantage. He imagined Daley tossing the knife from hand to hand, acting out images he had no doubt seen in crime movies. He further watched this play out in his mind's eye as Martin stepped behind Daley…

Martin kicks Daley's right leg from behind and Daley falls back into Martin. Martin reacts and pulls his arms around Daley which draws Daley's right arm inward while still holding the knife. Now they both fall forward and Daley lands on his right arm which ironically bends upward as it hits the floor first. And his neck literally pushes itself against the knife. Martin's weight behind the falling Daley is sufficient to prevent him from changing direction and the act is complete.

Jacobs was now ready for trial.

"Martin, you didn't stab Daley," Jacobs yelled to him across the threshold of The War Room as Martin entered the building for a briefing on

Tuesday evening. Josh Freeman was there as was Don McBride, the two having arrived just minutes before Martin. Josh was busy getting the coffee urn filled for this evening's discussions and Don was reading the *Miramichi Gazette* which lay open on the table in the kitchen/meeting room.

"I'm glad you think so, Reg," replied Martin. "But according to today's *Gazette*, the Chief Crown Attorney may beg to differ." He picked up the weekly paper sat at the table with Don. "I guess you've read the article, Don," said England with concern.

"Yes, I've read it," he said. "And this is what I think of it…" McBride tossed the paper in the garbage can beside the table. "Our Chief Prosecutor has a very large ego and he's certainly politically driven," MacBride added.

"This is the kind of thing I expected," said Jacobs, gesturing to the garbage can. The headlines were visible and they read:

MONTREAL LAWYER TO DEFEND ENGLAND IN MURDER CASE
TRIAL OF THE CENTURY TO START FRIDAY

Martin continued to read the article:

In an apparent desperate position, Martin England has hired the services of Mr. Reginald Jacobs, QC to seek justice for his war time underling in the "murder trial of the century." England has been accused of the stabbing death of Vincent Daley at the Chatham Legion Branch # 3 on December 23rd just past.

Martin served overseas with Captain Jacobs in the Italian Campaign during the period from July 1943 to early February 1945. The two spent most of their time "on loan" to *The Patricia Princess Light Infantry* while in Italy and they were then transferred back to the First Canadian 3rd Field Regiment in northern France in mid-February, leaving the Americans and Brits to claim final victory for the liberation of Italy from the Germans later that year.

Captain Jacobs returned to his posh corporate law firm, Devoe Jacobs MacLean in Montreal immediately after the war, and is now coming to the aid of his war chum. When asked by the writer what he thought his chances were of having Martin acquitted in this trial, he had no comment. The trial is scheduled to commence Friday, January 17th. Chief Prosecutor for the Crown, Harrison Miller QC promises a quick guilty verdict to the affair.

"The Crown will prove beyond any reasonable doubt that Martin England had been waiting since his return home for this opportunity to fatally harm Vincent Daley. When the prosecution rests, too will the Town of Chatham, knowing this dangerous individual has been brought to justice," stated the Crown Attorney earlier today from his residence at Riverside Drive.

Staff Reporter
Harold Jenkins

"Well, I guess you're in for a fight sir. This guy is pretty good at getting the public on his side," said Josh.

"The public be damned," exclaimed Jacobs. "We'll fight this in the Law Courts, not the court of Public Opinion." Jacobs was clearly angered by the article. Martin noticed. It was the first time he had 'cursed' in the presence of the Minister. *So what?* Martin thought. *Maybe this was exactly what they needed: get Reg's blood boiling a bit...*

Martin was also anxious to get his side of the whole affair out there. Jacobs had not yet explained to him why he now knew Martin had not intentionally stabbed Daley. Actually, the more Martin thought about it, the act happened so quickly, and it was so traumatic that he was unsure himself of what had actually occurred. He was confident though that Reg would explain everything at the appropriate time.

PART IV

THE TRIAL

Chapter Twenty

FRIDAY, JANUARY 17th arrived to the Town of Chatham and brought with it a major snowstorm which threatened to postpone the trial. A large group of media people representing several national outlets arrived the day before,. Much appreciated revenues went to the hotels and inns that had available lodging accommodation. A number of restaurants in the downtown area also welcomed the tide of new business that came their way as a result of the legal event about to take place.

Meg watched the snow falling from her bedroom window as she got herself ready for the trial. Her sister Rita had readily agreed to look after Jake while Meg attended the hearings; hopefully, it would not last too long. Rita's boyfriend Dave Jensen was also helpful, willing to take people here and there as required in his vehicle.

While Meg was very grateful for all the help, her feelings of despair surrounding their situation could not be held at bay. No matter how confident Captain Jacobs seemed about an acquittal, she knew juries could be misled. Maybe they would believe what the Prosecution would be asserting.

In addition to the pending perils of the trial, she was still bothered by Martin's mental state. As recently as only last night, Martin had experienced another nightmare. Her thoughts were interrupted when he had called her from downstairs. "It's eight-thirty Meg, we're running late." They all piled into Dave Jensen's car and they sped to the courthouse.

As they got out of the vehicle, they were confronted by at least a dozen reporters, all of them yelling questions. First at Jacobs, then Martin, and finally even Meg fell under the barrage as they hurried into the building.

Neither Martin nor Meg had ever been to an actual trial before. In fact, this was the first time either of them had actually been in a courtroom. The setting itself was intimidating.

When Jacobs entered the courtroom with Martin and Meg, he first directed Meg to a seat on the first bench behind the Defense desk. This would be her own seat for the duration of the trial and here she was in close proximity to her husband. Martin sat in the chair to the left of the desk as he faced the judge and Martin sat beside him.

In a couple of minutes, the Crown Attorney appeared with two assistants, and they sat at their designated desk. Except for the sound of papers shuffling and the odd person coughing, everything was silent. Not once did Harrison Miller look over to the Defense table. *He's nervous,* Jacobs thought. *Good.*

Soon thereafter, the usher opened the door to the judge's chambers and preceded a slight balding man into the courtroom.

"All rise," the usher shouted as the judge proceeded to his bench and sat perfunctorily while his name was announced as the presiding judge, along with the defendant and the case number. The usher directed everyone to sit.

Looking at the Defense table, the judge politely asked, "Mr. Jacobs, I assume you are here today representing your client, Mr. Martin England?"

"Yes, Your Honor" replied Jacobs.

"You are aware of the jurisdiction in the Province of New Brunswick I expect, and it will then go without saying that you know of the time limitation regarding your practice of law in our fine province."

"I am Your Honor, and I expect the one-hundred-day limitation to be adequate."

"Very well, sir." Judge Cripps now looked directly at Martin. "Mr. England," he said. "You have been charged with the unlawful killing of one Vincent Edward Daley, of the Town of Chatham. How do you plead?"

As earlier directed by Jacobs, Martin stood beside his lawyer and replied, "Not guilty, Your Honor," in an unwavering tone of voice.

"Has your lawyer counseled you in this regard sir? It is a most egregious charge, and I want to be sure you are fully aware of the consequences here."

"He did, and I am Your Honor."

"Very well then, we shall begin." He directed his question toward

Miller. "Counselor Miller, is the Crown ready to proceed with the case?

"We are Your Honor."

"Then let me first set a few ground rules, as it were. We shall begin with jury selection on Monday and hopefully the actual trial shall get under way by Thursday, January 30th. Given the time restriction placed on Mr. Jacobs, I expect the Crown to exercise expediency." Looking at his calendar, he said to both attorneys, "Gentlemen, since the clock began ticking for Mr. Jacobs on January 9th, that gives us until April 19th. Mr. Jacobs, somebody told me you were only planning on needing six weeks, is that correct?

"I believe so Your Honor," said Jacobs.

"And Mr. Miller?"

"More than adequate, I should say," Miller smirked.

"Another item I wish to address," stated the Judge. Jacobs could sense Judge Cripps had noted with disdain the smirk displayed by Miller. He also could tell the Judge was well aware of Miller's reputation as a headline-seeker. "I have not been oblivious to the heightened sense of gossip and media frenzy that appears to have been generated over this trial. I want you both to know that I shall have no foolish outbreaks in my courtroom during our sessions. Indeed, if the appropriate decorum is not observed, I will not hesitate in having the whole affair closed to the public and the press," he said, practically shouting. He banged his gavel on its pad.

"Court is adjourned."

Jacobs simply smiled and escorted Martin and Meg out of the building, dodging reporter's questions as they went to Dave Jensen's vehicle.

On the way home, Jacobs commented "That went well, Martin. I like the attitude of Judge Cripps at this point, though that may well change. So far, so good," he said.

Let the games begin, thought Jacobs.

Jacob thought jury selection in a town with a population of approximately four thousand people should be relatively easy. He figured he could use the personal knowledge of the Martin family, and maybe the Bradfords if need be, in the selection process. In Canada, the Crown was allowed six peremptory challenges while the defense was allowed ten. Normally, jurors were selected from a pool of fifty potential jurors. Jacobs was hoping Meg would know enough about the available selections to help in the process.

He devised a simple code to aid in this regard. A 'yes' required three light taps on the back of his chair. Conversely, if she potential witness turned out to be at complete odds to Jacobs's requirements, two taps would be the indicator. Only one tap meant she knew nothing about the person.

He specifically did not want witnesses who were known to be bullies, drank to excess, were assertive in their ways, held racist views, or were familiar with the elite crowd. Finally, anybody who had the least grudge at all against any of Martin's two families would be an automatic challenge in Martin's mind.

Chapter Twenty-one

THE SNOWSTORM that hit the town on Friday was quick to depart and continue on its way easterly to eventually dissipate in the great Atlantic Ocean. Nevertheless it packed a wallop, leaving a foot of snow in its wake. The main roads had been cleared by Sunday and the England family made their usual appearance at church. Reverend Don McBride, not one to hide behind his vestments when it came to taking a position on anything controversial, was quick to urge the congregation to offer their prayers for the acquittal of one of their brothers, Martin England.

Meg could not be certain, but she thought she noticed several glances from some people in the church that reflected anything but confidence. The looks appeared to be more of doubt, some of, maybe, *pity?* Even a couple of outright angry looks. The latter concerned her.

The biggest shock of all however, was what they witnessed the next morning when they were about to leave for the courthouse with Dave Jensen. On their front door, somebody had painted an awful picture of a knife in bright red paint, dripping with blood, as it were.

Martin began to rage and it took a lot of talking from Jacobs to calm him down. The courtroom was once again empty when they arrived, save for the court clerk, a bailiff, and a Court Reporter. Outside of the building however, again there was a scene of bedlam with reporter's fighting over a chance to ask questions of Jacobs, Martin, and his wife as they made their way into the building. Jacobs would only offer his standard 'No comment' as they waded through the media throng. All the others in Martin's party remained silent as instructed by Jacobs. The day was clear and bitterly cold, with temperatures hovering around the five degree level. The reporters would have dearly loved to be able to enter the courtroom and be on hand to witness the jury selection process, if only to be out of the cold, but Judge Cripps had prohibited them from doing so.

Once the Defense had settled at their table and the Prosecution had done the same, the Court usher again appeared from the judge's chambers and preceded Cripps into the main room. Once seated, Judge Cripps then had the group of potential jurors appear before the Court. Martin looked up as twenty people entered through the door to his far right. They ranged in age from their early twenties to their late seventies. There appeared to be an equal number of males and females, mostly white Caucasians. Some wore suits and ties, others dressed more casually.

The process of the jury selection began, and they appeared facing Martin in the traditional way. After a number of coded taps from Meg, Jacobs was able to finally end up with what he believed to be a reasonably fair jury selection.

At least the first round of the trial had gone their way.

Given the process had gone quicker than expected, Judge Cripps suggested they break for the day and they would begin first thing in the morning when both the Crown and Defense would present their opening arguments to the jury. The public and media would be present.

"All rise," declared the Court Usher as he entered the packed courtroom ahead of Judge Cripps who sat at his elevated seat, this time in a more imperialistic manner.

"Before we proceed," he declared, "I saw with great distaste in this morning's Gazette, this violation of the Defendant's personal residence," and here he held the weekly rag high with the picture of the vandalism on display to the room. "Rest assured the person or persons responsible for this act will be punished once exposed, and I shall not be lenient in handing down stiff sentences for this senseless action.

"Mr. Miller, if you are ready to present your case, please proceed."

Harrison strode regally to the front of his large desk and faced the jury panel. He wiped the annoying stray lock of hair from his forehead and proceeded to outline his case. He pointed to Martin with great disdain and he began his case.

"The Crown shall present a story of this man's resolve to murder the man who on several occasions had humiliated him in front of others. We will show through evidence that he prepared in advance for revenge against the victim, Mr. Vincent Daley. When the opportunity presented itself, he struck.

"The Crown will offer forensic evidence to prove beyond a reasonable doubt that the Defendant intentionally caused a fatal knife wound to the victim's neck. We shall also show with duly admitted circumstantial evidence, that on the night of December 23rd, 1946, the Defendant knowingly could have called in the assistance of our Town Police at the time the so-called robbery was happening at the Royal Canadian Legion. He did not, electing instead to confront the victim personally, thereby giving himself the opportunity to complete the commission of this most foul deed."

Finishing his opening remarks, he strode confidently back to his desk, all the while staring with anger and defiance at the Defendant. Martin held Miller's gaze stoically and never as much as shifted in his seat.

"Mr. Jacobs, you may now state your case, sir." said Judge Cripps.

Reg Jacobs then walked purposely to face the panel of jurors. He looked directly into the eyes of each of the members and walked back to his desk to stand beside Martin.

"Ladies and gentlemen of the jury. I should first confirm my relationship with Martin England. We are very close friends. More than that, we were comrades in war, having fought the Germans together in Italy and Holland. And I am the Godfather and namesake of their firstborn child, Jacob England.

"I am a corporate lawyer and I practice as a senior partner with my own firm in Montreal. This case represents my first criminal trial, so please bear with me. Notwithstanding my inexperience in these proceedings, when I heard of the assistance required by Martin at this time, I was only too pleased to offer my services, as inadequate as they may be." At this point Harrison could be seen rolling his eyes at the melodramatic approach being taken by Jacobs. Indeed, even Judge Cripps gave off a small smile as he listened to the attorney from Montreal get into his stride.

"I have closely examined the Crown's file in the matter before us today," Jacobs continued, "and frankly, once we have presented our side of the events that occurred on December 23rd last, we are confident you will agree this is a desperate attempt by the Crown to reach out to public opinion in an effort to convict an innocent man. Martin England's character could never allow him to conduct such an act in premeditation. You will find this was simply a case of self defense and more probably a dreadful accident. Indeed, Martin was trying to help the victim survive when his brother-in-law returned to the scene after the skirmish broke out.

"Always remember." He made eye contact with each of the jurors. "The onus is on the Crown to prove *beyond a reasonable doubt* that Martin England *intended* to cause the death of Mr. Daley that fateful night, and that simply was not the case."

He returned to his desk.

Chapter Twenty-two

By noon on the second day of the trial, jury selection had been completed and opening arguments had been finished by both sides. The trial would now focus on the presentation of evidence. The first to be heard would be witnesses for the Prosecution.

"Mr. Miller, please call your first witness," instructed Judge Miller.

"Thank you, Your Honor. The Crown calls Mr. Frederick Trainor."

Trainor, a sallow, thin-looking man of forty slowly made his way to the witness stand. He was sworn in by the Court Clerk and he took the witness chair, a slight tremor to his hands. Trainor was clearly ill and also nervous appearing before so many people.

"Please state your name and address for the court, sir," said Miller.

"My name is Trainor, Freddy Trainor. I'm livin' in Loggieville with my mother," he replied.

"Mr. Trainor, do you recall an event that took place at the Royal Canadian Legion Branch # 3 at Chatham on July 18th, 1945?"

"Yes sir. That was the day there was the fight at the Legion."

Shit, thought Martin, as Jacobs gave him a sharp glance, his lawyer silently asking him *What the Hell is this about?*

"Can you please describe the fight sir?" continued Miller.

"Well, John Norman, another friend of ours, was there with me. We was drinkin' pretty good, and John Norman, he took a swing at Martin. Martin then hit him hard and next thing ya know, Vince, the bouncer there, he come over to us and broke it up."

"Did the Defendant, Martin England, strike Mr. Daley?"

"Yeah, he hit 'em a good one. Old Vince fell on some ice and broken glass and then all hell, sorry, all heck broke loose and everyone was into it. Then the cops landed."

While Trainor was testifying, Martin was furiously writing on his legal pad which he now passed to Jacobs. Reg just finished reading Martin's notes as he heard Miller say, "Your witness Counselor."

Jacobs rose from the desk and approached Trainor in the witness stand.

"Mr. Trainor, you were a friend of John Norman, yes?"

"Yes sir."

"You went overseas with him from Halifax in 1939 and spent time with both Mr. Norman and the Defendant in England prior to the Italian Campaign?"

"That is correct."

"Your Honor," interrupted Miller. "I fail to see where this line of questioning is relevant?"

"Mr. Jacobs, please get to your point."

"Yes, Your Honor," Jacobs said. "Mr. Trainor, in the length of time you have known both the Defendant and the late Mr. Norman, is it safe to say they had a number of disagreements similar to the one you just described that took place July 1945 at the Legion?"

"They did, for sure," smiled Trainor, obviously recalling several such occasions.

"And did Mr. Norman carry a grudge against Mr. England for any of these minor spats?"

"Nah, they was nuthin' sir," replied Trainor. "Water under the bridge."

"Now Mr. Trainor, think back to that late afternoon at the Legion. Before Martin struck Mr. Daley, what had happened?"

Trainor appeared to be deep in thought, gazing at the floor. "Well sir, I think Vincent grabbed Martin around the neck right after Martin planted a punch on John Norman." This drew some laughter from the spectators and caused the judge to use his gavel to restore decorum.

"Thank you, sir. No further questions, Your Honor."

"Mr. Miller," the Judge looked at the Chief Prosecutor, who seemed to be speaking angrily with his assistant. "Do you wish to re-direct?"

"Uh, no Your Honor."

"Mr. Trainor, you are excused sir. Mr. Miller, please call your next witness."

Miller seemed a bit frustrated by the way Trainor was handled by Jacobs on cross examination. He was anxious to even the score with his next witness.

"The Crown calls Mrs. Eva Flaherty," said Miller. Everybody waited as a small, elderly lady slowly made her way to the witness docket where she was sworn and took her seat facing the crowd of people. Eva Flaherty was as sharp as a tack in spite of her age, and both her hearing and eyesight were in excellent shape.

"Mrs. Flaherty," Miller began. "I refer to the late morning of July 30th of 1945. Mr. Martin England had arrived at your residence on MacIntosh Street to paint a veranda, correct?"

"That is correct. His brother-in-law, John Bradford brought him to my place in his vehicle since Martin needed help getting his ladder there."

"Can you identify Mr. England, ma'am if he is here in this courtroom, and can you please point him out for the Court?"

Eva pointed to Martin. "That is Martin England." Martin smiled, gave her a nod.

"Very good, ma'am. Now was there another individual working with the Defendant that morning?"

"There was. Mr. John Norman was with him, God bless him."

"Can you please tell the court what you saw and heard when the two began their job on your veranda?"

"I saw John Norman from my kitchen window. I first noticed him going up the ladder to the roof of the veranda. I believe Martin had instructed him to clean the gutters of debris, because John Norman was perched on the edge of the roof, leaning over while he performed this task. Then I saw Martin begin to climb the same ladder. Just then I had to take the kettle off the stove because it was boiling. While I was away from the window, I heard what sounded like some arguing going on," she said. "I removed the kettle from the stove and went outside to investigate. When I got to where Martin was working, I saw John Norman lying on the ground and Martin was standing over him."

"Was Norman hurt?" asked Miller.

"I'm not sure," replied Mrs. Flaherty. "But he did rise up and said some cross words to Martin. He immediately left him to do the remainder of the work by himself."

"Thank you, ma'am," said Miller and returned to his desk.

Jacobs then rose and said, "A few questions, Your Honor," and he approached the witness.

"Mrs. Flaherty, did you hear what was actually said between the two men?"

"No sir."

"Did you witness Mr. England strike Mr. Norman at any time?"

"No sir."

"And how did Mr. England act when Mr. Norman left?"

"I don't know what you mean."

"Well, ma'am, was he mad? Did he say anything bad about Norman?"

At this point Jacobs was expecting an objection from Miller that he might be leading the witness but there was nothing.

"He said nothing to me about the incident, other than that John Norman was not feeling well and that he, Martin, would be back the next day to finish the job himself," she said.

"And did he?"

"Yes sir."

"And was the job to your satisfaction?"

"Very much, sir."

"Thank you, Mrs. Flaherty, that will be all."

"Mrs. Flaherty, you are excused," said Judge Cripps. "Next witness, Mr. Miller?"

Miller stood and frowned as he looked at his legal pad.

"The Crown calls Sergeant Richard Herman."

After Sgt. Herman was sworn in, Miller began his questioning. "Sgt. Herman, you are employed by the National Archives in Ottawa and you are responsible for the collection and distribution of records for all military personnel in the Canadian Infantry during World War Two, correct?"

"Well, I am employed by Library and Archives Canada. My department is responsible for the collection, maintenance, and release of

Canadian Armed Forces Personnel records."

"Very well Sergeant. I am in receipt of a copy of a file which I received last week from you in regards to the records for Corporal Martin England." He handed the copy to Sgt. Herman. "Is this the copy you sent, sir?"

Herman quickly scanned the document

"It is," he replied, and gave it back to Miller.

"If it pleases the Court, I would like to enter this file as Exhibit "A" for the Prosecution," and he also provided a copy to Jacobs. The Judge and Jacobs read their copies and the Judge gave his copy back to the Prosecutor.

"I have no objections, Your Honor," said Jacobs when he finished reading the file.

"Sgt. Herman, I refer to page 3, paragraph 2 of the report. It states here that Corporal England, along with two other people, one a non-commissioned officer and the other a man of rank. These other names are redacted. All three were arrested in London on the night of March 12th, 1940 for stealing a bus? Can you please elaborate?"

"Sir, the three were inebriated at the time and never really made it that far with the vehicle. They ended up spending the night in one of the local jails, and a fine was paid. There was only nominal damage to the vehicle and nobody was hurt."

"And this was not the only incident of alcohol abuse?"

"No sir, there are a total of 4 such cases, all occurring while Corporal England was stationed in the U.K."

"Regarding the personnel record of the defendant, was there ever a promotion to a higher rank?"

Jacobs jumped from his seat. "Objection, Your Honor. What possible connection can my client's rank in the army five years ago have to do with the alleged crime that he faces today?"

"Sustained. Counselor, please confine your questions to the matter at hand," agreed Judge Cripps.

"But Your Honor, we can show relevance as to the irresponsibility of the accused."

"Mr. Miller, being irresponsible is not a crime, at least not in the context of the matter now before us. Please proceed."

Miller had to accede to the Judge's demand. "No further questions, Your Honor," he grudgingly replied.

Jacobs approached the witness. "Sgt. Herman, in the document you have provided the Court, is there any information that has been specifically omitted, other than the redactions of the two other people in the bus incident? In other words, is this all there is available regarding my client?"

"That is correct, sir."

"Thank you, Sergeant. I have no further questions," and Jacobs returned to the Defense table, giving Martin a huge grin. Martin was not sure what had just transpired, but whatever it was, it was pleasing to see the captain in a good mood once again.

The Judge then spoke. "It is now four-fifteen. I think we have accomplished quite a bit today. Let's adjourn and resume in the morning." He looked at the jury panel and once again gave them instructions, cautioning them to not discuss the case with anybody and to abstain from reading or listening to media accounts of the trial.

Chapter Twenty-three

WEDNESDAY, JANUARY 22nd, the third day of Martin's trial, commenced with the testimony of John Wilks, witness for the Crown and friend of the late Vince Daley.

"Mr. Wilks, you know the accused, Mr. Martin?" asked Miller.

"Yeah, I do," he replied.

"Were you present at a dance at the Legion here in town on New Year's Eve last year and did you witness the fight which resulted in the death of a Mr. John Norman?"

"Objection, Your Honor. Records from the inquest into that unfortunate incident indicate the cause of Norman's death was accidental," exclaimed Jacobs.

"Sustained," Judge Cripps agreed. "Be careful in your choice of words, Counselor."

"Mr. Wilks, please tell the court what you observed at the time of the *accident,"* and here Miller snidely used his fingers to define air quotation marks on the subjective noun. At this, Judge Cripps slammed his gavel on his desk.

"Mr. Miller, you are coming extremely close to being held in contempt!" said the Judge. "Continue with your witness but I do not wish to have to warn you again regarding the decision of the inquest. Proceed."

"Please tell the jury what you witnessed, Mr. Wilks," stammered the Chief Prosecutor, brushing the ever-present stray lock of hair off his forehead.

"Like I told Frankie Comeau earlier, England hit Vince, Vince fell against Norman, and Norman fell down the stairs, causing his death."

"Objection, witness is not an authority and cannot state the cause of death," said Jacobs in a tone expressing exasperation.

"Sustained," added Cripps, clearly becoming agitated.

Miller tried a change in his approach. "Why, in your opinion, did Mr. Norman fall?"

"Objection. The Crown has not qualified the witness as to his expertise in such matters. Again, the inquest into the whole sordid affair was quite conclusive, Your Honor," said Jacobs, now sounding bored with this tiresome rebuttal.

"Gentlemen, please see me in my chambers," shouted Cripps. "The Court will take a short recess." He pounded his gavel and rushed into the room behind his bench.

"Harrison, I know what you're trying to accomplish here, and it won't wash,," shouted Cripps when the three were seated in his chambers.

"Judge, I have a witness who was standing right beside Vincent Daley when the accused struck him. He saw him fall against Norman, and we know that's what caused Norman to fall down the stairs."

"And I shall strenuously object to such testimony, Your Honor," said Jacobs. "The Coroner's Inquest held in this matter clearly cites the resulting fall of Norman as an accident. To infer otherwise at this time is not permissible. In other words, while the decision may have been challenged at the time, there is a three-month time window under which the challenge was to have been rendered, and that time has obviously expired."

"Jacobs is correct Harrison. Now this is definitely the last time I want to discuss the pitfalls of Mr. Wilks's testimony. Unless you have another avenue to pursue with him, I strongly suggest that you move on to a new witness."

Miller looked like a child of seven or eight who had just been caught by his mother with his hand in the cookie jar. "Yes, Your Honor," he conceded, again pushing the stray lock of hair from his forehead.

When they returned to the courtroom, Judge Cripps excused the witness and instructed Miller to call his next witness.

"The Crown now calls Mr. Roland Marsh," said Miller.

Marsh was a man of fifty-five or so, extremely large around the middle, with a slight wisp of white hair circling the mid-circumference of his otherwise bald head. He wore a thin moustache and his bulbous nose was lined with reddish tell-tale veins of alcohol abuse. Dressed in a shiny brown suit with a short, wide, yellow tie, he was the image of the actor, W.C. Fields.

"Mr. Marsh, on the night of September 5, 1946 you were at your place of employment, that being the Miramichi Exhibition Building, correct?"

"That is correct. I am the Manager at the Exhibition Building," replied Marsh.

"Did you observe the accused there that night?" asked Miller.

"Yes sir, Mr. England was there with his wife and another couple."

"I see, and can you tell the Court what you observed Mr. Martin doing, please?"

"Well, I heard several people arguing over by the picnic tables they have set up outside of the dance hall entrance, you know? So I looked over that way and I seen the accused there, grab hold of Vincent and, ah, he threw him over his back! Awesome, it was awesome! A big man like Vincent being tossed by that little guy!"

Judge Cripps intervened "Mr. Marsh, please restrict your response to simply answering the questions posed by the lawyers here!"

"Yes, Your Honor," replied Marsh.

"I have no further questions at this time Your Honor," said Miller.

Jacobs moved to the witness stand and asked Marsh, "Sir, did Mr. Daley have anybody else with him at the time he met up with the accused?"

"He did, sir."

"And who was that?"

"Sir, he was with the Wilks brothers, Everett and John."

"Thank you. Now, you state Mr. England was there with his spouse, Meg, and another couple. Who were they?"

"I don't know their names. They was a couple of darkies. The guy plays ball with the Ironmen I think."

"Sir, I believe the man's name is Josh Freeman," He spoke sternly to the witness because of his use of the derogatory racist term. "And," Jacobs continued, "he is a friend of my client's. He is here in the courtroom. Could you please stand, Josh?" Josh rose from his seat. "Is this the man you observed with Mr. England?"

"It is," replied Marsh.

"His name again sir, is Josh Freeman. Would you not say he is an athletic looking individual, fit as it were, capable of handling himself?"

"Objection Your Honor, as to relevance and credibility. Surely Mr.

Marsh is not able to attest as to Mr. Freeman's physical condition on the night in question."

"Sustained. The jury will disregard the question. Continue Mr. Jacobs."

"Then Mr. Marsh, will you tell the court what Mr. Freeman did to assist his friend in what appeared to be a confrontation against a much larger opponent than himself and two others?"

"Ah, he did nothing," said Marsh.

"Nothing?" said Jacobs, in an incredulous way. "Surely Mr. England asked for some help or at least seemed at some point in need of assistance?"

"Nope, Vincent made the mistake of stepping in front of Martin's wife, grabbing her arm to block her way when she was leaving, and Martin simply tossed Daley at that time."

"In other words, Martin was protecting his wife?" said Jacobs.

"Objection, leading the witness," Miller was fully off his chair.

"Sustained," shouted Judge Cripps. But the inference had already been made by Jacobs and it did not go unheard by the jury. "Mr. Jacobs, you are starting to try my patience with these tactics. Be careful."

"Yes, Your Honor," replied Jacobs, contritely. "No further questions."

"The Crown calls Mr. Delbert Wrigley," said Miller, resuming the questioning of his witnesses.

A short man in his late sixties approached the witness stand. Delbert Wrigley was a Fingerprint Analyst with the RCMP Forensics team from their Detachment in Fredericton, N.B. His credentials were impeccable and his tenure of some thirty years with the RCMP was a testimony to his expertise. He exuded confidence as he took his seat, a copy of his file in hand. He wore a sharp grey pinstripe, three-piece suit over a crisp white shirt and a maroon bow tie. His short-cropped grey hair was parted in a precise line down the centre of his skull and he wore a pair of pince-nez glasses to complete the appearance of a very meticulous individual. After Wrigley had been sworn and his credibility was thoroughly established, Miller began his questioning.

"Mr. Wrigley, I draw your attention to page four of your report, paragraphs four through six," said Miller, once the Fingerprint Analysis Report had been submitted as evidence, and copies distributed as required. "You state here that four prints from the Defendant's right hand have been lifted from the bottom of the stiletto's hilt, or handle, correct?"

"Correct," replied Wrigley. *This was a no-nonsense guy,* Jacobs noted, simply from the tone of his voice.

"You go on to indicate several prints from both of the victim's hands were also lifted from the knife, from both the upper and lower regions of the hilt?"

"Yes."

"Now Mr. Wrigley, please clarify your comment that a single print of the accused was taken from the top of the knife handle," said Miller.

"The statement speaks for itself, Counselor. It is what it is. One print belonging to the accused on the top of the knife handle, four of the same man's prints on the bottom."

"But Mr. Wrigley, how did they get there?" asked Miller. "I mean, obviously the accused must have held the knife thusly?" and here Miller had held the stiletto in his right hand toward the witness with the thin, cutting portion of the blade pointing downward and his fingers covering the top half of the handle.

"Objection, Your Honor, Counsel is asking for speculation," said Jacobs.

"Let me rephrase, Your Honor," said Miller. "Mr. Wrigley, is it possible the accused could have left his print on the knife handle by holding it in this manner?" and again he demonstrated with the knife to the witness.

"Yes, certainly possible," said Wrigley.

"Your witness," said Miller, returning to his desk.

"Mr. Wrigley," asked Jacobs, purposely taking his time getting to the witness box. "As to the four prints from my client's right hand on the bottom section of the knife handle," he emphasized the word 'bottom'. "Would that not be consistent with the accused leaving these prints when he removed the knife from the victim's neck?"

"It would," replied Wrigley.

"Now, as for the single print on the top part of the handle," continued Jacobs, emphasis on the word 'top', "could this have occurred if the knife had been grabbed by the accused in a defensive struggle?"

Wrigley took his time, his mind apparently envisioning such a scene. "Yes, I can see where that would have been possible," he conceded.

"No further questions at this time Your Honor," and Jacobs returned to his desk.

Martin was ecstatic on the drive home. "That was excellent work today, Captain. Things are going well for us, wouldn't you say?"

"Let's not get ahead of ourselves, Martin. We still have the possibility of dealing with another one or two more witnesses. Besides, a lot of their case depends on the mindset of the jury panel. They can surely make it look like you were well prepared for this clash with Daley. No way could you predict a time, but they'll make it look like you premeditated the act of homicide."

Jacobs began listing items with his outspread fingers.

"You had, One: Capacity for the act lending to premeditation. After all, you *are* self-trained in the art of *Tae Kwon Doh* and you're no stranger to violence considering your tour with the military in Italy across Europe to Holland.

"Two: Opportunity. You were willing to exercise patience in your desire to meet up with him in a hostile confrontation sooner or later and you did. This is a small town, too many opportunities exist and it was bound to happen.

"Three: Motive. Revenge is a strong motivator. You were, remember, humiliated in front of your friends on occasion. As well, revenge for the cause of John Norman's death in your mind, could also be considered."

"I see what you mean," said Martin, his elation had now vanished. The trial was beginning to have its effect on Martin. There were just too many emotional peaks and valleys. Sometimes he was positive things were going to work out absolutely perfectly for him; and then, in a matter of minutes, Jacobs had a way of presenting a different viewpoint to the case which made him look as guilty as sin!

Jacobs could sense Martin's frustration and simply said to him, "Lighten up soldier. I've got a few tricks left to play," and he left it at that.

~ * ~

That night, Martin once again had his visitor. The lovely Italian Senorita came to him in his dreams. He was sitting at a table in an outdoor setting at a cafe in Tuscany, enjoying a break from the battle they had just completed at Saint Fortunato. Out of nowhere, Captain Jacobs had appeared with the Senorita, and he had introduced Martin to the Senorita. But something was horribly wrong. When the beautiful lady turned his way, Martin was horrified to see a stiletto was protruding from the side of the beautiful lady's neck.

Chapter Twenty-four

THURSDAY AND Friday it snowed beyond belief. A huge low-pressure system had moved in as usual from the north-west, burying the town in three feet of heavy snow, followed by freezing rain. The temperatures then took a nosedive to twenty-six below, making it impossible to properly clear the local streets until late on Saturday. The trial was postponed until Monday, January 27th, and by then, speculation amidst the town gossip mongers was running overtime.

Rumors were abounding in the community from the sublime to the ridiculous. In one case Jacobs had heard from somebody that Martin had learned his martial arts skill while in the Army overseas. Apparently he had been taken prisoner by the Nazis and a Japanese fellow-inmate had given him lessons personally. In yet another scenario, Martin was informed by a friend that a rumor was making the rounds regarding his lawyer. Apparently, Jacobs was a secret agent for the British Commandos no less, and he was instrumental in teaching Martin the craft.

When the trial resumed, the Chief Prosecutor was anxious to win some points. For the most part Miller had failed so far to grab any real great headlines that would cement a feeling of guilt in the minds of the jurors. Time was running short. But he still had a couple of witnesses left he was hoping would help his cause.

"The Crown calls Mr. Ricky Wei," Miller intoned on Monday morning. The crowd watched as a robust young Asian man walked to the witness stand. He was thin and wiry looking and moved with the grace and efficiency of a well-trained athlete.

"Mr. Wei, please tell the Court what you do for a living," asked Miller of his witness once Lee was seated in his chair.

"I own *Miramichi TKD Arts,"* answered Wei. "We provide training classes on weekday to peoples who maybe want to learn *Tae Kwon Doh* art of self defense."

"I see, and do you have the accused, Mr. England, enrolled as a student in your class?"

"Yes. Mr. England is good student. I say best student I have."

"Why is he your best student?"

"Mr. England very quick to learn TKD. Also, he want to teach others the skill."

"But Mr. Wei, how, in your opinion, was the accused so easily able to become adept at this skill? Does a teacher's level of proficiency not normally require years of training and practice?"

"For most people, it take long time. For a few, it can happen quickly," he said.

"How long did it take you?" Miller was getting rattled, Jacobs could tell.

"I study art of TKD in Japan as young boy, many years ago. Come to Canada in 1930 and still practice. I enjoy," Wei stated proudly, a big smile on his face and it was obvious the crowd enjoyed his enthusiasm.

"Mr. Wei, did you notice anything special about Mr. England? Was he obsessive in his desire to learn the…."

"Object. The witness has not been qualified as a psychologist nor as a psychiatrist, Your Honor," said Jacobs.

"Sustained," said the Judge. "Mr. Miller, please rephrase your question," he added.

"Mr. Wei, did Mr. England ever say anything to you about wanting to hurt anybody with this skill?"

This was a dangerous move on the part of the Crown. Unless Miller was aware of something specific that Martin had said to Wei that might infer intent regarding a future act against the victim, he was treading on thin ice.

Mr. Wei thought for a moment, then began. "Mr. England, he say one time to some guy here in town that he want to show him how he could help him get girlfriend to, you know, like him more," he laughed shyly as he said this.

Miller was now interested. "Yes? Please continue," he added.

"But I don't think his friend want to hurt the girlfriend," he added with a puzzled look. The courtroom then broke into a roar of laughter. Even

Judge Cripps had to contain himself from laughing as he lightly admonished the spectators.

"No more questions," said Miller, clearly frustrated with the witness.

"Mr. Jacobs, do you wish to cross examine the witness?"

"No, Your Honor," chuckled Jacobs.

Miller was clearly agitated as he consulted his notes. *Surely his next witness would prove more successful*! the prosecutor thought.

"Your Honor, the Prosecution would call Dr Wilbert Hennigar to the stand," said Miller.

Hennigar approached the witness stand, took the oath, and was sworn in. He fingered his nicotine-stained moustache as he got settled in his chair and a thin film of perspiration formed on the bald man's forehead. Jacobs studied him closely. *The man's about to make testimony that is probably quite ambiguous–*, he thought. *He is eager to please the Chief Prosecutor, but knows what he is about to say will be challenged. Interesting...*

"Your Honor, I have before me Exhibit "B" which is the Autopsy Report on the victim as prepared by this witness, Dr Wilbert Hennigar. Mr. Hennigar, can you confirm for the records this is the same copy?" and he handed the document to the coroner.

Hennigar looked at the document and said " Yes sir, that is my signature and I prepared this report." The document was then entered into the court records and copies were provided to the witness, the Defense and the judge.

Before beginning, the Prosecutor took the stiletto from the evidence table and held it in front of the witness. "Sir, please refer to page five of your report, beginning at paragraph three. You make specific reference here to the fatal wound in the neck of the victim. You describe it as being consistent with this knife entering Daley's neck in a downward movement with the cutting edge of the knife facing down, like this. Am I correct?" asked Miller, demonstrating the movement to Hennigar.

"That is my opinion, yes sir."

"The knife severed Mr. Daley's right carotid artery and caused death which would have occurred within seconds to a maximum of, maybe two minutes?"

"That is correct. Death actually results from a lack of oxygen to the brain." Hennigar was totally in his element at this point. He gravely looked at the crowd and stated "The heart pumps blood to the brain through the carotid arteries. One of each is located on each side of the neck. The blood carries the necessary oxygen to the brain and when it was severed, the brain was starved of this life necessity. Unconsciousness would have occurred in seconds, death within two minutes."

"I see," said Miller. "Now, in your expert opinion, in order for the knife to enter Daley's neck in this position, how could this have happened?"

"Again, in my opinion, there would have to be force exerted against his neck in a downward direction, with the cutting edge of the blade in the downward position, as you earlier demonstrated."

"How many years have you been performing autopsies, Dr Hennigar?"

"I'm in my 34th year as Coroner for the County of Northumberland," he replied.

"And can you approximate the number of autopsies you have conducted over this period of time?"

"Gosh, sir. Quite a few. A safe bet though, would be over three thousand."

"That's amazing, Doctor. And of all of these post-mortems, how many of them would have involved knife wounds?"

"I can't be certain of course, but again a conservative estimate would be perhaps twenty percent of them, or say, around six hundred."

"And finally, Doctor, of these approximately six hundred wounds inflicted by knives, how many would you be able to say were due to the victim actually *falling* on the weapon?" Again the air quotes for the term 'falling'.

"None sir."

"Your witness, Counselor," Miller said as he walked to his desk, a smug look on his face while Jacobs could not help rolling his eyes in exasperation. Jacobs approached the witness.

"Doctor Hennigar, I am impressed with your memory and for the sake of brevity, let us assume your numbers are correct. Can you tell me,

Doctor, how many of the deaths you have detailed over the years were caused by snake bites?"

"Ah, there were none, sir." Mumbling could now be heard coming from the crowd of spectators.

"Really, Doctor? Then how about deaths due to spider bites?"

Miller jumped up from his desk. "Your Honor," he yelled. "What possible relevance is Mr. Jacobs planning on achieving here? I am clearly at a loss," objected Miller.

"I am tending to agree with the Crown, Mr. Jacobs. Please get to relevance with Doctor Hennigar's testimony," added Judge Cripps.

"Certainly, Your Honor. Doctor Hennigar, just because you have never encountered a death that had been caused by a snake bite certainly doesn't mean they do not occur, would you not agree?"

"Yes, but__,"

"Then can you not stipulate that a death due to an individual falling on the weapon can indeed occur, even though you have never seen such a case in your vast experience?"

"I find it extremely difficult to see how it could have happened."

"Your Honor, if I may indulge the court with a brief demonstration?"

"Your Honor, I object. We are taking Mr. Jacobs' speculations too far."

"Overruled Counselor," said Cripps. "I just allowed a demonstration from you with this witness. To quote an old adage, *What's good for the goose...* proceed Mr. Jacobs."

Jacobs gestured to Martin, led him to stand in front of the jury. "Here Martin, you stand in front of me." Martin did and Jacobs gave the stiletto to him. "Now hold the knife in your right hand with the cutting edge facing in the 'down' position and your arms held in front of you." Martin did as instructed.

"Now, you have stated you had just received a small cut of the knife from Daley on your left hand and you moved quickly behind him in the position I now am replicating," and Jacobs, acting in the role of Martin, jumped behind him. Martin who was acting out the role of Daley.

"You then kicked Daley's legs out from under him like so," and he mimicked doing this to Martin who began to let himself fall to the floor of the Courtroom, now fully into the role play.

"At the same time, you wrapped your arms around Daley so as to enfold his outstretched arms against his own body, just as he was beginning to fall." Here Martin actually started to fall but Reg held him up. "I daresay we will find some of your blood on the left arm of Daley's shirt as a result of this.

"When Daley was falling you grabbed his right hand for the knife with your own right hand and thereby left a print of your middle finger of that hand on the top of the knife handle." Jacobs pretended to be grabbing the knife now in Martin's hand.

"And also in the process of attempting to grab the knife, you fell with Daley while holding onto his hand. The same hand that held the knife, and it was bent downward." Here he demonstrated by bending the knife towards Martin's neck while it was still in his hand. "And Daley landed on the knife as you landed on Daley." Martin was now lying on the floor, holding the stiletto against his neck. Jacobs bent over, and gently took the knife from him, helping him to his feet.

Jacobs was out of breath. He walked over to the evidence table and gingerly placed the deadly weapon there. Then he walked slowly back with Martin to their desk. The crowd sat in stunned silence for several beats. One could have heard a pin drop.

Judge Cripps then broke the silence by suggesting the court be adjourned for lunch. "As a matter of fact," he then added, "I understand we may be in for another snow storm later today. Let us then err on the side of caution and adjourn for the day. That will give us all time to get home safe and sound. I am encouraged with the fast pace in which this trial is proceeding, so we have some time to spare."

Chapter Twenty-five

THE STORM that fell on the Miramichi area on Monday, January 27th, was another monster. It came roaring in from the west and deposited a total of eighteen inches of snow, only to be immediately followed by another three inches of freezing rain.

The streets of Chatham were clogged solid for two days, and everything in the small town was at a standstill. Reporters milled about in the local hotels and inns, speculating among themselves as to what could be expected from the Defense witnesses scheduled to appear as soon as Court resumed.

Everybody in the town was talking about the demonstration provided by Reginald Jacobs on Monday. When the *Miramichi Gazette* got around to publishing their weekly issue after it had been delayed by the storm, the headlines read:

STORM HALTS TRIAL AMIDST DEFENSE DEMO
By Staff Writer, Harold Jenkins

After a highly charged demonstration by Counselor Jacobs, Judge Cripps adjourned the trial against Martin England as another unusually large winter storm battered this small town in Northumberland County, N.B.

The large group of spectators which has been drawn to the trial every day since it began, was silenced by a dramatic demonstration between Jacobs and his client, Martin England, who is accused of murdering Mr. Vincent Daley on the night of December 23rd, 1946.

The trial thus far has been centered on evidence being presented by the Crown. Chief Prosecutor Harrison Miller, QC felt he had sown the final seed of undisputable doubt after the testimony of his last witness, Wilbert Hennigar, Chief Medical Examiner. Hennigar had just spoken to evidence from his autopsy report which at first blush seemed to solidify a guilty verdict against the accused.

In Hennigar's opinion, the only way the wound to Daley could have happened as it did, was "through the downward force of the blade" as just earlier demonstrated by the Crown.

Then, in a performance befitting the great Mr. Gable, Jacobs stunned the audience in the Courtroom with a demonstration of his own, to offer an alternative cause of death. Had Daley fallen on his own dagger as the Defense Counsel suggests?

Despite strong objection from the Crown regarding Jacobs's so called 'theatrics', Judge Cripps overruled the objection citing turnabout is fair play, since he had allowed the Crown a similar demonstration in the minutes preceding the Defense cross- examination.

Jacobs will now try to further his case in defense of England as he will bring forth a series of witnesses for the Defense once the trial resumes, which we assume shall be tomorrow, Thursday, January 30th.

Harrison Miller, angrily tossed the local paper into the garbage can beside his desk as he readied himself for the defense presentation to begin. He realized he was in a difficult position. What he presumed initially would be an open and shut guilty case against England was suddenly not so open and shut. It was possible Jacobs had managed to drive a nail of reasonable doubt into the minds of the jury with his cute demonstration on Monday. He would have to look for an opening with one or more of the Defense witnesses and attack ruthlessly.

The Court usher entered the courtroom and began his customary preamble to the proceedings.

"All Rise. The Honorable Judge Robert Cripps is now presiding in the King's case of The People vs. England, docket number 67.

Judge Cripps quickly entered the court and sat on his seat. "Please be seated," he said. "Mr. Jacobs, are you ready to call your first witness?" he asked.

"Yes, Your Honor, the Defense calls Mr. George MacDiarmid," replied Jacobs.

George MacDiarmid was well known in the town. He owned and

operated his family convenience store in a prime location on Wellington Street. He was considered to be a fair, honest, and hardworking man by all accounts.

"Mr. MacDiarmid, I refer to the afternoon of May 25, 1946. I note in a statement prepared by you that you had occasion to witness a fight that day between my client, Martin England, and Mr. Vincent Daley. Is that correct sir?" commenced Jacobs.

"It is."

"And can you tell the court, in your own words sir, what you recall about that incident?"

"Well, Martin had just purchased a package of cigarettes and was about to leave when Mr. Daley and his friend, one of the Wilks boys, came into my shop.

"Daley immediately started berating Martin and accused him of causing John Norman's death at the Legion on New Year's Eve, earlier that year. Martin was clearly eager to get home, indicating they should just forget about it. Daley would have none of that, and he went so far as to insinuate Martin was also responsible for the loss of his employment at the Legion.

"In a matter of seconds, Daley threw one unexpected punch which floored Martin. Daley and Wilks then left the shop, laughing. Martin was very upset but I talked him into standing pat. I then shared a few drinks with him from a pint I keep on hand," he said, while grinning at the crowd. "Martin then left for home, a short walk up the street, and I only hope he didn't get into too much trouble with the missus because of me," and the spectators chuckled.

"Your witness Mr. Miller," said Jacobs.

"Mr. MacDiarmid, you say Mr. England was very upset when Mr. Daley and his friend left your store. In fact, he was so upset he needed several drinks to calm himself down? "

"Well, I wouldn't say he was that upset, sir. Maybe for a short while, but……"

"Thank you, Mr. MacDiarmid, no further questions, Your Honor."

"May I redirect, your Honor?" asked Jacobs.

"Go ahead sir," said Cripps.

"Mr. MacDiarmid, how many drinks did you serve Mr. England that afternoon?"

"Three, as I recall," said George.

"And over what period of time did this occur?"

"He was at my store until some time after nine. I remember I was late closing, since I normally close shop at nine pm sharp."

"So, he would have been there for approximately five hours. Was he staggering when he left?"

"No sir."

"What was discussed during that time, Mr. MacDiarmid?"

"Sir, that was the remarkable thing. At first, Martin was upset, but more embarrassed than anything, I would say. I was expecting him to rant and rave about getting even with Daley, or maybe claiming he was, you know 'sucker-punched' or something. But after a drink, we got around to talking about the Ironmen baseball team. Martin was looking forward to playing for them. That's all we talked about."

"No further questions, Your Honor," said Jacobs.

"Anything further on cross?" Cripps asked Miller.

"No, Your Honor," said Miller, clearly frustrated.

"The Defense calls Dr Michael Moar," said Jacobs.

Dr Moar approached the stand. He was a tall, handsome man in his early fifties who sported a full head of jet black hair, save for a dash of silver on each sideburn. His moustache was pencil thin and he had piercing dark blue eyes. He took the witness seat with confidence and displayed a charming smile in the direction of the jury.

"Dr Moar, how long have you known the accused?"

"I met Martin during a small interior painting job he was completing at our residence on May 27th, last."

"What were your impressions of Mr. England, Doctor?" asked Jacobs.

"I was quite impressed with the man. I should say I arrived home early that day, unexpected by Martin. My wife Dorothy had left him with the key to the house with instructions to lock up when he was finished, and to leave the key under our doormat.

"I watched while he did his work, unaware of my presence. It was necessary for him to remove several bottles of liquor from a cabinet in order to paint it and I did not say a word as he placed each bottle on the dining room table. For a while, I thought he might take a break and help himself to a drink of scotch. He did not, and I was thereby impressed."

"Did you have occasion to speak with him at all?"

"Yes sir, I introduced myself and then offered him a drink, in fact. This, however, he declined on the basis he had to get home to his wife. It was a nice gesture, and I was glad to meet the man. Furthermore, I was very satisfied with his work and I was quick to call Doctor Blake the next day to thank him for referring Martin to me."

"No further questions, thank you Doctor," said Jacobs.

"I have no questions for this witness, Your Honor," said Miller.

"The Defense calls Josh Freeman," said Jacobs.

Josh then approached the witness stand. He was the epitome of an athlete: lean, long muscles like those of any long distance runner or swimmer. He had an easy stride up the aisle. Anyone could see he was a man who was confident in his body and his mind.

"Mr. Freeman, you say in your statement that you moved to the area from Boston with your family, your father being stationed here at the Chatham Air Force Base, correct?" asked Jacobs.

"Yes sir," replied Josh.

"Bit of a change from Boston, I would venture, eh Josh?"

"Well sir, the winters can be cold, but the summers are nice. Plenty to do if you like the outdoors." He was smiling at the jury now.

"How do you know the accused?"

"Martin started to play third base on The Chatham Ironmen ball team when he returned home from the War," said Josh. "I'm a pitcher on the team and we struck up a friendship immediately."

"I see," said Reg. "Were you with Martin at the Exhibition Dance the evening he had the set-to with Vincent Daley in the early fall of last year?"

"I was there with him and his wife Meg. I was with my girlfriend."

"Please tell the court in your words what you saw that evening."

"We were outside the dance hall sitting at a picnic table, just relaxing and drinking our Ginger Ales. Martin was having a smoke," and here he looked accusingly at Martin. "I've been after him to quit those things," he said half admonishingly.

"Just then a car rolled into the same area where we were sitting and it was Vince Daley and his two chums. Daley started right off insulting us and Mrs. England."

"What did he say?"

"He, ah, called me Martin's 'black playmate'. He told Meg she was a real looker and invited her into the building for a dance with a 'real man'. At that point Martin suggested we leave and he led the four of us toward the exit of the driveway. Then Daley stepped in front of Meg and raised his arm, he may have grabbed her, blocking her way."

"What did Martin do at that point?"

"He very neatly tossed Daley over his back. He explained to me afterwards that it was a move he had learned at the *Tae Kwon Doh* class he was enrolled in that summer. In fact, he has since started teaching the sport to me."

"Was Daley upset?" asked Reg. Then quickly added, "And the court will please excuse my bad pun!"

Josh chuckled along with the spectators. "As Mr. Daley was being helped back to his vehicle, he called out to Martin and told him he would 'regret it!'," said Josh.

"Tell the court Josh, have you ever heard Martin say anything in a threatening way about Vincent Daley?"

"No sir," said Freeman. "Never."

"No further questions, Your Honor," said Jacobs.

"Nor do I Your Honor," said Miller. Jacobs could see Miller was fuming inside, unable to gain anything on cross from the witnesses the Defense had so far presented.

"Your Honor, the Defense requests a short recess so that I may confer with my client?"

Judge Cripps granted the request, and Jacobs huddled with Martin while the court was cleared. He led Martin to a small vestry available in the building for such purposes and when they got settled at a desk, Jacobs looked seriously at him.

"Martin, as you know I've been reluctant to put you on the stand to testify on your own behalf. It's a move that a defense counsel seldom employs because it opens the accused up to difficult questions. It has on many occasions resulted in people being convicted, and I have remained fearful that this may happen in our case. Yet, the question of why the police were not called immediately that night at the Legion remains unanswered.

"I can easily relate an explanation to the jury right now, if you so wish. But in good conscience, I have to advise you that it would look much better coming from the defendant himself. So, I'm of two minds on this matter. What do you think?"

Martin looked thoughtfully at his captain and long time friend. "I think I should get on the stand and end this right now. I'll be okay, Reg," he added.

"Then let's do it," said Jacobs and they re-entered the courtroom.

When the judge brought the trial back to order, Jacobs stood and in a loud, confident voice stated "Your Honor, the Defense calls Martin England to the stand." A general hubbub of murmurs and surprised tones emanated from the crowd as Martin made his way to the witness box. He duly took the oath and got settled, looking in a serious manner at the Jury Panel, making eye contact with each of the twelve members.

"Mr. England," began Jacobs." You are here in the witness stand of your own accord and you have signed the necessary documents for the Court to allow you to speak on your own behalf, correct?"

"Yes sir, that is the case," said Martin.

"Then Martin, there are really only two questions I have for you. The first is, why did you not call the local police at the moment you and John Bradford went into that room and saw the three men in the act of thievery?"

"Well, sir," Martin replied, "Everything just happened so fast! Before I knew it, Vincent Casey was circling me with a knife. At that very point, the two Wilks boys appeared to be afraid of what was about to happen and they quickly decided to leave the scene. It was at that time I was concerned about the safety of my wife and sister, who were waiting for us at the entrance to the Legion. There is only one way out of the building from where the bar area is located and the women would have been waiting right in the path of the fleeing Wilks brothers.

"So I asked my brother-in-law, John Bradford, to check on them and call the police, which I understand he did."

Jacobs waited for a couple of beats, allowing this information to sink into the minds of the jurors.

"Then Martin, my second question. Did you at any time, either since you first ran into trouble with Vincent Casey, or in fact during the last fight with him, harbor any 'malice aforethought' regarding his demise, or in other words premeditate his murder?"

"Never sir," he said. "My only thought was of self-preservation."

"Your witness, Counselor," Jacobs proclaimed and walked to his desk.

Miller fairly flew out of his chair at the opportunity of questioning England.

"Mr. England, *really* sir," he commenced, in a seemingly exasperated manner. "You would have this court believe that you never once planned the fatal outcome of Mr. Daley after having developed a very contentious relationship with him since the very week you first arrived home? I find this extremely hard to believe."

"Objection Your Honor," said Jacobs. "The Crown is badgering the witness. Does he have a question for my client?"

"Sustained. You are at the stage of being argumentative, Mr. Miller. Please proceed."

Suddenly, Miller realized a very large part of his case was mainly built on the previous fights the accused had incurred with the victim. He was hoping the jury would see England as the perfect person on which to lay a charge of premeditated homicide. It was not going to be that easy, so he decided to take a different approach.

"Mr. England, we have heard evidence to the effect that you joined the Miramichi TKD Martial Arts club. Apparently you wanted to be able to teach this art to a friend?"

"Well, yes sir, but that___" Martin began to reply.

"Just answer the questions, yes or no, sir," said Miller.

"Yes," said Martin, testily.

"And I believe you became very proficient at this art of *Tae Kwon Do?"* again the familiar use of his air quotes.

"That requires a subjective answer sir. I presume I was considered proficient since I was granted a teaching certificate by the owner of the Club, Mr. Wei," Martin finished.

"Is TKD not considered a lethal art or a 'deadly weapon'?" asked Miller.

"No sir, it is not," said Martin. "That is an American legend. It was__"

"Your Honor, please instruct the witness to restrict his response to a yes or no answer!"

"No, Mr. Miller. You have ventured into this form of dialogue without knowing the answer. As a teacher, Mr. England is considered to be qualified on the so called status of the practice as a 'defense weapon' and I am interested in hearing his full response. Mr. England, please continue," said Cripps.

"Yes, Your Honor. As I was saying, the assertion of the art of TKD, indeed, many of the Martial Arts, as being deadly or lethal weapons, started as a myth in the USA with the entry of Japan into World War Two. It is simply not the case. There is no country that has ever registered any of the Martial Arts as deadly weapons."

Miller was once again becoming rattled. He brushed the errant lock of hair off his forehead and tried another tack.

"Mr. England, are you telling the court here that you joined Mr. Wei's class with the sole purpose of wanting to teach the art of TKD to a friend?"

"No, not only that," said Martin.

Aha! thought Miller. Now he was getting somewhere with the accused. "And what other motivation did you have, may I ask?" and he smiled out at the courtroom, anxiously waiting to hear England have to admit he took the course to be able to exact revenge on Daley.

Unfortunately, as soon as he turned to see a smile on Martin's face, he once again realized he had made a mistake, and probably a costly one, at that. He was now only too aware of one of the Golden Rules of a solicitor: *Never ask a question of a witness for which you do not know the answer.* Martin began his response.

"Well sir, I am an alcoholic. And yes, it is true that I have not had a____" and at this point he was interrupted by Miller.

"I am finished with this witness, Your Honor," and he turned to go back to his desk.

"Hold on, Mr. Miller. Mr. England, please remain seated where you are. I would be interested to hear what the witness has to say in his defense. Please continue with your response, Mr. England," Judge Cripps again added.

"Yes sir, as I was about to say, I decided to quit drinking on the day of that run-in with Mr. Daley at George MacDiarmid's store last spring. But it has not been an easy battle," and he began to hang his head. Then with renewed determination, he looked up and leveled his gaze at the jury and continued.

"I go to AA Meetings here in town on a regular basis and I am told that an effective way of dealing with the disease is to have another 'habit'. I chose TKD and it appears to be working for me." Martin said this in a very matter-of-fact manner, more to the court than to the prosecutor. He was immediately awarded for his candor with a polite round of applause from the crowd.

After Martin had returned to the Defense desk, Jacobs then stood and directed a statement to Judge Cripps.

"Your Honor, we had earlier intended to have several other witnesses appear before the Court. At this time however, we do not feel this to be necessary. With respect Your Honor, the Defense now rests."

There was a general hum throughout the audience as they took this news into account. Several reporters ran out of the room in order to make calls to their editors.

Judge Cripps banged his gavel three times before the crowd settled down.

"Very well, Mr. Jacobs... Ladies and gentlemen, we have spent pretty well a full day here. I believe we can now adjourn until tomorrow at which time we shall hear closing arguments, agreed?"

Both Jacobs and Miller nodded in agreement and gathered up their documents, putting things away in their briefcases as they prepared to leave.

As Jacobs made his way outside the courthouse with Martin, Meg, Dave Jensen, and Mr. England in tow, they were once again accosted by several reporters.

"Counselor," asked one of them, "you seem to be quite confident of an acquittal at this time, yes?"

"We have felt confident about the eventual outcome of this farce since the outset. Mr. Miller has based his entire case on a great deal of circumstantial evidence, hoping that the media and public opinion would sway in his favor. Martin England is innocent," he proclaimed. "The good people of the Miramichi realize this and will not fall for this game of political ambition by Counselor Miller." By this time the small group had reached Dave Jensen's vehicle and Jacobs simply climbed into the front passenger seat and closed his door on the three reporters standing in the snow covered street. Jensen put his car in gear and he drove away with Martin, Meg, and Mr. England in the back seat. They were all staring ahead, wordlessly trying to contain their smiles.

Chapter Twenty-six

Northumberland County
Courthouse,
January 31st,1947

CLOSING ARGUMENTS were about to be heard from both the Crown and the Defense. The first to present their case was Harrison Miller for the Prosecution.

"Ladies and gentlemen," he began as he addressed the jury. "You have heard from the Prosecution how Mr. Vincent Daley had several run-ins with the accused before his life was brutally ended on December 23rd of last year.

"We have illustrated how Mr. England went so far as to gain the knowledge of Martial Arts skills no less, and then laid in wait for an opportunity to occur where he might use such a weapon against Daley. Chatham is a small town. Anyone could have predicted these two opponents were going to clash at any given moment, and clash they did!

"You have also heard the testimony of the Chief Medical Officer. Clearly, the fact the victim's knife wound happened as it did could only be the result of either: a.) the accused directly stabbing the victim, or, b.) by the accused bending the victim's hand while he held the knife so as to cause a self-inflicted wound, as it were.

"Do not be swayed by the fancy demonstration conducted by the Defense!

"Lastly, and most important: the big question remains... why did Martin England not simply call the police immediately when it was determined there was a crime in process? I suggest it was because that would have deprived the accused from achieving the goal he had been planning since his first altercation with the victim. It was purely and simply a case of premeditated murder. It is now your duty as citizens of the province to uphold the laws of a great nation and find the defendant guilty as charged."

Miller walked slowly back to his desk. His thoughts were on the last question he had asked Martin yesterday, and how the crowd had actually applauded his response. He was beginning to wonder if that same applause would ever be for him, if and when he sought the higher political seat he so coveted.

It was now time for the closing rebuttal from the Defense. Captain Reginald Jacobs, QC stood in front of his desk. He was about to refer to his legal pad which contained copious notes he had been taking during Miller's closing arguments. Instead, he placed the pad on his desktop and strode over to the jury panel, hands free.

"You have heard from the Crown how my client has been plotting the demise of Mr. Daley since the second he was accosted by him on his first week home from the War. That was simply not the case. Ladies and gentlemen, Martin England was finished with death on the day he left Holland. All Martin ever thought about from then until Mr. Daley's awful accident, was how much he was looking forward to providing a good life for his wife and child." Here he looked appreciatively at Meg seated behind her husband.

"Martin, like too many of our veterans, suffers from an abuse of alcohol. And that, in turn, is a direct common result of having witnessed too many horrific events you could never, ever, imagine. Your comrades dying in front of you, creating scenes to be etched in your memory for decades to follow, maybe forever.

"So, he sought a way to forget these images which, unfortunately, was through alcohol. And he ended up fighting with Daley that first week he was back home, and several times thereafter as Daley kept running into him. Miller was correct. This is a small town and it was bound to happen. I suspect when we delve further into Mr. Daley's past, we'll probably find a history of alcohol abuse on his part as well. Unfortunately, Vincent never sought help. Instead he sought a way to save face in front of his friends, so he goaded Martin into the final confrontation he had with him.

"He could not have known of Martin's new found ability in the

Martial Arts field of self defense. Ladies and gentlemen, this was a tragic accident, nothing more. And yes, it would have been great had Martin been able to contact the local police prior to everything else happening. But that was not possible.

Before you retire to consider this case, Judge Cripps shall be instructing you regarding your options and other matters. But remember this: the onus is on the Crown to prove guilt *beyond a reasonable doubt*. And this they have clearly failed to do."

Jacobs then walked back to his chair beside his client. He wore a sad, world-weary look and gently pressed Martin's arm in a gesture of comfort.

The judge then proceeded to instruct the jury. They had only two options, really. Either find Martin guilty of intentional homicide or acquit him totally of the charge.

The confidence Jacobs had displayed yesterday to the reporters outside of the courthouse was not present today as they went home. Inside, Jacobs was mindful of other trials he knew of that had ended badly. This would not be the first time in Canada an innocent man might be sent to prison. So it was with more than a little angst that Jensen and his three passengers approached the England residence.

Just as Jensen was driving into the lane, he saw Rita come running out of Martin's house holding little Jake in her arms. Jacobs, Meg, and Martin were quick to exit their friend's vehicle and they looked in alarm at Rita.

"They just called from the courthouse," she cried. "You have to go back. The jury has already returned with a verdict and Judge Cripps wants you back in Session." The three of them climbed back in Jensen's vehicle to join George. Jensen ran the vehicle around in a tight swerve in the small lane and he quickly sped back to the Courthouse.

On the way there, Martin was also having his own thoughts about the outcome of the trial. What did this very early return of the jury mean? Could it be a good sign for him? Or something dreadful. What would happen to Meg and Jake if Martin had to spend the rest of his life behind bars? Who would look after them? Before he knew it, they were at the all too familiar entrance of the Courthouse.

He took Meg's hand as they entered the building and he leaned over to her saying, "Whatever happens, Meg, I love you so much. Thanks for believing in me."

"We'll be okay, whatever the outcome, Marty," she replied.

"Hey Martin," some reporter shouted, "what do you think the jury has in store for you?"

He just kept walking.

When they took their seats at the Defense table, Jacobs and Martin stood with the rest of the people in the courtroom as Judge Cripps once again entered the room. Everybody sat down following the judge, and the jury was called back into court. Martin and Jacobs watched the solemn faces of each juror as they filed into their seats. It was impossible to tell from the jurors what their decision had been.

"Ladies and gentlemen of the jury, have you reached a decision?" asked Judge Cripps.

"We have Your Honor," said the Jury Foreman.

"The accused will now stand," intoned Judge Cripps.

"Members of the jury, in the case of The Crown vs. Martin England, what say you, Guilty or Not Guilty?"

The jury foreman stood and pronounced "The members of this jury find the Defendant, Martin England, Not Guilty Your Honor."

Cripps had to shout to be heard above the uproar. "Ladies and gentlemen, thank you for a job well done. You are now dismissed. Martin England, you are released. Go in peace."

The next day, *The Gazette* headlines read:

ENGLAND ACQUITTED IN MURDER TRIAL
By Harold Jenkins,
Staff Writer, The Miramichi Gazette

The jury panel of six men and six women were only out of the courtroom for ten minutes today before returning with a unanimous verdict of Not Guilty in favor of local war veteran Martin England.

England had been on trial stemming from charges of murdering Vincent Daley on the night of December 23rd, 1946. The jury listened to two separate accounts of how a knife wound happened to result in Daley's death. In what would be the crux of the case for Martin England, the 12 member jury decided to believe the version as presented by the Defense. This had the victim falling on his own weapon while holding it during an attack against the accused.

No doubt their decision was helped by the articulation of Defense Counsel Captain Reginald Jacobs.

Harrison Miller,_QC attempted to convince the Jury panel that England had in fact harbored feelings of revenge against Daley after several previous encounters with him. Miller insisted England had joined the Tae Kwon Do club as a means of gaining knowledge of this 'lethal weapon' as he termed it, and thus enable himself to exact his revenge. His efforts to sway the jury toward that end however, were in vain.

After a unanimous Not Guilty verdict, the crowd of spectators at the Courthouse today broke into wild applause as Martin England and his Defense team hugged each other with joy. The Chief Prosecutor was not available for comment at the time of going to press.

Jacobs finished reading the article in the *Miramichi Gazette*. The trial was over, Martin England's innocence had been declared, and all was well in the England household. But despite the aura of well being, there were mixed feelings being shared by all. Reg Jacobs had completed his task of successfully defending Martin and it was now time for him to leave and return to his law practice and his own life in Montreal.

John Bradford offered to drive Reg to Moncton for his plane trip back and Martin was going along as company for John on the drive back.

They discussed fishing on the Miramichi, Martin's future with his painting business, and the prospects for the Chatham Ironmen Senior Baseball team.

They arrived in time for Reg to buy himself a drink at the Airport Bar before his flight departed and he bid his two friends a fond farewell.

Jacobs promised to keep in touch and then he was gone.

Chapter Twenty-seven

THROUGHOUT THE rest of that winter Martin struggled with his business, only finding several small jobs. They were fortunate they still had two boarders at the house, the telephone company workers. The Province was switching over to rotary dial models, and the extra income allowed them to eat healthy, if not extravagantly.

Then the ensuing two years brought little in the way of added fortune or income for the Englands. Martin continued to work at various house-painting jobs in the area, and while some people suggested he should advertise more, grow the business, and hire more staff, he did not have the confidence nor the capital to take it to a higher level.

In June of 1950 James told Martin one day that they were hiring painters at the Ammunition Depot in Renous, NB where he worked as a fireman. After a short interview in July of that year, Martin was hired on. At least he now had regular hours of employment, his wages were average and he was able to make ends meet. This was a good thing, since the telephone workers had just finished their contract with NB Tel. Meg's income from the roomers ceased.

Martin got settled on his job at the Renous Depot and life went on. While it was a source of steady income, it was not at all interesting nor did it leave any room for advancement. He rode the bus each morning from Chatham to work, then back home, a forty minute ride each way. In the winter time, he was leaving and returning in darkness, and overall it was becoming quite mundane and boring. Martin yearned for something more exciting in his life, but there was little he could do about his situation given his limited education and finances.

The Christmas of 1950 was sparse yet they managed. Jake continued to grow and the young boy provided the England house with plenty of love and laughter that definitely would not have been there without him.

Then in the late spring of 1951 his father had another stroke. Just before that unfortunate event, Meg had decided to put her high school course of Junior Accounting and Clerical Work to use.

She had taken up employment at a local garage as a bookkeeper where she could walk to work. Their next-door neighbor looked after little Jake during the day for a nominal fee, so it had been working out okay for them financially. But now, with George England having suffered another stroke, he was going to need somebody to attend to him full time since he was totally confined to his bed.

In the end, it was Mattie Bradford who came up with the idea that seemed to help everyone out. She decided to sell her property in the lower end of town and buy a place that had just become available only two blocks from the Englands. Ever since the awful incident with Vincent Daley several years ago, the Legion had lost its appeal. John Bradford was especially loathe to live and work in the building that harbored such bad memories.

Therefore, it was with a certain amount of relief when John and Becky agreed to move in with Mattie and they brought their daughter Helen with them. This allowed Mattie to give the necessary care to George England, so they moved George over to Mattie's. With the experience John had gained at the Legion tending bar, he decided to open a small convenience store in the back end of the house. From there he sold cigarettes, magazines, milk, bread, eggs, and the like to local clients.

Things went along well over the next year until tragedy once again struck the extended families. First, Martin's father had a final stroke which took his life one night in May 1952. Then the following month, with the families still grieving over George's passing, John's wife Becky died while giving birth to a beautiful baby girl.

A heavy cloud of doom and despair settled over both families as the summer approached.

PART V

ITALY REVISITED

Chapter Twenty-eight

AFTER MARTIN lost both his father and sister within months, Meg had a sick feeling that his battle with alcohol was about to be severely tested. As well, other events seemed to conspire against him: his close friend Josh Freeman had returned to Boston in May of that year when his father had been relocated to Boston; a month later, Reverend Don McBride had taken a new position with the Presbyterian Church in Saint John; and finally, with his two closest friends now gone, Martin no longer had the same desire to play ball, and so last month he had quit the team.

Lately, Meg noticed he was beginning to spend a lot of time by himself. During the last week in August, 1952, Meg's fears became a reality. This was the week that the town of Chatham held its annual late summer fair. Relatives from both sides of the family were home from Maine and Massachusetts, and the Bradford and England extended families were attempting to thoroughly enjoy themselves.

This, of course, included sitting out on warm nights on the back porch of Martin's home late into the evenings, picnics at the beach down on the Shore Road, or treks to the Exhibition grounds to see the horse hauling contests, the harness races, and the usual sights at the fair.

Inevitably, somebody would have a bottle to pass around and it was only a matter of time before Martin was back into his old habit. By the time the fair had ended, and all the relatives had gone back to the States, the damage had been done. Martin was now drinking as much, if not more, than he had in the past. It was extremely difficult and sad for Meg to see Martin waste all of that time and effort he had spent breaking away from his habit. And the worst of it was, Meg knew Martin was once again experiencing some recurring dream about an Italian lady who owned a vineyard, and another character who was a German officer...

Martin was not a good drunk, if ever there was such a thing. He became morose when he drank, tending to get nasty and argumentative. Sadly, those to receive the brunt of his foul moods were usually those closest to him: Meg, his immediate family members, and even his six-year-old son, Jake.

Friday nights were the worst. On payday at the Renous Ammunition Depot after the bus dropped the workers off at the terminal beside Ben's Lunch in Chatham, several of the men, including Martin, would immediately go to the liquor store, the Legion, or a local bootlegger. Martin would end up arriving home by cab after dark with one or two of his pals, staggering loudly into the house. Meg would then be put in a situation where their limited groceries would have to be shared with his inebriated cronies.

The arguments would then begin in the kitchen while one or two of Martin's pals lay asleep on the family couch in the den. Oftentimes the next morning, Jake would come downstairs to find strangers snoring away in drunken stupors in their living room high back chairs. ⸗

Meg was reaching the end of her rope. It was taking all of her hard earned income to keep the family afloat, since Martin's pay mostly all went to his drinking requirements. Jake would be starting school in a week's time and she wanted to be there for him when he came home at noon for lunch, and again at mid afternoon. This meant she would have to give up her job at the garage, or at the very least see if she could arrange with her employer to work on a part-time basis. And if that option didn't happen, she wondered if it would even be worth her while, going in to work for only a couple of hours each morning.

One Friday night in early September, Meg decided to have a serious talk with Martin. Before his crony Fred Trainor got settled on the den couch, she sternly told him she needed to speak with her husband in private and it would be better if he went home to his mother right away.

Martin was already quite drunk and after Fred had left, he was quick to start their regular Friday night argument. "What the hell was all that about?" he demanded.

"We need to talk Martin," Meg calmly stated. "Jake starts school on Monday and I've made arrangements at the garage to resign. I want to be home for him at noon and mid-days."

"So, big deal. Quit, then!" he shouted.

"It's not just that, and you know it. The little money I've been making has been going to our grocery bills and winter clothing. It seems most of *your* pay cheque is supporting your drinking habit." She stopped a beat, let this sink into his head, then continued. "Starting Monday, I want you to quit as well. Quit drinking. You did it before, Martin, and you can do it again," Meg pleaded.

"Yeah, that's so easy for you to say," Martin argued. "You have no goddamned idea what it's like to have to ride a bus every day for forty minutes, only to go to a job that you hate. I put in an absolutely boring day at work, ride the bus *another* forty minutes to get home and then look forward to having a recurring nightmare every other night. It's driving me crazy, Meg. Can't you understand?" he shouted.

"I understand that you need help Martin. And I'm not a professional, but I think you need to see that doctor again in Montreal, what's his name, LeBlanc?" she asked.

Martin looked hard at Meg. "I can't afford to go to Montreal, Meg. But let me think about what you've said." He was tired and he just wanted a drink. But as he strode off to the back shed to be by himself with the pint of rum he kept hidden there, he felt the familiar pangs of guilt wash over him.

He hadn't mentioned it yet to Meg, but in addition to the nightmares and flashbacks, he was also starting to hear voices now. They came to him out of the blue, not frequently, but now and then: *Go to the shed Marty, you know what you want to do, what you must do, so just do it! Get the rope. The rope, Marty. Just do it for, for their sake!*

He didn't see or hear Meg standing behind him as he sat on his father's old saw horse, staring across the shed at a spool of rope hanging on the wall. He held his head in his hands and he began crying. Meg came over to him and held him gently in her arms. "We're going to get help, Martin. Leave it with me. Come back into the house, it'll be alright."

But of course it wasn't alright. Again that night Martin had pieces of the same dream return to haunt him. The beautiful lady with a dagger protruding from her slim throat, all the blood; the German officer laughing while Captain Jacobs turned to face Martin and level his gun at him. "I'm sorry it has to end this way, Martin," said Jacobs as he fired his pistol!

Martin awoke with a loud cry and was relieved to find Meg holding him again. "Martin, while you were sleeping I telephoned Captain Jacobs. He said he would get home to see us within the week. He said he had some news for you that might help. Let's go back to sleep."

Chapter Twenty-nine

REG JACOBS hung up his phone with a worried look on his face. His wife Peggy noticed his concerned manner and asked him if everything was okay. He told her there was no problem, but he was probably going to be away for a week or so. A client needed counseling in New Brunswick and it involved politics. He knew this was a boring subject for his wife of only two years so it made the lie a bit easier to state.

He had just finished speaking with Meg England. Jacobs now allowed his mind to return for a moment to that day in a Tuscany villa in the autumn of 1944. Little did he know then how the effects of that incident would haunt him for the next eight years. It was time to make things right for Martin, his close friend and aide during the war. First however, he needed to call another player into the game, his other close friend, Dr Michel LeBlanc.

"Good evening Michel, it's Reg calling, how are you?"

"Just fine, Reg," said LeBlanc. "To what do I owe the honor of a call from my good Captain?" he added jokingly.

"Michel, I was just speaking with Meg England, the wife of my friend and a former patient of yours, Martin England."

"I see," Michel said, suddenly very serious.

"Doctor, might you be able to free up about a week of your time to help me with something? I'm afraid it relates directly to our Tuscany affair of '44….," Jacobs left the implication unsaid.

"When are you thinking, Captain? I guess I can be available right away for something as serious as this."

"Excellent! In that case, I'll pick you up in the morning and we'll catch a flight to Moncton. We can discuss our plans along the way," he added cryptically. Reg then made a second call, this one to Colonel Francis Saunders at his home in CFB Kingston, Ontario. Before doing so, he ensured the door to his study was closed and locked. On the fourth ring, the telephone in Kingston was picked up.

"This is Saunders."

"Colonel sir, I apologize for the late call. This is your former Captain, Reginald Jacobs calling from my personal line in Montreal. Do you have a minute? It is important sir!"

~ * ~

Twenty minutes later, Reg went to his bedroom. Peggy was asleep and he was careful not to wake her. He lay beside her as his thoughts returned to the villa outside Veragno, Italy and the days leading up to the awful event that day in October 1944. He had held a secret from everybody since that time, including Martin and indeed, his own wife.

It was necessary, since he was forced to do so under the Official Secrets Act of 1939. The law however, had since been amended whereby the Crown had the discretion to waive any penalty in the event of either intentional or accidental disclosure by parties hitherto, and such waivers were largely dependent on the length of time that had lapsed. In this case, it was now eight years. *Was that enough?* He was about to find out...

Chapter Thirty

WHEN JACOBS and LeBlanc arrived at the Moncton Airport at 11:15 AST the next morning, they were met by a Sergeant Clarke as they waited for their luggage. "Sir, I have been requested by Colonel Saunders from CFB Kingston to escort you and your associate to CFB Chatham, courtesy of the Armed Forces," said Clarke after introductions had been made.

"Well Sergeant, this is great. We appreciate the lift. Please thank the Colonel for us when you're speaking with him," he said.

"You can tell him face to face in a couple of hours, sir. He's catching a flight to the base in Chatham as we speak," said the Sergeant.

Well, well, thought, Jacobs. *This is getting interesting...*

The drive from Moncton to CFB Chatham was uneventful, and both Jacobs and LeBlanc went immediately into the men's room at the Officer's Mess once they were in the building. Jacobs was drying his hands on a towel as he spoke to LeBlanc. "Michel, I don't know what Colonel Saunders is doing here, so we'll have to play this by ear. Time will tell whether or not he's on our side in this. Let me take the lead, okay?"

"Sure Reg, no problem there. I'm just a small player in this deal, and I'd like to keep it that way," he said. They left the wash-room and went into the bar area. A tall, bald-headed individual in full uniform approached them as they entered, his hand extended, a smile revealed perfect dentures beneath a short-clipped grey moustache.

"Captain Jacobs, good to see you after so many years. And Captain LeBlanc, you as well. The years have been kind to both of you, I see," the Colonel said, giving them an appraising look.

"And you too, Colonel. But let's limit the use of honorifics," Jacobs said with a wry smile. After all, both he and LeBlanc were now retired officers and preferred to be addressed by their civilian names. "Call me, Reg," he said.

"Likewise, sir," said LeBlanc. "I prefer to be called Michel."

"Very well, gentlemen, let's first get a drink and you can tell me what this business with Martin England is all about."

They sat in high-backed maroon leather chairs located in a bar that would have given any of Jacobs's regular drinking establishments in Montreal a run for their money. The bar was empty, save for the bartender who kept discreetly out of earshot. The only background noise was the soft clicking of billiard balls and the odd bit of muted laughter from a room some distance away. Saunders raised his hand to the barkeep who was at their table in seconds. As soon as their drinks arrived, Saunders continued.

"Reg, England is the same young man who unwittingly became entangled in the adventure we put you guys through while you were in Veragno, am I right?" asked the Colonel.

"That is correct, sir," said Jacobs. "The man is not in good shape. In fact, I'm not sure how much you know, but he's been suffering from mental fatigue ever since returning from the War in 1945. He has had his share of problems related to the illness, as Michel here can attest. In addition, most recently he underwent a trial in which he was wrongly accused in the *stabbing* death of a man in the area here." Jacobs emphasized the word 'stabbing', and he continued.

"Actually, I was able to defend him in my capacity as Defense Counsel and we won his acquittal two years ago. I had thought things were going to be okay for Martin after I left him when the trial was over, but I was incorrect in my assumptions. His wife called me last night and told me his condition has worsened. She said he is constantly being plagued by recurring nightmares of something he calls the 'Tuscany Terrors'. Michel, maybe you can jump in here and tell the Colonel some of the story from your perspective."

Michel gently put his drink on the table and began his part.

"Sir, as you know, I was also on loan at that time to *The Princess Pats.* I was called to the scene of the incident in Tuscany by yourself, which was after you had spoken with Captain Jacobs, as I now understand. As part of my medical training, I was quite well versed in the practice of therapeutic hypnotism. You requested my expertise at that time to assist Corporal

England and I was able to help," LeBlanc said.

"Yes, Michel. I became aware of this special talent you had and decided it might be an opportune time to put it to use. It is not every day that somebody is put in a situation where they must kill another human being in the defense of a superior officer. And I am glad you were on hand and available in that event," finished the Colonel.

"However, sir," Jacobs now cut in, "England is now experiencing bits and pieces of the episode in the form of flashbacks. Most of these occur at night when he is sleeping, but he also has day visions of the same images. They are tormenting him, driving him to drink. His marriage is in jeopardy, and worst of all, he has just started to hear voices inside his head, encouraging him to commit suicide."

"Then Captain LeBlanc here should immediately help the man once again. Surely, through hypnosis he can make him forget the episode? I don't see a problem, Captain," said Saunders. *He was back to using army rank again*, Jacobs noted

"Colonel," said LeBlanc, giving a side glance to Jacobs. "You don't fully understand. Hypnosis is a therapy, but it is only *one* part of a full regime of various steps in a full program to treat the illness. By itself is not a cure to what is afflicting Martin England. He needs more than a band-aid, sir."

"I was told last night by Captain Jacobs here that Corporal England has been successful in forgetting a number of other incidents that happened over there. He said you were the one to accomplish this over a number of sessions with him in Montreal a couple of years ago. Why can't you do the same now?" The Colonel asked. Both LeBlanc and Jacobs could tell his attitude had changed somewhat.

"Yes sir, that is correct," continued LeBlanc. "I believe the post-hypnotic suggestions I gave to Corporal England that night certainly helped him forget about it. Yet it was bound to come back to haunt him... the fight he incurred with the local man here involved a knife. That man was accidentally stabbed in the neck and died. What better incident to 'trigger' the memory of the Tuscany affair? Sir, he must be properly treated," LeBlanc insisted.

"Then by all means Captain, treat the man," shouted Saunders.

"Well yes but you should know, Colonel, it will be necessary for us to fully disclose the mission we were on at that time in England," stated LeBlanc. "If he is not aware of *why* he had to kill the Senorita, and *why* Reg was there in the first place, then chances are his mind will not accept the therapy. Oh, he'll have temporary relief and, like the other incidents, he may even go for several years before they recur. But I can guarantee they will return."

The Colonel then rose from his chair and assumed an imposing posture.

"And you should be aware, Captain, that we are still under the governance of the Official Secrets Act of 1939. Christ, we can be prosecuted for such disclosures. Therefore, you are hereby under strict orders to keep this to yourself." The Colonel was now clearly outraged at this perceived subordination.

By this time, however, Jacobs had heard enough. He stepped in front of the Colonel and got into his face. "All right, Saunders, let's cut the bullshit."

He held up his index finger under the Colonel's nose.

"In the first place, we, meaning Doctor LeBlanc and myself, are retired from the Forces. We are no longer under your goddamn command!"

His middle finger joined the index.

"Secondly, Michel was right. You didn't give a shit about the well-being of Martin England in October of 1944, and you sure as hell don't give a shit now. Your main concern is keeping the lid on the incident that happened in Tuscany."

Now Jacobs's ring finger came into play.

"Lastly, if Michel in his expert opinion, says Martin must now know the full truth in order to be free of his demons, then that is what is going to happen. Corporal England saved my life that day, and I will *not* leave him now in this condition. I know a thing or two about the law and if I have to Colonel, I'll take this to the goddamned Supreme Court of Canada. Let's go, Michel," and they left the Colonel standing alone in the bar while they called a taxi from a house phone in the lobby.

Meanwhile, still smarting from the verbal assault from Jacobs, the Colonel went to a phone at the bar. "Sergeant, listen carefully. I want you to contact Colonel Jim Fraser, CFB Trenton. Tell him I need to speak with him here in person, like yesterday!"

When the connection had been made, Sergeant Clarke spoke with Fraser in Trenton. He spent five minutes on the phone with Fraser, then returned to Saunders and passed on his message to him. "The Colonel was not happy sir, but he will be here on a ten-fifteen flight later tonight."

Christ, thought Saunders. *This business could open up a real can of worms...*

He went back to the bar and ordered another drink

~ * ~

When their cab entered the England driveway, Meg ran out to greet them. "Oh Reg, it is so good to see you again," said Meg as they held each other warmly.

"You never change with the years, Meg. It must be this great Miramichi air. Say, this is my good friend, Doctor Michel LeBlanc. You've heard me mention him before, and how he has helped Martin."

"Of course, Doctor, it's so nice to meet you. Both of you come into the house, I have Reg's favorite meal in the oven and you'll both want to spend some time with Martin before we eat. He has taken time off work ..." she was near sobbing.

"Meg, how is he?" Jacobs's tone was serious. "It didn't sound good from your call..." he left it open.

"You'll see Reg," Meg said, in a sorrowful tone. "Come on, let's go in."

The woman sounds defeated, thought Reg. *It must be bad.*

Chapter Thirty-one

AS REG and Michel were ushered into the kitchen, a figure appeared from the adjoining den. It was Martin, but Jacobs was stunned at what he saw. His friend had lost at least twenty pounds since he had last seen him. Martin approached them looking like a walking skeleton. But more shocking were his eyes, red-rimmed and sunken in his pale, thin face. He looked like one of the POWs they had come across outside Auschwitz in early '45. Reg was momentarily at a loss for words.

"Martin, good to see you," he stumbled. It was an awkward greeting.

"And you, my friend," Martin responded. "I know you're uncomfortable seeing me like this. I'm sorry to bring you here." He turned his attention to LeBlanc. "Doctor, I'm glad you're here with Reg. I assume you've met Meg?" He made an attempt at a smile, his eyes watering. It was a sad sight.

"All right," said Reg, stepping into the moment. "Martin, where's my favorite Godson?"

"Ah, he's upstairs playing with his toys, Reg."

"Go tell him I'm here and that I have something for him. While you're there, Marty, have yourself a shower and shave, okay?" He came closer to Martin while Meg was busy tending to a salmon baking in the oven, and he placed his hands on Martin's shoulders. Quietly, he spoke to him, "We're here to make you well, soldier. It's going to be okay."

Martin left them and in a couple of minutes, Jake came bounding into the kitchen and ran over to Reg's open arms. He picked the boy up, held him high in the air, then he crumpled on the floor.

"Oh! Ow, ow! I've hurt myself! I think I've broken my back… it's all Jake's fault. He's getting too big for me." When Jake turned to his mother with a worried look, Reg grabbed the boy and started tickling him in abandon, the two of them rolling around on the kitchen floor together.

Finally, Reg got up and reached into his suitcase. His hand came out holding a hardcover book that had a large picture of a pirate on the jacket. It was one of the classics, Treasure Island, by Robert Louis Stevenson. "Here you go, Jake," said Reg. "I heard you like pirate stories?"

"Yeah," said Jake, in awe. "Gee, thanks Uncle Reg," and he ran off to look at his gift.

By the time supper was ready, Martin had finished making himself look more presentable. At least he was clean-shaven, his black hair was shining and lustrous, and he now walked with a purposeful stride. They ate their supper, and Meg was pleased when the three men all accepted second helpings.

"Mrs. England, I can't remember the last time I had such a great home-cooked meal," said Michel. "Martin, with a cook like this I don't understand why you aren't at least twice as big as you are..." then he immediately realized he had made a verbal faux pas. "Oh, God, sorry Martin, I wasn't thinking," he looked contritely at his friend.

"No problem, Doc'. I understand," he said. "I know I've been neglecting my health lately. I guess it's part of the problem, you know."

"Right! Speaking of, when do you want to start therapy, Martin?"

"God, Doc, as soon as you want. I'm ready whenever you are."

"Do you want to do this here in private? I've discussed it with Reg and if you want, we can have Meg sit in on the preamble and the briefing. We think it's important and it may be helpful if you're both privy to the full story we are about to relate." As he said this he looked with raised eyebrows at Reg.

"Exactly, Martin. Meg, maybe we should wait until Jake goes to bed though, if that's okay?" said Jacobs, looking aside at Jake in the den who was absorbed in his new book.

"By all means," she said.

It was only six pm so the group of adults decided to have a card game in which Jake could be included, *Crazy Eights*. After an hour of card-playing in which Jake had managed to be declared the overall Miramichi Crazy Eights Grand Champion, he gave Jake a silver dollar he had been carrying. Meg gathered up the cards while Jake went back to reading his book.

"Reg, I swear you're going to spoil that child to death," admonished Meg. "And by the way, I saw you playing right into his hand on several occasions."

Reg only winked at her and they all moved into the den once Meg had taken Jake to his room. When she returned, she sat beside Martin and Reg addressed them.

"Folks, this is going to sound very dramatic, but what we're about to tell you must stay between the four of us only, at least for a while. Are we agreed?" he asked.

The couple looked seriously at each other and they both nodded and gave their promises. They were clearly intrigued.

"The reason for this is simple. What occurred in October of 1944 in Veragno, Italy with Martin, Michel, and myself is restricted under The Official Secrecy Act. The three of us could be brought up on charges for unlawfully disclosing certain information. However, Michel and I both strongly feel that Martin must know the full story of what happened in order for his mind to heal. It will all become clear as we go through several sessions with you Martin. And you, Meg, are an integral part of his future care-giving. So, you are included. Now, where should I begin, Michel?"

"Reg, why don't you relate the full story of the weeks leading up to the final meeting with the people involved and then finish with the incident itself. When you're done, I can work with Martin and have him relive the experience under hypnosis."

"Very well, Michel," said Jacobs as he looked seriously at Meg. "Meg, it all started right after we finished what we could at the Battle of Rimini in September, 1944. The Germans had been driven a bit further north, but their morale was still strong, and they had dug in at the Gothic Line. By that time our troops had been cut in half by having to send many of our men to participate in the D-Day exercises. We were exhausted. Our group, *The Princess Patricia Light Infantry* under the command of Colonel Frank Saunders, had established quarters outside of the town of Veragno in the south-central part of Italy.

The warm Tuscany sun was a welcome relief from the cold rains and the full-force fighting that had started in the northern part of the country.

We took every advantage of the furlough," Reg smiled at the memory.

He began his story...

In September, 1944, Jacobs and England were on loan to the Princess Patricia Light Infantry...

Reg was with this group when he had first met up with Dr Michel LeBlanc, a fellow Canuck from Montreal who had entered the Forces as a commissioned officer like himself. As with Martin, Reg and the doctor became close friends, but due to circumstances, rank and file separations, Michel had never met Martin until later...

The Princess Pats' were charged with assisting the 8th Army in driving the Germans north out of Italy and their help was particularly needed by the 4th British Army and several Divisions of the 1st Canadian Army. The latter had met with a stubborn German defense on the night of September 19th. The Allies were down in numbers by one-half and were near exhaustion but they persisted in driving the enemy as far north as the Gothic Line. Here the Germans were able to solidly dig in and were awaiting support from their troops in North Africa, while the Allies awaited the arrival of the Americans.

Meanwhile, the 'Pats' had been given a much needed rest and they were deployed south to the Tuscany area in late September. The heavy rains had started north of them, and mud was a constant problem causing vehicles to be bogged down, and morale was low. As such it was with a good deal of relief when Jacobs and Martin were able to relax a bit in this beautiful area of the country, even if it was for only a short time.

On the second day in their new surroundings, Reg and Martin were enjoying a warm, sunny day in a café on a side street in the town of Veragno. They were sitting at an outside table when they heard a commotion inside the restaurant. A woman was yelling and they noticed a British infantryman giving a beautiful lady a hard time. The man was clearly inebriated and Jacobs, with Martin, intervened before the situation got too ugly. As a result, the grateful woman invited them to her villa outside the town that day for a late dinner and the three took off, Martin driving the Captain's jeep.

She was a vintner, a single lady who was quite successful in her trade and the object of many suitors in the town. Her father had left her his vineyard two years previously when he had passed away. Her name was Senorita Madellena DeFranco and her beauty and wealth were the talk of the Tuscany region.

Very quickly, from what Martin could tell, it seemed she had captured the heart of his Captain. A sensuous smile here and there, a slight flip of her hair, or an outright flirtatious grin. They were all signs to Martin she was definitely in the process of seducing Jacobs and Martin felt uncomfortable in seeing this. But, hey. Jacobs was a single man, so if he wanted to have an affair with the Senorita, who was Martin to deny him this natural desire?

Over the next two weeks, now into October, they continued to visit the Senorita's vineyard in the Tuscany Valley, with Martin always accompanying the Captain. Martin knew it would probably end soon but he was a willing companion to Reg on their regular visits to the villa. He was aware Reg and the Senorita had held private moments in various parts of the villa while Martin simply enjoyed a walk by himself among the grapevines and the rolling landscape.

One day in mid-October, such a day occurred and frankly, it again made Martin feel awkward. After an hour, he was becoming irate, waiting outside the villa, feeling the fool. He decided to again take a stroll alone through a section of white *Pinot* on his return to the villa. It was then that he spotted an open Mercedes-Benz roadster approach from the north in a hurry, raising a cloud of dust from the dry unpaved road that led onto the property.

Not knowing why, Martin remained out of sight from the figure in the vehicle and he watched as it stopped in front of the main building. A uniformed officer quickly leapt out of the car and ran into the house. *What the hell?* thought Martin. Unless he was seeing things, the man was definitely wearing a German uniform. He decided to check it out and followed discreetly behind the officer.

Martin deftly crept closer to the entrance of the villa, then he entered the building and snuck down a hallway that led to the main parlor where he could faintly make out people talking quietly. As he hid behind an armchair in the hall, he could clearly see his captain sitting on a sofa alongside the Senorita, drinking a glass of red wine, oblivious to the fact that a German officer was somewhere in their presence.

As he watched the two from behind a large wing-backed chair, Madellena rose and left the parlor. She was now heading directly toward him. Unseen, he held his breath behind the large chair as she passed by him and continued into the kitchen. Martin was undecided as to what he should now do. He was about to go to Jacobs and advise him of the situation, but just then the German appeared out of a side room off the hall and ran to Madellena in the kitchen, holding her in his arms.

It quickly became apparent that the two were lovers. They spoke insistently in German to each other, and at several points in their conversation they each looked anxiously back his way toward the parlor where Reg was sitting with his back to them.

Martin was about to alert his captain when Madellena and the German walked out of the kitchen, she carrying a bottle of wine, and they strode past Martin as he again hid behind the large chair in the hall. Now smiling, the two entered the parlor and greeted Reg where he sat. Martin could not believe what he was seeing. *Did Jacobs know the German?*

As Martin secretly watched them, the Senorita then poured wine for the three of them and wistfully spoke of better days to come when "this awful fighting would be finished."

After finishing his drink, the German looked at his watch, excused himself and bade them goodbye, saying he had a long and dangerous drive ahead. It was necessary to get back to his battalion.

When the German left, Martin entered the sitting room, pretending to have just returned from his walk in the vineyards.

"Martin, there you are," said Jacobs. "We were just talking to a friend of Madellena's. Perhaps you ran into him on your way back, no?"

"Why no, sir," said Martin. He wondered what kind of game Reg was playing. He also wondered how far he should play stupid about this. Maybe he should simply report the whole business to the Commanding Officer of the *Princess Pats.*

"You're looking awfully serious, Martin. What's on your mind, my friend?"

"Nothing, sir. I'm just tired. Maybe we should be getting back to the camp, okay, sir?"

"Sure thing. Why don't you throw our gear into the jeep and I'll be right along." While Martin was outside in the jeep, he watched as Jacobs held Madellena closely and he could hear him telling her he would be back the following evening.

"I promise to have some interesting information for you then," he said, then he kissed her goodbye.

~ * ~

On the drive back to Veragno, Martin decided things had gone too far and it was now time for them to talk. "Sir, with all respect, I must ask you to explain your relationship with the Senorita."

Jacobs looked sternly at Martin. "Corporal, pull the jeep to the side of the road." When he did, Jacobs looked at him very seriously. "Listen, I don't have to explain a damn thing to you, but in consideration of our relationship over the past five-and-a-half years, let's just say this is an 'affair of the heart'. We are two single adults who are attracted to each other and, who knows? Maybe we can make a life together after the war is over."

No mention was made of the German officer. Martin would now be caught in a lie if he were to tell Jacobs what he had witnessed back at the villa. Besides, if his Captain was indeed a traitor, now was not the time to bring anything further out into the open. He decided to hang on to this bit of knowledge and see if he could find out anything more if he did indeed, go to the authorities.

"Of course, you are correct, Captain, and I apologize for prying," he said to Jacobs, hoping the captain would believe him.

"Nonsense, Martin," Jacobs said. "Let's forget about this. But just so you know, I did tell Madellena that I'd bring her a certain present tomorrow. So I won't bother having you tag along with me then. Besides, I hope to be staying overnight," he said with a wink. Martin felt he was saying this as a way of hiding something. He was quite certain there was some form of conspiracy underfoot, and at that moment he decided he would follow Reg secretly tomorrow night in an effort to learn more.

~ * ~

The following night there was no moon. In addition, a light cloud cover provided Martin with all the darkness he required as he followed Jacobs in a jeep he had borrowed from a New Zealander comrade in the Princess Pats Regiment. He had also made sure to bring his service hand gun, a Walther P38. His headlights had been turned out as a precaution, and the open Tuscany landscape allowed him to maintain a distance of approximately a quarter of a mile from his quarry.

Fifteen minutes later he parked his jeep on the far side of the villa after Jacobs had gone into the house, and he crept silently along the outer wall of the building under the eave of the veranda roof. He moved stealthily, situating himself beneath a window which he determined was directly under the sitting room, hoping to see Jacobs with the Senorita in familiar surroundings. He was not disappointed when he saw them again sitting together on the sofa, sharing a carafe of wine. But oddly out of setting, Jacobs had spread a document on the coffee table. It appeared to be a map and now Martin was highly intrigued.

Suddenly, the same German Martin had seen yesterday entered the room from the kitchen, carrying his own glass of wine, smiling warmly at Jacobs and offered him a pleasant greeting. The window under which Martin was hiding was closed and he could not hear what was being said. All he could do at this point was sit and wait, silently fuming with what he had witnessed.

He remained hidden under the parlor window for what seemed an eternity. Every now and then from inside the house he could hear muted laughter and he was tempted to simply barge into the room and demand an explanation. Yet he waited, his anger building.

As he crouched in place, he sensed movement beneath him. Looking down, he saw a huge, tan-colored spider that had crawled beside his left boot and was now beginning to move up his leg. *Jesus!* If there was one thing Martin feared and despised, it was spiders. This species was a large Brown Recluse known in Italy as the *'violini'* because of its distinct markings on its dorsal area, similar to a violin. More significant, it was venomous!

Martin could no longer stand to watch the arachnid approach his middle torso area and he jumped quickly in an effort to brush it off his groin. Unfortunately, in the process his foot hit a rake that had been leaning against the outer wall of the building. It clattered on a metal bucket as it fell. In a matter of seconds the German officer had come outside to investigate.

When the German approached Martin, he was surprised to see a young infantryman with the iconic Canadian Maple Leaf insignia on his uniform, pointing a pistol at him. Martin silently gestured toward the doorway of the villa and he led the German inside. As Martin entered the room behind him, Jacobs stood in shock to see his aide holding the German officer at gunpoint.

"Martin, what the hell are you doing?" he shouted. "This is Lieutenant Kelerring. We are friends for God's sake."

"I can see that," said Martin sarcastically. "Sir, how could you?"

"Now wait, Martin. You don't understand," said Jacobs as he edged closer to the sofa which separated them.

Unknown to Martin, Jacobs had removed his own sidearm when he had arrived, and it was now lying within easy reach on the sofa. At that moment the Senorita, who had earlier left the parlor, now called from the kitchen, "Who wants more wine?"

Martin was distracted by the sound of Madellena's voice, and Jacobs, taking note of this, grabbed his own weapon off the sofa in a quick motion and held it a foot from Martin's face. He now had the upper hand over his aide. One hand at a time, he carefully pulled his leather gloves from his inside jacket pocket and put them on, smiling menacingly at Martin.

"Martin, place your gun down and I'll explain everything," said Jacobs. When Martin hesitated to do as he was told, Kelerring immediately drew his own Luger. Jacobs walked over to Martin who was too stunned by what was happening to react, and Jacobs hit him viciously with the butt of his pistol on the side of his head. Martin fell to the floor, toppling over behind the sofa, barely conscious. Jacobs retrieved Martin's pistol and placed it under the webbing of his own belt.

The German suddenly shouted at Jacobs. "What is happening here, Jacobs? Were you planning a double-cross against me? Shoot this man immediately," yelled Kelerring.

Jacobs again trained his gun against Martin. Martin, barely

conscious, stared down the small bore of his friend's Beretta semi-automatic.

"I'm so sorry it had to end this way, my friend." Martin's world collapsed. He closed his eyes as he realized his best friend was a traitor who was about to kill him. The sound of the shot in the small sitting room was deafening to his ears.

When Martin opened his eyes he was looking at the body of the German officer as it lay on the floor of the parlor. He continued to feign unconsciousness, watching behind his barely-closed eyelids as the Senorita now came into his limited view. She had apparently managed to quietly enter the room from the kitchen, and had crept behind Jacobs who was standing over the German, his smoking Beretta pointed at the fallen officer.

He watched in horror as the Senorita pulled a very long stiletto from the folds of her serape. She snuck up soundlessly closer to Jacobs and wrapped her left arm around Reg's neck, pressing the point of the dagger against his carotid artery with her right hand.

Calmly, she frog-marched Jacobs toward the body of Kelerring where he lay on the floor. She pushed Jacobs down and knelt with him in a kind of operatic dance move, all the while keeping the knife pressed against his neck. She pulled the Luger from Kelerring's death grip and swung it in the direction of the Captain at the same time as she flung the dagger away from herself.

"Throw your weapon behind you, Captain!" A knowing look came over Jacobs's face as he reluctantly threw the Beretta aside.

"A tragedy, no?" said Madellena as she took careful aim at the captain. "Three lovers, one of them a jealous officer of the Allied Forces, another a senior German Officer. Both in love with the beautiful Senorita. You shot him when you arrived here tonight to find us in '*flagrante delicto*'. You thought you had killed him but as you turned toward me, he was able to find the strength to fire a fatal shot at the man who was about to steal his love away…

"The authorities will respond to the call that I am about to make and find this pistol returned to his hand. Yes, I will wipe my fingerprints off of it first. That is, of course, after I shoot you. And I will also be sure to fire a shot after you are dead from this gun while it is in Kelerring's hand. The local police will be sure to find traces of gunshot residue on his hand. Do you not like my plan, Captain Canuck?" she said with disdain. "You Canadians are all so naive," she sneered.

In her free left hand, the Senorita then held the map with drawings that Martin had seen Jacobs looking at earlier. Martin was still in shock and confused, trying to take all this in, pretending to lie unconscious on the floor behind the sofa. The Senorita continued, "I will then take this information to my German friends in the North and be paid handsomely. That should cover all the bases I belie___ " Her words were abruptly cut short by the stiletto that suddenly appeared from nowhere and entered her throat,

Unseen by Madellena, Martin had managed to crawl behind the sofa where he had found her weapon lying on the floor. Without giving it a second thought, he had picked it up by the blade and threw it unerringly at the vintner. End-over-end the stiletto had sailed through space toward the neck of the Senorita where it found its mark, immediately killing her.

Jacobs hurried over to his aide who was standing still, his mouth agape, a shocked expression on his face. Jacobs first examined the side of Martin's head where he had struck him, then he looked closely into Martin's eyes and spoke to him.

"Martin, listen carefully to me. You are in shock. I am sorry I had to hit you, but you would have been killed otherwise. I shall explain everything to you later. Right now we have work to do, and we don't have much time."

Jacobs removed the knife from the Senorita's neck, wiped it clear of prints and placed it in the right hand of the dead German. He also replaced the Luger in Kelerring's holster. He then took the map and papers from Madellena and put them in his briefcase. His eyes scanned the room and not finding the object of his search, he went into the Senorita's bedroom. In minutes, he was back with the German's valise which he threw with his own briefcase to Martin and told him to put them in the back of his jeep.

While Martin was outside, Jacobs called their base camp and asked for Colonel Saunders. He spoke hurriedly to his superior when he came on the line.

"Colonel, this is Captain Jacobs. I am at the villa and we have a problem. Our two targets have been terminated but there is a complication with one of our own people." He waited while Saunders absorbed this coded information. "Yes sir, my aide. Yes sir, I understand," Jacobs replied as he listened to the response from the Colonel. "We'll be here when they arrive and all will be fine, sir. Trust me," he said.

When Martin returned, Jacobs returned the Walther to him and told his stunned assistant to sit in the sofa. "Okay, my friend, our people are on the way. Right now, I want you to lie down and rest." As Martin was getting settled on the sofa, Jacobs poured a full glass of *grappa* and gave it to Martin, telling him to drink it. "Our military doctor will be here soon and he'll treat you for that head wound," he said.

Martin had not spoken a word since he had been struck by Jacobs with the pistol. He was still in deep shock over the events he had seen, and in which he had taken part. Jacobs was confident his doctor friend would be able to help, and he was grateful Saunders had provided his assistance.

By midnight, the situation at the villa was under control. Jacob's friend, Dr. Michel LeBlanc, had arranged to be driven to the villa by a colleague who had immediately returned to base after dropping him off. Martin had been treated for his head wound, and LeBlanc had given him a light sedative which would enhance his receptivity to hypnosis. They then took him into the Senorita's bedroom where the doctor placed him under a deep trance. Carefully, he left him with the suggestion that he would not recall a thing about what happened at the villa that evening, period. He would only vaguely remember going for a drive in the jeep he had borrowed from his Kiwi pal. Not where he went, who he saw, nor what he did.

Leblanc then drove him back to camp in the borrowed jeep and dropped him off at his quarters. In the meantime, Jacobs had stayed behind and waited until the local authorities had arrived. He explained to them the tragic event that had unfolded while he was visiting the Senorita: a German officer had arrived upon the scene. He was unknown to Jacobs who was out of uniform at the time, but it seemed from their ensuing argument he was a suitor of Senorita DeFranco. In a jealous rage, the German had pulled a stiletto from the inside of his tunic and stabbed her, then ran at Jacobs. Jacobs however, already had his own sidearm drawn and was able to successfully defend himself. End of story. He was terribly upset, but what else could he have done?

The local constabulary took all this information with a grain of salt, but he was not about to arrest a senior officer of the Allies under suspicion of any wrongdoing, certainly with the evidence that was in front of him. Jacobs was released without further questioning. The police chief, Alfonzo Vitelli, even said to Jacobs that the lady had been playing with fire now for quite a while. "A sad tale with a tragic ending," he had exclaimed.

Jacobs had driven back to their Base quarters outside of Veragno where he had met up with Colonel Saunders. Saunders now drew on his cigar while Jacobs gave him a brief synopsis of the events that had occurred that evening.

"I don't have to tell you how important it is this affair be kept secret, Captain," he warned.

"Sir, my assistant won't remember what happened last night," he said.

"Very good. I take it Doctor LeBlanc has done his thing?" he asked.

"That is correct, sir."

"I have taken the opportunity to advise Colonel Fraser about what happened," said Saunders. "So, get this straight, Captain. There are to be no leaks, understand? We want this kept quiet. You, LeBlanc, and Fraser are all that know about what happened here. That will be all." Jacobs was dismissed.

At the time, Jacobs wondered why the Colonel seemed so adamant about any word of the killings not getting out...

Chapter Thirty-two

BY THE time Jacobs had finished his story, it was almost nine pm. Martin and Meg were spellbound "I know you have questions," Jacob said. "Fire away." Martin shook his head, clearly at a loss. "Reg, why didn't you tell me I was responsible for the death of the Senorita?"

Jacobs explained the restrictions placed on himself and Michel via the Official Secrets Act. "Michel and I both felt the easiest way to do that at the time was to induce a memory loss in your mind. Now that eight years have passed, I believe we can argue. We have a right. Indeed, I believe we have an *obligation* to disclose this information to you now."

"Why were you there at the villa, Reg?" asked Meg. "Did it have something to do with the documents you retrieved that night?"

"Good questions, Meg," he said. Then to himself, *in for a penny, in for a pound,* he proceeded. "Yes, I was on an undercover mission. We were aware the Senorita and the German were operating together. She was using her connections along with her sexual prowess to gain highly confidential information from various 'clientele' that she could then pass on to her German friends... data about our troop movements, future operational plans. I was playing her game. As a double agent, I was hoping to gain information from *her* about the exact whereabouts of the German troops. Any data I passed on to her was bogus. Oh, at the outset, I was allowed to give her some minor details that were factual, but the rest was all made up."

Everything was coming together for Martin in bits and pieces. "So, now that we know this, and we're not about to disclose it to anyone, why the big problem?" Martin asked.

Martin hesitated, looking at Michel. "Well, I wasn't intending to bring this into our conversation, but now you may as well know the full story. There are two Colonels in the Canadian Armed Forces who were also a part of this 'plot': Colonel Francis Saunders and Colonel James Fraser.

They particularly do not want any of this getting out. Somehow, I think they've managed to use the scheme to their own financial advantage. Trust me, they will be fighting against any legal attempts I may take to get disclosure.

"I do remember seeing their names on some document somewhere that might connect them to this. It's quite possible the two colonels may have been acting for Senorita DeFranco and Kelerring as a source of referrals for them. It would be easy for them to arrange for any of their elite friends to spend time at the villa and relax in her 'charms' as they say."

Michel ventured it would now be a good time to proceed with further hypnotic therapy for Martin, so they softened the lights in the den. In no time at all, Martin was in a deep trance. With all the information Michel now had, he was easily able to have Martin relive the self-named Tuscany Terrors firsthand under a controlled environment.

~ * ~

"Three, two, one…wake up, Martin," Dr. LeBlanc softly spoke to Martin when the hypnosis session was complete. Martin's eyes opened and he looked around at everyone in a serious way.

"How are you feeling, Martin?" asked Meg.

"Meg, you're here. I feel very good. At least, much calmer," he said, hesitating, looking in awe at everyone. "More importantly, I see now why I've been so afraid of confronting that event. Hell, Reg, we were up against it there, weren't we," he exclaimed.

"We were, Martin. You saved my life, my friend."

"So, Reg, let's get it all out. Now I understand that you were at the villa on a secret mission. But how did all that come about? I know we first ran into Madellena at the cafe in Veragno, but what enfolded after that?" he asked.

"Okay Martin. You may as well jump all the way in on this, and you too, Meg. After our little skirmish with the Brit at the cafe, and our subsequent visit to Madellena's villa, it was necessary for me to report this to Saunders. I was immediately requested to attend a meeting with him and Colonel Fraser. I was told they had been aware for some time of this extortion plot she and the German had formed. It was suggested this was now a good opportunity for me to act as a 'double agent', in the role as her suitor.

"I now believe though, that Saunders and Fraser had already given the Senorita and the German a small amount of information they knew about upcoming troop movements in order to gain their trust."

Meg now brought in a tray of fresh coffee, and Jacobs continued.

"A plot was hatched whereby I was to gain what information I could by a certain date. At that time, I was to take the German as a prisoner of war and bring him to our headquarters outside Veragno. However, and this is important, I was told the Senorita was not to know about this," Reg emphasized.

"Why was that necessary, and how were you supposed to accomplish that?" asked Martin.

"The Colonels knew once she found out we had Kelerring in custody, she would use her relationship with them as leverage, you know, she would start spilling the beans and they were obviously afraid word would get out about their part in the game. So, I was told to continue to play along, let her think her lover was safe, inform her Kelerring had the info from me that he needed, and he was anxious to get it to his superiors. I was to provide her with a false telegram from him, confirming this to her, and that he would be in contact with her by the end of November. Also, that he loved her, blah, blah.

"As to how I would capture him, I was simply going to wait for him to leave the villa the morning after that fateful night and follow him until the right opportunity arose where I would be able to confront him alone on the highway. It was not foolproof, but it was conceivable."

Michel then entered the conversation, "And all that time the two Colonels were setting you up, just so they could get in on some quick cash. They probably had a plan or two to extort things from her at a later time," said the doctor.

"Correct," said Reg. "When the incident happened that night at the villa, it was perfect for them. But they had to be sure Martin here would not be able to relate anything, since, as we now suspect, they were probably involved in the plot with them."

"So, they needed Michel to have him forget everything through hypnosis," said Meg, getting into the conversation. "Reg, they *must* have been involved in something shady," she added. "But can you prove it?"

"Not without evidence, Meg," Jacobs replied. It was going on eleven and they all felt the best course of action at this point was to get a good night's sleep and tackle the problem in the morning.

As he lay in bed, Jacobs was struggling with something. It was a thought he had about some form of evidence they could use, something he had seen or heard that night in Tuscany at the villa that was bugging him. It had obviously escaped him. Then he had another thought. *Maybe if Michel took him back to that time and place again through hypnosis?*

He'd ask the doctor in the morning.

Chapter Thirty-three

"SAY MICHEL, are you able to hypnotize anybody you want?" Jacobs asked when they had finished their morning coffees and breakfast.

"I think so, why do you ask?"

"I'd like to be hypnotized."

"Well, maybe. But I don't know if you're smart enough," joked Michel. Realizing Jacobs was serious, he added, "We'll try, c'mon."

They had removed themselves to the den while Martin and Meg took Jake for a walk. Jacobs told Michel specifically what he was looking for, something he had seen or maybe it was something somebody had said the night things had gone dreadfully wrong at the villa. Michel decided to start at the point where he had arrived at the scene himself…

He had treated Martin, and they had gone into the Senorita's bedroom. Michel then hypnotized Martin, and he had driven him back to base Headquarters near Veragno. Jacobs had stayed behind in the villa.

The local police arrived. They seemed to reluctantly believe everything Jacobs told them, and the person in charge, Police Chief Alfonzo Vitelli, was indeed sympathetic with Jacobs. He said to Jacobs that the woman was well known in the area for the grand parties she threw. The Chief had even said himself that he knew it was only a matter of time before her antics would come to this type of tragic ending. In fact, before leaving, the Chief asked Jacobs for the names of the two Colonels presently in command of the troops stationed outside Veragno.

From this segment of his hypnosis, Reg was able to recall the data that had escaped him. He realized it was the police Chief in Veragno, Chief Vitelli. He had written the names of the colonels into a notebook. *Why?* It would be an expensive trip to Tuscany, but by God it would be worth the price if his intuitions were proven correct. First things first.

"Buona sera., Police Chief Vitelli?" asked Jacobs. He had obtained

the number of the Veragno Police Department from the long-distance operator and had her call the station.

"*Lui non e qui,*" the voice said.

"Ah, *parla inglese?*" asked Jacobs.

"*Si, si,* a little," replied the voice.

"*Buona.* Where can I find Chief Vitelli," he asked.

"Well, I notta too sure. He either up, or down," a small laugh. "*E morto!*"

"He died?" asked Jacobs.

"*Si, e morto,*" said the voice, now somber.

"*Grazie,* I am sorry." Jacobs ended the conversation.

"*So much for that,*" exclaimed Jacobs to himself when he hung up the phone in the den and went back to the kitchen where the others were sitting.

"I was hoping to be able to speak with Chief Vitelli in Veragno just now. Thanks to the hypnosis I just went through, I was able to remember that night in the villa in greater detail. The Chief of Police arrived on the scene, and I recall him saying to me he was not surprised with the fate of the Senorita. Apparently, he suspected she was involved in an extortion ring of some kind along with the German. I am sure the Chief had some information on her and he maybe even had the names of some of her victims, or other players involved. Unfortunately, he died, according to his Sergeant that I was just speaking with."

"That's awfully coincidental Reg," said Michel. "Did he say how or when he died?"

"Ah, no. My Italian is not sufficient to carry on a conversation. Frankly, I was too embarrassed to continue."

"Maybe something bad happened," said Michel. "It's just a feeling I have, Reg. Tell you what. I have a friend in Florence I keep in touch with. Why don't I get him to check the local obituaries in Veragno to determine when the Chief died. Then we can go from there, okay?" He received permission from Meg to place a person-to-person ca-ll to his friend in Italy.

Later that evening, the Englands received a long-distance call from a mister Pasqual Savante in Florence, Italy asking for Michel. In minutes, Michel went back to the others. "Listen to this," he said. "It seems our Police

Chief had a rather unfortunate and odd accident in early March, 1945. Just before the Americans were able to breach the Gothic Line, he was found in his vehicle in a gorge off the highway going to Florence. Apparently, the brakes on his car failed and he ended up driving off a steep embankment, resulting in a broken neck."

"No kidding," said Jacobs. "I think your hunch is paying off Michel. The timing of that accident just so happens to coincide with the approximate date the Canadians departed from that area for Northern France.

"What does your friend Pasqual do for a living in Florence, Michel, and do you think he might be up for a visit from a couple of Canucks?"

A huge grin spread over Michel's face. "Pasqual is an investigative newspaper reporter Reg, and I believe he would be delighted to have visitors from Canada."

"Then I suggest you call him back and make the necessary arrangements. I believe a little detective work is in order. And by the way, Meg. I'm keeping track of these calls, so don't be worrying about the expense."

Martin and Meg were happy to see some progress being made on a couple of fronts. The hypnosis provided by LeBlanc was certainly helpful in raising Martin's spirits and his self confidence. Through therapy he was able to determine the reason for a lot of his frustration and self doubt. And it now appeared Jacobs and LeBlanc might be able to uncover some connection between the two Canadian colonels, the Senorita Madellena, and her German lover, some eight years ago.

Reg and Michel wanted to get an early night's sleep since they were going to be leaving on a long trip tomorrow. Just before going to bed, Jacobs said to Martin, "Well my friend, we may be getting closer to some answers regarding Saunders and Fraser. How are you feeling?"

"Like a huge weight is being lifted off my shoulders. For the past year up until now, it's been like I've been walking in a thick fog. I think it is finally clearing, Reg and it's a great feeling," he said.

"We're headed for Italy in the morning. You and Meg take care and say nothing to Saunders or Fraser, okay? We should return in a week or so. Goodnight my friend..."

Martin was so thankful to have this man as his friend. He shook his hand warmly and said "Thanks Reg. You two be careful over there."

After Jacobs and LeBlanc had retired for the night, Meg joined Martin in the kitchen. "Well Martin," she said. "It's a lovely, warm fall evening, and I can see a beautiful Harvest Moon hanging over the swing set." She took his arm and pulled him toward the kitchen door.

They were sitting side by side on the swing his father had built a number of years ago. It still worked perfectly.

They sat on the wooden bench seat, arms around each other, and stared up at the night sky. Every major constellation was visible to them along with the full moon that fully lit up the backyard. At that moment, for the first time in a long while, their minds were only on the love they shared, and Martin was once again at peace.

Chapter Thirty-four

ON FRIDAY afternoon, three-thirty local time, the Douglas DC-3 landed on the hot tarmac at Peretola Airport, Florence, Italy. It was a blistering 94 degrees outside and in a matter of minutes, Jacobs and LeBlanc were soaking in their suits. They were met at the concourse by a short, stout man who appeared to be in his late thirties. He had black, curly hair and wore a small black moustache in the current Clarke Gable style. His white shirt stretched at the middle as he greeted them warmly.

"Pasqual, the Rasqual!" shouted LeBlanc, in an obvious familiar greeting. He gave his friend the obligatory European double-cheek kiss. "Please say hello to my good friend Reg Jacobs here."

"*Ciao,* Pasqual!" said Jacobs.

"*Benvenuti a Firenze,*" Pasqual welcomed Reg to the beautiful city of Florence, and Reg knew right away he was going to hit it off with the little Italian.

When they had their luggage in hand, they walked to Pasqual's year-old Fiat, and drove to his apartment in the city. Along the way, they marveled at the restorative work that had been accomplished since they had last been here only eight years ago.

The Germans had been driven from Florence in late July 1944, but not before they had blown up many of the beautiful bridges and buildings there. Prior to that, the Allied Forces had also contributed to the horror of the War, dropping bombs that killed over two hundred civilians and causing much destruction as well. So, it was with great sadness yet wonder and admiration that Reg and Michel viewed the breathtaking city as they drove to Pasqual's place.

Michel's friend lived in a small three-bedroom apartment in the heart of the city. It was only a block from the Basilica di Santa Croce, the famous burial site of Michelangelo, Galileo, Rossini, and Machiavelli. The building was situated on Lungarno delle Grazie overlooking the peaceful Arno River.

Once they got settled with three glasses of ice cold *limoncello*, Pasqual impressed his visitors with a serving of antipasti consisting of cold hams and chicken. His main course of chicken piatta then followed.

"Good Lord," Reg exclaimed after they finished the meal. "That's it, I'm moving in here, Pasqual and there's nothing you can do about it," he joked. "You're treating us like royalty. One day we'll have to pay you back. Have you ever been to Montreal?" he asked.

"No, much to my regret. My friend has been insisting I visit him for some time now, but work…" his voice tailed off.

"You must learn to enjoy life, Pasqual," admonished Michel. "After this, you must definitely allow us to reciprocate in kind."

"Very well, Michel," agreed Pasqual. "Now what brings you to my beautiful city with such urgency?" he asked, as he filled three snifters with *grappa,* the excellent Italian brandy.

"As we talked a bit about it on the phone, we're here to further investigate the circumstances surrounding the death of the Veragno Police Chief back in 1945. We'd like you to arrange a meeting for us with the man to whom you spoke. I believe he was the Chief's Sergeant at the time of his accident?"

"Si, that's correct. Sergeant Frenetti. He has since taken over the former Chief's position," replied Pasqual. "Let me make a quick call and see if he is available."

Five minutes passed as Michel and Jacobs sat on a balcony that overlooked the wonderful view of the Arno flowing westward towards its ultimate union with the Mediterranean. The little Italian interrupted their reverie. "Capo Frenetti is at his office, and he would be pleased to meet the gentlemen from Canada," Savante said.

"Well done, Pasqual," said Jacobs. "Which newspaper are you with?" he asked.

"I am with *La Nazione.* We have been around since 1859, and we lean toward moderate Liberalism."

"Before we are through here, we may be in a position to provide you with a great story for your paper, my friend," said Jacobs. This was greeted with a huge smile on the face of the rotund Italian.

"Ah, senor, that would make my day. Things have been somewhat slow the past few months. I could use a good story," he said.

As it turned out, the police station was only a five-minute walk east along the Lungarno delle Grazie. When they reached the station, the three men were led to a spacious office where a tall, muscular man greeted them warmly.

Pasqual made the introductions and said "Capo Frenetti, my friend Doctor LeBlanc is here from Canada with his associate Mr. Reginald Jacobs. They are here in connection with something that happened locally in early 1945. He believes the incident is tied to the untimely death at that time of your former supervisor, Capo Alfonzo Vitelli," he said, all the while speaking in rapid Italian. Jacobs and LeBlanc were at a loss.

"Si, Senor Jacobs. We speak on the telephone, no?" said the Chief in his broken English.

"Yes, Chief, please forgive my poor Italian. Thank you for seeing us today. I realize you are a busy man, so it may save us time if we use Doctor LeBlanc's friend here as an interpreter. Is that alright with you?" he asked, looking at Pasqual as he said the last part.

Through the translation of the story from Pasqual, Jacobs was able to determine the present day Chief Frenetti indeed thought there was something odd about the accident of his boss. He knew him to be a particularly cautious driver and a person who took meticulous care of his vehicle.

Unfortunately, at that time there was a lot of confusion happening with the Americans in town after the liberation from the Nazis and the ongoing battle further north of the city at the Gothic Line.

Jacobs asked Frenetti through Pasqual if there had been any other people he may have seen around the Senorita or her German friend.

"Ah, Senorita Madellena DeFranco," exclaimed the Chief, a mischievous gleam in his eye. "There were so many around her. She was like a bitch in heat."

"Any rich or important people?" prodded Jacobs.

"Bah! *Only* the rich and important," came the reply.

"What about any foreigners? People from the Allied Forces?"

"Una momento, Senor," he said. The Chief left the office and was gone for maybe ten minutes. When he returned, he carried a file folder that was perhaps a half-inch thick. He spoke in Italian to Pasqual who then translated for him.

"The Chief remembered there was a file on the Senorita that his former boss had compiled. While you are here you may read through it if you like." Jacobs was suddenly like a six-year-old kid at Christmas.

For the next fifteen minutes, Jacobs and Pasqual sat completely involved with the contents of the file folder while the police chief and the doctor talked about all the construction that had been accomplished in the city over the past eight years.

When he was finished, Jacobs asked the Chief if he might be able to have his assistance, if necessary, in a case on which he was working. Jacobs told Chief Frenetti he had some more work to do on the case first, and then he would contact him regarding his proposal. They left the police station and went back to Pasqual's apartment to further discuss the matter. But after having another glass of grappa, they all felt too exhausted and decided to get some sleep. Jacobs would explain the file in the morning.

~ * ~

The weather in the Miramichi area of New Brunswick was not quite as temperate as it was in Florence. A low-pressure system from the east had settled over Northumberland County the previous day and it matched the dour mood of the two colonels as they sat at the Officer's Club on Friday evening, September 12th.

"So Jim, what did your source have to say on the matter?" asked Saunders.

"He said it was something an experienced lawyer might be able to take in hand. The problem is, there has never been a precedent set around the issue. In all likelihood, if we continue to follow the Official Secrets Act ruse, it will come back to bite us in the ass. As you know, there was never a valid decision made by anyone higher up the food chain back then to authorize our claim as an official secret, as such. So, we'd need to go into this on a bluff. You want to do that against Jacobs?" said Colonel Fraser.

"Not me," said Saunders. "But I know somebody who might."

~ * ~

Harrison Miller's living room telephone rang rudely at eight-oh-five pm in his home on Riverside Drive in Chatham. It was a cold, wet night and he had no immediate plans for the evening. Still, it was bothersome to be interrupted in the middle of his quiet time. His wife had driven to Newcastle to visit with her mother, and he had the house to himself.

That was all to change. The call was from Colonel Saunders, and he wanted to see him on something important. Suddenly he was dressed for the wet weather and going out the front door. *This could be a big break*, Miller was thinking as he drove towards the air base. Saunders carried a lot of weight in the province, not to mention the municipality. And when he implied to Miller that he might have some work for him in the near future that involved putting an old foe of his behind bars, he was intrigued. *He'd soon find out*, he thought. He pulled into the entrance gate at the Base and showed his ID to the Master Corporal on duty, then sped toward the Officers Club.

Miller found the Colonel sitting with another officer in a plush leather sofa that was the color of a deep burgundy Claret. The two rose to greet him and Saunders then introduced the Crown Prosecutor to Colonel Fraser.

"Harrison, Jim is here visiting us from CFB Kingston. We're having a small problem I thought you might be interested in helping us with. You may even get some payback on that lawyer from Montreal who you argued against five years ago and lost. I think it was the People vs. England murder case. His defense lawyer's name was Jacobs."

"Yes, I had some very weak witnesses going into it," Miller said. "The blood work expert, for example, was incomp__," and he was curtly cut off when Colonel Fraser interrupted him. "We can discuss that later counselor, but right now we need to know if you want to take something on for us, yes, or no?"

"What would that entail?" asked Miller. Saunders could tell he was practically salivating at the idea of getting even with Jacobs, but he was still somewhat timid, knowing this was probably something complicated.

"How about a breach of information under The Official Secrets Act 1939, which could very well take you to the Supreme Court of Canada?" replied Fraser.

Miller's eyes widened and his jaw dropped a fraction. The two officers could see he was hooked. "Sir, I think that would indeed be an honor," Miller replied.

"Very well, Miller," said Saunders. "Put some kind of requisition together in writing for us as to what you require. You know, things like the data surrounding the details of the breach, the principals involved, that kind of thing. We'll check with our people and put it all together for you, then you can do the necessary research and get warrants drawn up that you will be issuing against those involved." *This is child's play,* thought Saunders. He continued.

"At this point, other than a Medical Officer who was with him overseas, we believe the only party given the details of the incident is Jacobs's friend and former aide. In fact, the very man that was acquitted in your trial here five years ago. Martin England." Saunders was guessing at that, but it would certainly stir the pot.

This was too good to be true, thought Miller as he left the Officers Club. His mind was filled with thoughts of how to expedite this opportunity, and what had to be done to get things moving. First, he knew he had to call the Provincial Deputy Attorney General to ensure charges could indeed be laid against Jacobs and any others involved in the breach.

He had a somewhat loose relationship with the existing AG, the Honorable John B McNair, mainly because of his own father, Harrison Miller, QC, Sr. It was a good opportunity to make up for the loss of the England trial in 1947, which in fact McNair had personally initiated. So, he decided he would present the case to the Attorney General as soon as he received the dossier from the Colonels. *Speaking of which, what could their motives be behind this?* he wondered.

But his mind could not focus beyond the benefits and gratuities that would accrue to him should he be successful in convicting Jacobs. There was nothing as shameful and unpatriotic as the improper disclosure of information under the Official Secrets Act. He would like nothing better than to exact revenge against that uppity lawyer from Montreal for having humiliated him in their last meeting. And of course, he was not unmindful of the favorable media coverage if such a trial could be implemented. Miller decided to wait until Monday morning before calling the AG in Fredericton.

~ * ~

Meanwhile, the two Colonels again sat in their plush leather high-back chairs, sipping brandy and smoking cigars. Saunders twirled his snifter of VSOP, warming it under his nose before taking a small drink of the liqueur.

"So, Jim, what do you make of this Crown Prosecutor Miller?"

"I see a greedy politician," offered Fraser. "But no matter, if he can get the job done, so be it," he added.

"Copy that, Jim," said Saunders. He was thinking about the meeting he had with Jacobs back in October of 1944 concerning the Senorita. It was clever how they had led the captain to believe he was part of an undercover plot for the Allies in an attempt to gain information from the owner of the vineyard and her German lover. How naive Jacobs was...

"Colonel," said Fraser. "Please tell me again, but are you certain Jacobs had no idea we were involved in that game with the Senorita? We made a lot of easy money from the scam, but hell, it certainly isn't worth getting court-martialed over."

"Hey, don't worry Jimbo," said Saunders. "Jacobs doesn't know about our involvement; nor does he have any way of finding out. After all, it was eight years ago and the main players are dead. Even that old Chief of Police, Vitelli, who was starting to get too close to what was really happening, is also kaput. Too bad about his car accident," he said with a small chuckle.

"I don't want to hear anything about that," said Fraser. "You said you knew a mechanic in the area that would do some work 'on the side' as you put it. Whatever else he did is between you and him."

Let Fraser think what he wants, thought Saunders. If push comes to shove, he'll quickly remind the Colonel the both of them are equally involved in the Chief's mishap. He wasn't supposed to die, just become immobile until the troops were deployed to France. Hey, sorry Jim, shit happens.

But that was all history, and now it was threatening to haunt them. Colonel Frank Saunders was not a man to allow others to control his destination. He took things in hand and that was exactly what he was about to do now. The Crown Attorney would do their bidding and Jacobs might be convicted. And if that didn't work, he'd have to come up with another idea. He simply would not allow the information from the 1944 incident at the villa in Tuscany to see the light of day.

After the death of the Senorita and the German, and following the cursory investigation by the Veragno Police, Saunders and Fraser had made a clandestine visit to the property. The safe that Saunders and Fraser had discovered in the vast wine cellar of the villa was a godsend. To the officers' surprise, the small safe contained a total of just over five-hundred thousand U.S. dollars, all in used currency.

When the two Canadian colonels left Italy the following spring, they had opened a joint account at the Swiss National Bank in Geneva under false names.

"Relax, Jim. Everything is under control," he said to his friend, taking another sip of his brandy.

Chapter Thirty-five

BY THE time Saunders and Fraser had left the Officers Club and Harrison Miller, Jr. had returned to his home, it was around ten pm on Friday, September 12th. With the difference in time zones, it was six am on Saturday the 13th in Florence, Italy. Pasqual Savante was playing excellent host to his two Canadian visitors and Jacobs was describing to them the contents of the file he had viewed the previous evening at the police station.

"From what I can gather," Reg said to the two, "the former Chief started to look into the business with the Senorita and the German officer more carefully right after their deaths at the villa."

Jacobs took a bite of his toast with a sip of the outrageously strong coffee, and he continued. "He had heard from another local source there were two senior Canadian officers making regular visits to the vintner's villa. He found out their names from me that night at the villa and he had subsequently queried Saunders at length about his relationship with the deceased senorita. I was not aware of that.

"Unfortunately, there wasn't much more in the file. Nothing came from his talk with Saunders. I saw in the file, however, there is a separate notation about one of his constables having followed Saunders one day to a vehicle repair shop. The constable gives the name of the shop as *Autocarrozzeria Giglio* located on Via Artenia in the extreme Southeast end of the city." Jacobs told the two he had an uneasy feeling about the notation.

"Gentlemen let's go pick up Capo Frenetti and make a visit to the Giglio Repair Shop," he said. "Pasqual, along the way you can explain to the Chief what we now know and what we are looking for."

This could be the break they were seeking.

Within a half hour the four of them were approaching the shop in Pasqual's Fiat. This area of the city was dominated by warehouses, several small cement plants, a couple of rundown garment factories, and a low-income rental complex. Everything here was in need of repair and the buildings were in direct contrast to the beautiful charm and wealth only several blocks away.

They entered the shop and were met by a plump man of fifty or so. A heavy black beard covered his face which was otherwise quite florid around his forehead and nose. The building was in bad condition and a noxious odor assailed them. It seemed to be emanating from a toilet next to the owner's office.

During what seemed to Jacobs to be a very unfriendly discussion, Jacobs observed Capo Frenetti holding his nose and pointing at the door of the nearby toilet. After the talk with the owner had ended, Frenetti explained to Jacobs and the other two men with him that the owner would now reluctantly allow them to look at his records. They would have access to the records of his business from the day the former Chief had followed Saunders to this address, up to the present day. He went on to say he had to prod the owner somewhat concerning the state of his washroom facilities, and a visit from the local building inspector might occur if their records were otherwise not available. To that end, the four of them went into the owner's office with a number of file folders.

To save time, and in the interests of accuracy, it was agreed Capo Frenetti and Pasqual would look through the files, given their command of the language. Jacobs told them what to look for. It was a tedious job, like looking for a needle in a haystack, but after almost two hours, with only one file folder left, Pasqual got lucky.

"Aha," he exclaimed, "what have we here?" and he showed a piece of paper to Jacobs. It appeared to be an invoice for some work done on a 1943 Lancia Ardia sedan. The vehicle was registered to Capo Alfonzo Vitelli and the specific work completed was for an adjustment to the owner's brakes. Somehow, the shop had managed to get possession of Vitelli's vehicle to tamper with the brakes, but how?

Frenetti immediately called the owner over and asked to speak with the mechanic who had completed the job. However, the owner just shook his head and told him the worker in question had left not long after that date, which was March 6, 1945.

"*Dove e andato?*" asked Frenetti.

"*E tornato a casa sua in Germania,*" said the owner.

Frenetti then began to translate "He ret___" but Jacobs cut him off, saying "Yes, yes, but where in Germany?"

"*Hai un indirizzo?*" asked Frenetti.

"*No, vive con suo padre, da qualche parte nel Villaggio de Gettsbrieg.*"

"May I see the invoice please?" asked Jacobs. He looked carefully at the handwritten invoice and saw it was signed in the way a young, uneducated person in their teens would tend to write, the last name clearly legible as Friessen.

"Herr Friessen?" asked Reg as he pointed at the invoice he now held before the owner.[2]

"*Si,* Rolf Friessen," said the owner.

"*Grazie,*" said Jacobs and they left the shop with a bit more information on hand.

"Okay Capo let's go back to your office. Pasqual, ask the Chief if we can use his telephone to call the directory assistance operator for Gettsbrieg. We may get a break."

Once they were back at the Chief's office, Frenetti very quickly established there was indeed one Herr Grigor Friessen living in that small village. They were also able to obtain the address for him.

Jacobs knew a direct confrontation with young Friessen would not work. The young man who had tampered with the brakes on the Police Chief's vehicle would certainly never admit to any wrongdoing. Nor would he be forthcoming with information as to any talks he may have had with a Colonel in the Canadian Military at that time.

Jacobs and his team needed help, and it had to be legal. Once again, he sought assistance of Capo Frenetti. Would the Chief be able to obtain the cooperation of the police in West Germany in arresting this individual?

~ * ~

The small village of Gettsbrieg was in the south of West Germany, just across the border from Zurich. It was a drive of approximately four hundred and fifty kilometers from Florence, and one of the most beautiful panoramas Jacobs and LeBlanc had ever witnessed.

At the border crossing just after Zurich, the four of them had to present their passports and finally they were in West Germany, the newly created section of former Nazi Germany after the War.

Upon arriving at a pre-designated area outside of the village of Gettsbrieg, they were met by two German police cars which had driven from Munich. They discussed the situation at a picnic table just off the Autobahn and the German officers were fully briefed and prepared for violence.

The small house was located at the south end of the village. Nobody was around when the three vehicles rolled up to the gate and the four *Polizisten* had announced their presence. Immediately, a stooped man in his early seventies came out of the small structure to meet them, staring at them in wonderment.

"Good day Herr Friessen. We wish to speak with your son Rolf," demanded the superior officer.

"Rolf is fixing his car out back," said the old man. In a minute the officers had surrounded the small cottage-like structure and the younger Friessen was placed under arrest without incident. He fearfully looked at his father as he was placed in the police vehicle as they took off for the twenty-minute drive back to Munich.

Once at the Munich police station, Capo Frenetti took over the questioning of the suspect. It did not take long to determine what they were looking for. The team discovered the young Friessen, acting under the direction of a Canadian senior military officer from Veragno, was told that the former Police Chief Vitelli would be attending a ceremonial dinner in honor of the Allied Forces on the night of March 4, 1945.

The young mechanic was to sneak under the vehicle while it was parked in the lot of the Town Hall on the night of the ceremony. He was to weaken the brake line so that any amount of extra force on it would result in the line breaking. For this he was paid five hundred lire, and he was told to leave the area soon thereafter.

The brakes on the vehicle were supposed to fail before the owner took it into mountainous country. It was to be a delaying tactic to allow the Canadian officers sufficient time to be transferred out of Italy with their troops before the Veragno Police Department had finished their investigation into the deaths at the villa. According to Friessen he had immediately left Italy after the job and was not aware of the death of Chief Vitelli.

"Why did you make up an invoice for repairs to the vehicle?" asked Frenetti.

"I'm a notta too sure," responded Friessen. "But thata was a parta the jobba with the Canadian officer," he added.

Jacobs thought about this bit of information. No doubt Saunders was thinking ahead. At the time, he was probably confident the Veragno Police would be checking with local garages to see if the vehicle had any work done on it recently. Essentially, Saunders was getting ahead of any suspicious questions regarding the 'accident' by leaving the invoice as a ruse.

The police would then assume faulty work had been completed by the garage, and of course, the mechanic would have left the country by the time this was discovered. It was rather shoddy work on the part of Saunders, but then with all the confusion with the Americans entering the fray and the fact the Canadians would be long gone, the two Colonels didn't think they'd be detected. Jacobs was fuming. It was really upsetting him now to know he had been duped by the two.

It rankled the captain that two of his own had dropped to that level and beyond, knowing they were directly responsible for the death of Chief Vitelli. And now they were trying to keep him and his friends silent about what happened at the villa on the basis it would be contravening The Official Secrets Act.

He took the German police aside and asked them for their assistance to bring the two Canadian colonels to justice. Perhaps young Friessen could be persuaded to provide them with testimony, at least against Saunders, in exchange for a lesser charge or some other form? The police agreed to talk with their supervisor and let them know. Their work in Germany was done, and they left.

After returning to Florence, Jacobs got in touch with the military Judge Advocate General in Ottawa who quickly determined that cases of improperly disclosing information under the Official Secrets Act were indeed rare. Reg was gratified to find that before any judge would hear such a case, they would need plenty of evidence. The plain fact of the matter was that even if Saunders were able to convince a judge an official secret had been breached, eight years had now lapsed. The JAG was sure that would probably be sufficient time to have the case dropped. Armed with this information, Jacobs was anxious to get back to New Brunswick on familiar ground.

It was payback time...

Chapter Thirty-six

Chatham, New Brunswick
Friday, September 21

JACOBS AND Michel would never match the wonderful food, and hospitality afforded them by Pasqual, but at least they were able to provide the journalist with an excellent story for his newspaper. Capo Frenetti was looking forward to coming to Canada to testify, however Reg would first need to speak with the authorities at home in order to initiate charges against Saunders and Fraser. In that regard, he was about to experience an ironic turn of fate when he and Michel arrived in Chatham on Friday, September 21st.

Just after six pm, their taxi pulled into Martin England's driveway. They had hardly made it into the kitchen when a police car rolled after them and Constable Harold Dennings loudly knocked on the door. By this time, Martin had just finished greeting Reg and Michel. When he opened the kitchen door, Dennings was standing on the threshold.

"Dennings, what do you want?" Martin asked. Gone was his earlier cordiality with the cop. Constable Dennings ignored his former friend and instead focused his attention on the captain.

"Sir, I believe you are Captain Reginald Jacobs?" he asked.

"That is correct," said Jacobs. Already, he suspected what this was about, having seen the documents Dennings was holding. "I suppose you have some papers for me?" and he held out his hand.

"I do sir, and your friend here would be Dr Michel LeBlanc?" he asked as he handed one of the documents to Jacobs.

"I am," agreed Michel, accepting the remaining document. With that, the Constable left and both Reg and Michel began reading their packages. They started chuckling, soft and low at first, but their laughter gradually grew to the point where both of the men who had just been served with subpoenas were holding their sides and both roared with laughter.

Martin was joined by Meg and Jake. The three of them stood looking puzzled at their returning friends and Jacobs finally began to explain as he pointed to the subpoena he held.

"The reason we're laughing folks, is because ten minutes earlier, Michel and I were talking about having warrants drawn and issued by this same Judge against the two Colonels who are each named as plaintiffs against us in these arrest warrants. I mean, how ironic is that?" Jacobs laughed again. "You see, when we were in Italy, we obtained sufficient evidence, against Saunders at least, to have him arrested on conspiracy to commit murder."

After Jacobs and LeBlanc had freshened and they had taken their bags to their rooms, they were all sitting with coffees while Jake played with his toys.

"What about their threat here to charge you under the Official Secrets Act?" asked Martin, holding one of the subpoenas.

"We've already checked into that," said Michel. "No Judge worth his salt will take this on. To begin with, the so-called war time 'plot' of the Senorita and the German officer was a front, as was this whole business of having me act under cover.

"Actually, they were all involved in an extortion ring. They were black-mailing people to whom she had been providing sexual favors. The German, her real lover, sent clients to her, and so did the two Colonels. The German took pictures of some of them in the act... hidden tape recorders were used as well. It was quite a scheme, and unfortunately, I fell for it."

Reg then added, "So we'll play along with these warrants, but then demand to see the Judge alone in chambers. I've already been speaking with Judge Advocate Harold Phillips in Ottawa. One phone call to him by Judge Cripps will be all we need to have these cancelled. In the process, we may pick up some additional info."

~ * ~

Harrison Miller put the telephone back on its cradle and turned to face the two men who were sitting in chairs in his office. It was seven-fifteen on Friday evening and Saunders along with Fraser had arranged a meeting with Miller to see how things were going.

"That was Constable Dennings," said Miller. "The subpoenas have been served to both Jacobs and his doctor friend. That was a good idea, Saunders, having the England house staked out, "he added.

"Now that we know they've been served, what's the next course of action?" asked Fraser.

"I expect Jacobs will want to fight this in court. No way will he plead to a lesser charge of, say, improper disclosure of information. No, this Jacobs is a fighter, and I relish the upcoming trial!" Miller was excited. "So, gentlemen, I believe you were going to be providing me with a dossier outlining the actual breach?"

"Sure, sure, Counselor! Don't worry about that!" said Saunders. "We'll get you a copy of the directive from General Weisman in Ottawa. But a lot of it will be redacted." *Christ, this lawyer was really naive!* thought Saunders. "I'll get all the other details together, such as the time and place of the infractions. The complete file will be in your hands by mid-week," he finished.

When Saunders and Fraser returned to the Base and they were sitting at their usual table in the Officers Mess, they discussed their options in more depth.

"Jim, I don't want that business in '45 from Veragno to ever be reopened," Saunders said. "We're sitting on a tidy sum of money. But as you know, five hundred grand in U.S. cash in a safety deposit box wasn't really doing us any good. So last month I took a quick flight to Geneva and purchased Canadian Utility bonds with our cash. They're just as good as cash, but at least our money will be earning interest, okay?"

Actually, the value of the Canadian Bonds after applying a Foreign Exchange rate from US dollars, brought their value to $695,000 in Canadian dollars. Plus, the annual rate of return on the bonds was 5%, payable in detachable coupons every October 31st, each worth approximately $35,000. Frank planned to clip these each year by making a quick trip to Zurich. Finally, also unknown to Jim, Frank had purchased the bonds in 'bearer' format, meaning they were not registered in anybody's name. They could be cashed by whomever was in possession of them. There was no need for Jim to have to be involved with all that business stuff!

"I agree, Frank. What do you have in mind?"

"I don't think our Crown Prosecutor has even bothered to look into the rulings behind the Official Secrets Act, otherwise he'd know we have a non-existent case. But Jacobs is no fool. He'll certainly know this whole business is a s-cam! "I think the best we can hope for is one of two things: either Jacobs and LeBlanc can be bluffed into thinking they'd be better off settling this out of court, or we buy ourselves some time to think up something else. Either way, I'm going to create a few memos, maybe a forgery of a directive of sorts from *'General Weisman'*."

"Christ Frank, we can end up court-martialed!"

"Colonel, it's time you realized something. If we don't do something to stop Jacobs now, we'll definitely be spending the rest of our lives in prison. You understand? So get with the goddamned program!"

Saunders stood up and paced quickly out of the room. Fraser was left wondering how it had ever got to this point and what was in store for them now.

Chapter Thirty-seven

AS PROMISED, a large legal-sized manila envelope arrived by courier on Miller's desk just after nine, Wednesday morning, September 24th. The Crown Prosecutor opened the parcel with a great deal of anticipation and began reading the official dossier on the letterhead of General Morris Weisman, Canadian Forces Base, Uplands, Ottawa, Ontario.

The file read in part:

This dossier will serve to authorize the appointment of Capt XXXXXXXXXX and Doctor XXXXXXXXXXXXXr. as undercover agents with the Canadian Armed Forces, hereafter to be embedded in a conspiracy which has been formed by party (a.) Senorita XXXXXXX of XXXXXXXXXX, Italy and party (b.) First Lieutenant XXXXXXXXX of the XXXXXXX of the German Infantry stationed at XXXXXXXXXX, Italy.

Signed this 10th day of November 1944
General M Weisman
1st Canadian Army

Miller noted the names of the individuals had been redacted just as Saunders said they would, but Saunders had personally scribbled footnotes to the margins of the document identifying Captain Jacobs and Dr LeBlanc as the 'moles' first mentioned plus the names 'Madellena deFranco', and 'Ulrich Kelerring' as the other two redactions.

The document had two other attached pages which went on to identify the objective of the 'mole', which was to obtain vital data concerning German troop movements along the Gothic Line in the late Fall and Winter of 1944/45. The Senorita and the German Lieutenant were to be duped into thinking Jacobs was a convert to the German cause. *This was the stuff of movies!*

He called his Police Chief, Ted Reynolds, and asked him what was happening with the lawyer from Montreal and his doctor friend. Had they appeared yet in response to their subpoenas?

The Chief spat in his waste basket as he talked on the phone with Miller. "Not yet, sir. The warrant calls for a deadline of tomorrow, Friday September 28th."

"Let me know as soon as they appear, Ted," ordered Miller. He was clearly anxious to get the game underway.

Ironically, as soon as Chief Reynolds had replaced his phone on its hook, it rang again. This time it was Constable Dennings advising him that both Jacobs and LeBlanc had just landed at the jail and they were demanding a meeting with Judge Cripps. What should he do? The Chief said he'd get right back to him and immediately called Harrison Miller back. The telephone was picked up on the first ring.

"Sir, Jacobs and his friend are in my jail as we speak. They have demanded an audience with Judge Cripps. Do we have to comply?" he asked the Prosecutor.

Miller thought about this for all of two seconds.

"Leave it with me Ted. In the meantime, they are to be searched, stripped of their belongings, you know, the usual. And I want them confined in separate cells. No special treatment, right?" *Let then stew for a while in their cells for a while,* thought Miller. *He'd bring the big-shot Jacobs, Q.C. down a peg or two.*

That information was passed on to Constable Dennings at three twenty-five pm. Shortly after nine o'clock that night, Dennings informed the pair his Chief had endeavored to reach out to the Crown Prosecutor for direction in the matter of their request, but apparently Counselor Miller was away, and not expected back until after midnight. Some type of gala affair in Fredericton, he believed. He promised to get right at their request first thing in the morning.

Both Jacobs and LeBlanc had been in worse situations in their lives, especially during the Italian Campaign. As such and knowing where things stood in regard to the doubtful validity of the charge against them, they found the initial arrest process somewhat amusing.

After spending a night in a couple of 'drunk tanks' at the small town's local jail, they were getting annoyed. And by the time eight a.m. rolled around, and there was still no word from Dennings, Jacobs vowed he would spare no mercy in seeing Miller ridiculed to the fullest extent he could muster!

At noon they were served lunch by a sneering Dennings. "Hope you're hungry, gentlemen," he said. "Our chef made a special effort today for our distinguished guests!" he added. Their 'meal' consisted of a piece of stale bread, a bowl of what suspiciously appeared to be some kind of soup, maybe potato, and a glass of cloudy water.

When the tray was passed through the narrow slot in the cell door to Jacobs, the prisoner feigned mishandling it, and 'accidentally' dropped it all over the Constable's trousers and shoes, apologizing profusely.

Dennings reeled back, swiping at the mess on his front pant legs and cursed loudly. "I know that was no accident Jacobs, and you'll regret this," he said as he left the cell block area.

Reg knew Dennings would relate the incident to his Chief, but he didn't care. It was worth it.

It was close to seven, Friday evening. Dennings appeared with a sorrowful look on his face. "Gosh boys, but I'm afraid we missed both Crown Attorney Miller and Judge Cripps. Seems they were unavailable all afternoon. Unfortunately, their offices are now closed for the weekend and you'll have to wait until Monday to see the judge. But don't worry, we'll make sure you get lots to eat, eh?" and he left chuckling softly to himself while Jacobs and LeBlanc sat fuming in their individual cells.

For Jacobs and LeBlanc, it was not a pleasant weekend. Had it not been for Martin and Meg's company from time to time, along with her home-cooked meals delivered daily at the appropriate times, their stay would have been unbearable. Jacobs was confident Judge Cripps would probably not even want to hear the case. Nevertheless, it was cold comfort while they languished in their cells having to await Monday's arrival.

In the meantime, Harrison Miller was thoroughly enjoying the moment. The region was experiencing an unusually warm Indian Summer and today he had been invited for a game of golf at the Miramichi Golf and Country Club by Col. Saunders.

"Our friends spent the weekend as guests in our Town Jail," said Miller to Saunders as he eyed his approach shot to the 18th green. "I expect Jacobs will be ready to plead to a lesser charge when he's brought before the Judge on Monday. Damn, it surely makes me feel good to see that big city lawyers have to eat crow." His pitch rolled on the green, only five feet from the pin. When Saunders made his chip-shot, it took a backspin off the fringe of the green and rolled back into the trap.

Chapter Thirty-eight

HARRISON MILLER'S telephone screamed at him for the fourth time Monday morning. *Early* Monday morning. The Crown Prosecutor was very hung over and in a foul mood.

"This had better be good," he shouted.

"Counselor, this is Judge Cripps. It's eight a.m. and I have Captain Jacobs and Doctor LeBlanc in my office. Is that good enough? Report to me in person ASAP," and the phone was loudly hung up in Miller's ear.

Miller hurried as fast as he could to get dressed, and in his haste, he cut himself shaving. He then hurried out of his house with his fly undone. When he entered the judge's office on Water Street he was greeted by his Honor and the two men who had spent the weekend in the town's jail.

Both Jacobs and LeBlanc had arranged with Martin for a special delivery of fresh starched shirts, ties, and their business suits. Martin had gladly obliged, and he had even polished their black oxfords for the occasion. Jacobs and LeBlanc stood as Miller entered the office and offered their hands in greeting.

"Good morning, Counselor," said Jacobs. "I'm sorry we had to drag you here this early, however, we assume you'll want to move the case against us along as quickly as possible?"

"Ah, yes," said Miller, declining their offered hands. "But surely we could follow tradition and accept your plea in the normal manner, that is, across the street in the courthouse?"

"As you wish," ceded Jacobs, and he moved toward the door. "Let's go, Michel. Judge, see you in Court," he said, and as he turned aside from Miller, he gave the judge a meaningful look.

Within ten minutes they were all in the formal setting of the courtroom. The judge had donned his robes, and their session had started.

"So. Captain Jacobs, the charge against you and Doctor LeBlanc is that of committing a breach under The Official Secrets Act of 1939. I assume you intend to act on your own behalf in this matter, and I further assume you shall be acting as counsel for Doctor LeBlanc. Am I correct sir?" intoned Judge Cripps.

"That is correct, Your Honor. The charge however, if I may, is slightly incorrect. It should state "Official Secrets Act of 1911 *with Amendments of 1920 and 1939*," Jacobs stated, squarely looking at Miller, who was now beginning to get a queasy feeling in his gut.

"Uh, yes sir. I shall have my Court Clerk amend the summons appropriately," and he scowled at Miller. Miller simply raised his eyebrows to form question marks, and the judge proceeded. Miller sat back in his chair, feeling a bit better and very content to see Jacobs having to answer to the charge now before him, even if it contained a minor typo.

"Captain, this is a serious charge," said the judge as he again looked askance at the Crown Attorney. "How do you plead, sir?"

"Not guilty, Your Honor, for charges both against myself and my client, Dr LeBlanc," Reg stated.

"Very well, Captain. Now that we have formally entered your pleas, I believe we can dispense with certain formalities and cut to the chase in this matter." Judge Cripps now glared angrily at his Prosecutor.

"Counselor Miller, have you any idea what you are doing here?" asked the Judge.

Miller then stood up with his arms folded, clearly taken aback. "Your Honor, I resent that type of address and I strongly object to the manner in which you are apparently showing bias in this important case."

"Miller, go to a mirror and examine yourself, sir," Cripps replied in an exasperated tone. "You are a disgrace to the profession. Here you stand, half-dressed and half-shaved, and reeking of alcohol. Had you bothered to spend ten- or fifteen-minutes performing background checks on the Act now before us, you would have found that only two precedent cases have been heard since 1921. And both of these were dismissed by the applicable judges for lack of evidence."

At this point Miller began to cringe as he stood before the judge.

"Furthermore, *your* only tangible evidence in this case would appear to be a copy of a dossier from a 'General Morris Weisman', CFB

Kingston, Ontario," he held the document in the air, "which is purported to be a directive for Captain Jacobs here to act as some kind of undercover agent in a vague plot during the Italian Campaign. Am I correct so far, Counselor?" Judge Cripps was now yelling.

"Yes, Your Hon…," started Miller, but the Judge immediately cut him off.

"Counselor, I have tried for a half hour this morning, before calling you at home, to reach this General Weisman. THERE IS NO SUCH MAN!" he yelled, waving the document in the air. "Counselor, you have once again allowed your desire for instant media gratification to warp your judgment. Had you bothered to contact me earlier last week, rather than having these good visitors to our fair province spend the weekend in our jail, we could have easily foregone this nonsense. Captain, I believe you have some things to add?"

"Thank you, Your Honor," said Jacobs, and here he had trouble looking seriously at Miller. "Counselor Miller, I would like to enter charges against Colonel Frank Saunders, and one Colonel James Fraser. The judge is correct. Plain and simple, you were duped into bringing this charge against us. It was an attempt on the part of these officers to have you obtain guilty pleas of lesser charges. Or perhaps it was done to simply gain them more time to plan something possibly more sinister.

"You see, the two men were themselves engaged in an illegal extortion ring during our time overseas. Full details are all spelled out on the memo attached."

Miller looked up at the Judge, then said loudly, "Your Honor, this is preposterous. I have personally met the two Colonels, and I deem them to be men of honor. What possible evidence do you have, Jacobs, to support such a ridiculous charge?"

"As I have already explained to Judge Cripps, Counselor, Dr LeBlanc and I have just returned from Veragno, Italy last week. We spent a number of days there seeking out the truth from local sources. We shall be providing a statement from both the local Police Chief Frenetti and one Rolf Friessen, a young German mechanic who has confessed to having acted under the direction of Colonel Saunders to tamper with the former Chief's vehicle, resulting in the death of that man.

"So *you* will now have an opportunity to actually bring some real charges against somebody, Counselor. I suggest you start with contacting the Military Police at the base immediately, before both Saunders and Fraser have returned to Ontario."

Miller looked at the two clean-cut gentlemen standing before him and could not even summon up an apology. He was truly a beaten man as he stood in defeat with his head bowed, his eyes puffy and red, and a piece of Kleenex stuck to his upper lip where he had cut himself shaving.

Jacobs motioned to LeBlanc and they started to move towards the exit. As Jacobs was leaving, he turned back to the Crown Attorney and pointed to the opening at the front of his pants. "And it might be a good idea to hide Mr. Johnson there, Counselor. I believe the media are waiting outside to ask you a few questions," he said.

Miller looked down at himself and his face began to turn a beet red. This was absolutely the worst day of his life. He pushed the errant lock of hair off his forehead and cringed in embarrassment.

Just as Jacobs had said, a couple reporters hovered about the steps of the Courthouse as Miller made his exit and he was approached by them before he made it to his vehicle.

~ * ~

At noon, two MPs strode with purpose from the gatehouse at CFB Chatham towards the Officers Mess only two blocks away. They were fully armed and prepared for action as they set out to arrest Colonels Saunders and Fraser at the request of the Base Commanding Officer.

When they arrived at the dining hall, they were informed by the Mess Hall steward that the men they were seeking were not there. Further calls to their quarters went unanswered, and when the MPs checked out their PMQs, they determined they had both left, taking most of their belongings with them.

Chapter Thirty-nine

JACOBS, LEBLANC, Martin, and Meg sat in England's backyard swing enjoying the mid-afternoon sun, which this year was still unusually warm in its strength. Jake would be getting off school at any minute and Reg was anxious to see the lad before he and Michel left for Moncton. They had booked a late-afternoon bus trip that would enable them to catch their Air Canada flight 403 to Montreal, departing at eight forty-five this evening.

It had been another arduous trip to the Miramichi for Jacobs, but he was thoroughly pleased with the way everything had worked out for Martin and Meg. In the larger scheme of things, he was proud to have played a role in bringing justice to the family of a far-away Police Chief for something that had happened over eight years previous. Earlier, he had spoken by phone to Chief Frenetti in his inept Italian language and told him where things now stood regarding the case against the two Canadian Colonels. Frenetti was pleased to hear how successful things had gone, though Jacobs could tell he was a bit disappointed to learn he was now probably not going to be required to travel to Canada to give testimony.

And more than anything, Jacobs longed to return to Montreal to be with his wife Peggy. It would be nice to settle into his law practice once again. Even as boring as it could get by times, it would be a lot less stressful. He laughed to himself as he thought of spending the previous weekend in jail with Michel. His colleagues in Montreal would get a great kick out of hearing this.

His thoughts were interrupted by the sound of the telephone ringing in the house. Meg got up from the swing to go and answer it, but in no time, she was running back with a worried look on her face. Martin and Michel had been tossing a football with each other, and the now stopped when they heard Meg yelling.

"Reg," she cried. Jacobs could tell his dear friend was deeply concerned. "I have a call for you from a man by the name of Saunders. He says that it is important."

Jacobs suddenly had a very bad feeling. It was like he had been punched, and the air had left his body. He ran into the house, followed by the Meg, Martin, and Michel. He immediately grabbed the telephone, fearing the worst.

"Saunders, what's going on?" he demanded.

"Hey soldier, take it easy," he said. "I think you may be interested to know I have a little friend of yours with me. Wanna say hi?" and Jacobs immediately knew what he was about to hear.

"Hi Uncle Reg. I'm with your friend Colonel Saunders. He's taking me fishing and we want you to come. Can you, please?"

"Sure Jake, I'll be right there. Can you please put Colonel Saunders back on the phone?" A second later, Saunders's voice came back to him.

"You see Captain, we just thought you'd like to get a bit of fishing in before you returned to Montreal, what do you think?" Saunders said.

"Listen you bastard, if you so much as touch one hair on that child's head, so help me…."

"Save it Captain. Now take down this address: 1260 on the Napan Road. It's a farmhouse on the right going toward Baie du Vin. The owners here have been very hospitable to Colonel Jim and me. So far. Know what I mean? Get here by five pm and nobody gets hurt. And absolutely no police." The phone went dead.

As Saunders hung up the phone, he smiled at Jake and told him his Uncle Reg would be here soon. He then brought him into a back room in an old farmhouse. Jake was excited to hear Reg and him would soon be going fishing. The Colonel had even said they might be able to take a boat out onto the ocean and catch some really big fish. Reg's friend seemed to be a pretty swell guy and that big grey car he was driving when they met him on the way home from school was really neat.

But these warm feelings left him as soon as he entered the back room. He was surprised to see two older people lying on the floor with their hands tied behind their backs. They had old handkerchiefs stuffed into their mouths which were tied around their necks so they couldn't speak; and they sure looked afraid when Colonel Saunders and he came into the room. Then the other man that came with them walked out of the connecting bathroom and he was holding a gun.

Now Jake wasn't excited at all about the prospects of going fishing. He knew something very bad was happening and he started to cry.

"Jim, you know what to do," Saunders said to Fraser as he pointed at Jake. Colonel Fraser began tying a rope around Jake's wrists, and he told Jake not to worry, that everything was going to work out. When he finished tying his wrists, he put one of those old bandanas into his mouth and it smelled and tasted awful. He cried a lot more, but of course no sound was coming from his mouth.

~ * ~

When Reg put the phone down, he stared at Meg and Martin. "That was Saunders," he said. "They have Jake and they're using him and probably a couple of others that they're holding as hostages in the Napan area. They want me."

With that he went back to the phone and made a long-distance collect call, person-to-person for his wife. Martin overheard the captain as he calmly explained to her how he had been delayed. He told her not to worry, but he would be home as soon as possible. He then asked Martin if perhaps he could arrange for the loan of David Jensen's car. Next, he went upstairs to his room and opened his suitcase to retrieve the Beretta pistol he had brought back with him from Italy.

After a quick change of clothes into a pair of jeans, a black turtleneck sweater and a pair of hiking boots, he was ready to go after the two colonels and his namesake.

Before going outside he said to Meg, "You know I never for a minute thought this business would enter your lives as it has. For this I am truly sorry, Meg. But I promise you, I *will* get Jake back." When he turned to leave, he found Martin standing in his way.

"Captain, you know there is no way in hell you're going after my boy without me." The two just looked deeply into each other's eyes and Jacobs finally gave in. "Shit, get what you need and meet me outside." He looked at Meg as Martin was going upstairs and simply shrugged his shoulders as if to say, "*What can I do?*

216

~ * ~

It was approaching four-thirty when they left Martin's house in Jensen's Plymouth coupe. As they drove to their destination, Martin showed him a weapon he had brought back from Italy himself.

"Is that what I think it is?" asked Jacobs in disbelief.

"The very thing," said Martin. It was the German Luger that Kelerring had actually pointed at him all those years before. They continued to talk, and a plan was quickly outlined. Hopefully it would work. If not, they would be in a world of trouble.

~ * ~

Jake was in the same room as the older man and woman. They didn't appear to be hurt, but he couldn't tell for sure. They just stared at him as if they were feeling sorry for him. As soon as the man who had tied him up left the room, Jake started trying to free his wrists. The elderly farmers simply watched him twist and turn his hands behind his back.

While Jake kept busy trying to untie the rope on his wrists, he could hear the two bad men arguing in the front room. For some reason, Jake felt that the one who tied him up was not the *baddest* of the two. The other guy was scary though, and he'd have to watch out for him.

Saunders was getting tired of having to carry the full weight of their 'operation', as he now saw the kidnapping. He was certain Fraser was very close to giving them both up and he had come too far to allow that to happen. His plan was to force Jacobs to bring them to a foreign country. He had seen a boat resting on a trailer outside by the barn when they had arrived. The Napan River emptied into the Miramichi, which in turn flowed into the Atlantic. Perhaps they could make it from here to PEI, maybe catch a flight overseas or even Mexico? Even if they could get across the border to the U.S. it might be possible. *Where was that goddamned Fraser anyway?* he wondered.

"Fraser, get your ass in here," he shouted. Then Colonel Fraser came out of the kitchen where he had been raiding the fridge. Colonel Fraser took one look at Saunders and knew the man was falling apart.

"What's the matter?" Saunders yelled. "Don't tell me you're getting soft on me."

"Colonel, this isn't right," Fraser started to complain.

"Where's your gun, Jim? Is it loaded? Jacobs will soon be here, and we've got to be ready for him."

Fraser pulled his Colt .45 Semi, from the back of his pants and showed it to Saunders.

"When was the last time you fired that weapon, Colonel? In '44?"

"Well, no, Frank, I fired it at the range in Kingston in, ah, I think it was a few years ago."

"Jesus, Jim, just fire off a round outside now, dammit. You gotta make sure it's working, right? The enemy will soon be arriving."

Jim Fraser had always been easily cowed by his colleague. He thought it would be best at this point to go along with him, humor him a bit. So, he did as he was told.

In a matter of seconds Frank heard the sharp report from the Colt and stepped behind the kitchen door, pulling on a pair of leather gloves. When Fraser stepped into the kitchen, he said "It's working fine, but I___." His sentence would not be completed as the unmistakable click from the hammer of Frank's .38 Smith & Wesson came from behind him and filled his ears.

"I'll take the Colt now, Jim," said Saunders. "Nice and easy, my friend." When he had Fraser's gun, Saunders then walked Fraser over to the kitchen table. "Have a seat, Jim." Fraser settled unsteadily onto a chair at the table.

"I really didn't want to do this, Jim. But hell, I can't think of any other way," said Frank. Saunders was in a frantic mood, holding his head with both hands. Jim's Colt in his right and his own Colt in his left, both pressing against the sides of his head. He began crying softly now as he looked at Fraser.

"Frank, you don't know what you're doing," shouted Fraser. "Let me get you some help. It's not too late. Think about this Frank, for God's sake," he pleaded.

"Jim, you're just too soft," cried Saunders. He was now totally out of control. "You always were," he sobbed, and without further ado he brought Jim's Colt up level with his friend's head and simply shot him in the right temple. The sound of the semi-automatic going off was deafening, and Fraser toppled off the kitchen chair onto the floor, instantly dead. Saunders then bent over and placed Jim's Colt in his right hand.

There now, he said to himself. *Poor Colonel Fraser just couldn't live with what he had done to the boy and the old couple, so he had to shoot himself.*

He looked around the kitchen, his eyes wild. *Let's see, Jim's gone. Perfect!* He paced the kitchen floor, his hands striking his head insanely. What else? Oh yeah…

And now he headed for the room where his captors awaited.

Chapter Forty

WHEN JACOBS entered the long driveway at 1260 Napan Road, they heard two gunshot reports about a minute apart and they immediately jumped out of Jensen's coupe and ran to the farmhouse some distance away.

The house was eerily quiet as they cautiously went to the front door. Martin stood to one side as Jacobs entered first, both had their weapons drawn and held by their sides.

"Saunders!" Jacobs yelled. "It's me, Jacobs. Send the boy out!" Hearing only muffled cries, the two entered the kitchen. There, sprawled on the floor lying in a pool of blood that was only starting to coagulate, was Colonel Fraser, clearly beyond help. It appeared to be a suicide. They moved toward the room from where the stifled cries were coming. Upon entering they saw the two elderly owners of the property, each lying bound and gagged on the bedroom floor. Once Jacobs removed the gags from their mouths, they quickly identified themselves as Gerald and Joan MacDonald, owners of the property. They looked warily outside the bedroom window as Martin worked on their ropes.

When the MacDonalds were upright with their ropes and handkerchiefs removed, they told them Saunders had only minutes ago left the room through the open window that the farmer's wife now pointed out. They added that they heard a gunshot from outside, then two men arguing.

Mrs. MacDonald started crying, then she controlled herself enough to talk to Jacobs. "I heard the man who just left say to the other man, 'You are just too soft, Jim, but then, you always were.' The next thing we heard was another gun shot, followed by what sounded like a man falling onto the floor. Then that man came in here..." she finished and began sobbing again.

As Reg loosened the ropes on Mr. MacDonald, Martin held the lady by her shoulders and calmly spoke to her.

"Mrs. MacDonald, when Saunders left through this window, did he take my son with him?"

"No sir," said Mrs. MacDonald. "That boy was just so smart and brave. He managed to get the rope untied from his wrists and then he jumped out the window before the shooting started."

Jacobs told the farmer to immediately call 911 and have them bring an ambulance along with reinforcements. They both climbed out the window and began searching for Saunders and young Jake.

~ * ~

The corn field literally surrounded the farmhouse and barn as it sloped north towards the road and the river.

Saunders was in a rage. But he could see from the broken corn stalks where the boy had left a trail. Following it, he reached the edge of the cornfield and realized he was now on the Napan Road. *Which way did he go?* Saunders wondered. He was about to try his luck going west, thinking the boy would want to get home as quickly as he could, then he heard the distant sound of a branch snapping directly ahead of him. Jake had simply continued straight ahead, across the road, down over the bank toward the river. Saunders followed the path over the bank as well and yelled out, "Jake, come back, I'm not going to hurt you. Where are you?" muttering to himself, *you little shit.*

Jacobs and Martin looked around as they climbed out of the side window of the farmhouse. Realizing they were surrounded by a cornfield that both Jake and Saunders had run through, they followed the trail toward Napan Road. When they reached the bottom of the field, they had to make a decision. Somewhere dead ahead of them, Martin heard somebody yelling.

"Did you hear that?" he asked Jacobs.

"Yes, straight ahead! Come on," and they tore down the hill through brambles, deadwood, and alder bushes when they soon came to the river. At this point it was probably fifty yards wide, maybe eight feet deep, with huge boulders breaking the surface just about everywhere, creating a swift current. Martin knew there was no way Jake would have attempted to cross the river at this point. Looking east, the same conditions prevailed as did the way west. He looked east again for some clues and noticed several fresh footprints in the mud.

"This way," he shouted to Jacobs, and they were off once again.

Christ, this kid was giving him a hard time, thought Saunders. He paused to catch his breath as he plodded along the riverbank heading east. Ahead, he heard a sharp cry and knew it was the brat. It sounded like he had just hurt himself. Saunders resumed his objective, now confident that he would soon be rewarded.

Jake ran down a steep embankment when he heard the bad man calling his name. It sounded like the man was a few yards away from him, but he knew he had at least a good two minute headway. He bounded onward when suddenly his foot caught between two protruding rocks, and he felt a sharp pain in his ankle. He let out a cry and fell to the moist earth. He had to keep going, the man would soon be upon him. With every last bit of his strength, he rose and started toward a sharp bend in the shoreline. Maybe he could find a place to hide once he made it around the corner of the riverbank.

Saunders was not adept at what he was now attempting, which was to catch a young boy who skipped seemingly without fear along a treacherously slippery riverbank. As he rounded the corner at a point where he thought the kid had injured himself, he was suddenly confronted by the lad who now brazenly jumped up in front of him.

Saunders was so startled he immediately lost his footing, falling backward into the river. The gun fell from his hand into the depths of the stream and Saunders was forced off his feet by the rushing stream.

Young Jake watched in astonishment as Saunders was carried along in the swift current, banging into large boulders as he rolled this way and that, his arms akimbo, a horrified look on his face. Jake decided he was now out of immediate danger, so he followed his desperate cries along the bank of the river. In no time he became aware of a constant roar ahead of him and realized something terrible was about to happen.

The Gaspereau Falls in Napan. Last year his dad took him to this spot. He was looking for the point where the river fell in a sheer vertical drop of about thirty feet. There was a kind of wooden ladder-assisted ledge from which you could stand and get a good view of the falls. Jake now found it and he climbed up to a rickety old platform to wait for the bad man to appear.

Jacobs and Martin continued to frantically make their way along the riverbank, seeing here and there evidence in the form of footprints left by both Jake and his pursuer. Finally, they came to a sharp turn in the bank where Jake had fallen and they quickly spotted Saunders, clinging to a large boulder with both hands. Saunders saw the two men and yelled to them for help.

"Where is my son, you bastard?" replied Martin.

"He should be right ahead of you," shouted Saunders in return. "Help! I can't swim and I'm losing my grip!" he pleaded.

"Martin, go see if Jake is around the corner, I'll see if I can reach Saunders."

Martin then ran ahead around the turn in the bank. Here he spotted Jake on the look-off. Trembling, looking upstream toward the opposite side, he was trying to spot his enemy. Then he saw his father and he jumped off the wooden ledge and ran toward him, limping as he went. They held each other fiercely and Martin wept with joy. Then, through the roar of the cataract they both heard a loud shout and looked back to the brink of the falls. It was an unbelievable sight…

Saunders and Jacobs were together as they both fell headlong over the edge and plunged deep into a pool at the bottom of the falls, narrowly missing two jagged granite rocks. After what seemed an eternity, Saunders rose to the surface, spitting and coughing only ten feet in front of them. Martin jumped into the pool to gather him up and he dragged the colonel to the nearby shore when he heard Jake yelling at him.

"Dad! Dad! It's Uncle Reg, behind you…"

Martin spun around and saw the captain floating face down on the water. He dropped Saunders and quickly swam to his friend and pulled him back to the shore's edge, one arm around his neck while swimming a half-stroke with the other. Soon he had Jacobs laid out on his back and he quickly applied CPR chest compressions. Thirty seconds later, Jacobs began coughing and finally, Martin was able to rest. In the meantime, Saunders also began coughing and he gradually sat up on the bank a short distance away from them.

"Jake, look after your uncle. I'll attend to Saunders," Martin said. When his son's back was turned, Martin walked over to Saunders and hit him with a solid right on his jaw, knocking the colonel unconscious. In the distance they could hear approaching sirens as the sun slowly sank in the west.

Chapter Forty-one

"GOD MEG, that was the best roast beef dinner I've ever eaten," declared Jacobs.

"And I second that," shouted LeBlanc. It was Tuesday, October 2nd and they would soon be leaving on the bus for the Moncton International Airport where they would catch their Montreal bound flight. Jacobs would be returning to his corporate law practice and Dr LeBlanc would be resuming his psychiatric clinic while continuing his research with the problems being experienced by veterans from the last two great Wars.

Jake was sitting between his mother and father at the table across from his uncle Reg and his new friend, Doctor LeBlanc.

"I hate to see you leave, Reg," said Martin. "And Doctor, you've been such a help to me. When will we see you two again?"

"Maybe I can get Peggy down East next year," offered Jacobs. "You'll love her Meg. She's your type," he said fondly.

"Reg, promise we'll get to meet her," said Meg. "And Doctor LeBlanc, we owe you so much. You must come back to visit us again soon. Don't even bother writing in advance, you're welcome any time."

"Martin, I'd like to hear from you from time to time," said Michel. "As I mentioned, remember to remain patient with this thing. It will be with you for a long while, maybe even forever. But the main thing to remember is this illness can be managed. You've shown that to be the case. And I'm only a phone call away, okay? In the meantime, I promise to keep in touch with you regarding any new methodology our research group comes up with. There will be a lot of study into this illness in the coming years, trust me," LeBlanc said.

Jake came to his father's side and asked him if he wanted to throw his football with him in the backyard. As the taxi pulled into their driveway to pick up Jacobs and LeBlanc, the four of them were wrestling playfully among the fallen leaves in the warm, early autumn evening.

Meg stared at them from her kitchen window as they frolicked on the lawn.

The taxi driver had put their bags in the trunk of his car, and he called to them. Jacobs and LeBlanc got into the car, and they backed out of the driveway, waving goodbye as they left. Jacobs looked back when they were just out of the lane to see Martin and Meg standing on either side of young Jake, their arms around him as they too waved goodbye. Jacobs wiped a tear from his eye.

He would be back.

EPILOGUE

IT WAS early evening, Halloween, 1952. In the twilight, Jake, dressed up in costume as a pirate, crossed Water Street and continued along the sidewalk, enjoying the feel of the dead, dry leaves brushing against his legs as he waded through them on his return home. He had a large shopping bag partially filled with various types of candy.

Jake was pleased with the goodies he had managed to collect, and he was now looking forward to making the rounds of the several blocks of his own area which his mom had designated as safe for him.

He was walking through Elm Park, the Town square so named for the numerous mature elm trees that decorated the town centre along with a number of cenotaphs and a central bandstand. Halfway through the park, he spotted a group of older boys who were gathered around one of the park benches where a man lay sleeping. They were pointing at the man, running around him, snickering and laughing, and Jake could tell they were *up to no good*, as his mom would say. As he neared them, one of the boys, the tallest, spotted Jake and yelled out to the others.

"Hey guys, look. Here comes Jacob," His name was Freddy Young, and he was known in Jake's circle of friends to be one of the town bullies. There were three others, and though a couple of them were okay, he knew they would probably side with Freddy if push came to shove.

"Whatcha got in the bag, *Jaaacob?*" teased Freddy. Jake knew some of the boys liked to call him by his full name rather than the nickname he preferred.

"None of your business," countered Jake. He had just decided he wasn't going to be bullied by Freddy anymore!

The group of young boys had been teasing the old man and Jake felt sorry for him. The man wasn't hurting anybody, so why did they have to pick on him? Freddy, the leader of the pack, now approached Jake with his hands held out before him, palms up.

"Hand it over, Jaycup. I think you have some candy for us."

"No way. Leave me alone."

Just then, the man that had been laying on the bench rose unsteadily and staggered over to where the boys were gathered.

"What's goin' on here?" he slurred. Jake knew from previously seeing his father in that same condition that the man had been drinking.

"Ah, why dontcha mind yer own beeswax, you old drunk," shouted Freddy. "Hey guys, let's get some candy from Jacob then finish what we were gonna do to old Drunken Duncan."

Duncan 'Dunc' Dickson was a vet from the first World War. He had seen action at Vimy Ridge and many other smaller battles. Bill was just another casualty of Shell Shock who had sought relief from his mental problems through alcohol.

His true story and his many acts of bravery and honor in battle had never been fully told. Alcohol had been extremely consuming his faculties and prevent any such reputation to flourish. Instead, he had become a man to be avoided, shunned. Over the decades his war medals had been lost, stolen, or pawned away.

Dunc saw young Jake being bullied and something inside stirred him to action.

"You leave this boy be," he said to Freddy.

Freddy then stepped close to the teetering old man and pushed on his chest. "Who's gonna make me, Drunken Duncan? You?"

"*I* am," yelled Jake, who was standing right behind the bully. And when Freddy turned around, Jake had to jump up to hit him because he was much shorter than the bully. But hit him he did. Blood spurted immediately from Freddy's nose, and it surprised him so much that Jake had time to land another punch, this one to the bully's mouth. At that point Freddy fell down holding his hand against the blood pouring from his face as he slowly struggled to his feet.

"Aw c'mon you guys," he muttered. "He ain't worth it," and the four crept away from Jake who looked like he was ready to take them all on if that was necessary.

"You're quite a scrapper, young fella. I think those boys were about to do me harm. But like most bullies, that guy was mostly talk. What's your name, anyway?" asked Duncan.

Jake told him.

"Would you be Martin England's boy?"

"Yes sir."

"Well, I know your daddy from AA. He's a good man and it looks like the fruit don't fall far from the tree," he said. The old man thanked Jake, and he staggered away.

By the time Jake got home, it was almost dark. His father was setting the table for supper when he saw the different look on his son's face as he came into the kitchen.

"Hey Jake, what's up?" he said. "I see you got yourself some candy already."

"Hi Dad. Yeah, I got this at the 'shell outs' down at Hachey's and Lounsbury's earlier," and he opened the bag for his father who had started to take some of the store-bought candy bars from the bag. His favorite by far was the O'Henry bar.

"Say Dad, who is the guy in town they call 'Drunken' Duncan?" Jake asked.

"Why do you ask, Jake?" Martin stopped unwrapping the O'Henry bar and gave Meg a look who had also stopped her work with her fudge when she overheard Jake's question.

"Well, I spoke with him on the way home in the park. Some older boys were teasing him and I, uh, kinda got in a fight with one of them."

"Oh yeah? Protecting Bill, eh?" said Martin. "You don't look like you got hurt," he ventured.

"Nah, that Freddy Young is just a bully. Once anybody stands up to him, he really gets just as scared as anybody else, right? Anyway, Mr. Dickson said he knew you from AA. He said you were a good man, Dad, and that the fruit doesn't fall far from the tree, whatever that means," said Jake, his eyebrows forming question marks.

Martin just smiled and said "One day we'll have a good talk about the fruit from the tree, and Dunc Dickson while we're at it. In the meantime, why don't you run upstairs and get washed for supper. Then afterwards you can go out and get yourself some more candy."

"If it's okay with you guys, I think I'll just hang around the house tonight and see if I can guess who some of the younger kids are when they come all dressed up in their costumes."

"Sure, that'll be fun. Mind if I have another one of those O'Henry's?"

~ * ~

"Martin England, stop that right now," yelled Meg. "You'll ruin your supper. Hurry setting that table, and Jake you get washed. The kids will be here soon."

After they had eaten, Martin spotted Monday's issue of the *Miramichi Gazette* lying on the counter. The headlines blared:

SENIOR AIR FORCE OFFICER SENTENCED
Crown Attorney Resigns

Judge Robert Cripps today sentenced Colonel Francis Blair Saunders of CFB Kingston, Ontario to life imprisonment following guilty verdicts received earlier last month on six charges including first degree murder, unlawful confinement, kidnapping, conspiracy to commit murder, and the fraudulent production of a military dossier.

Saunders had been initially charged with the homicide of his colleague Colonel James Peter Fraser on Monday, September 29th of this year…the story continued, describing the kidnapping, the death of Colonel Fraser and the ultimate capture of Saunders, ending with…

Saunders, who is now 63, will not be eligible for parole under current law for another 25 years minimum, and will probably never see freedom again.

(See also Page 2 re: Crown Attorney Resigns)

Martin flipped over to the secondary report.

Chatham, NB October 29, 1952
Staff Reporter

Harold Jenkins

CROWN ATTORNEY RESIGNS

Crown Attorney Harrison Miller, QC announced his retirement today after hearing the life sentence handed down by Judge Cripps following last month's trial of Colonel Frank Saunders (See Main story Page 1)

Miller had been duped by Colonel Saunders into laying a charge under The Official Secrets Act. Saunders had attempted to have Jacobs convicted under The Act thinking he might be able to keep his own involvement in an extortion ring from previous activities while he was in Italy in 1946/47 under wraps.

However, the Crown Attorney's opponent, Reginald Jacobs, once again proved he would outsmart him and the Montreal attorney was able to produce evidence from authorities in Veragno, Italy only last month that would put Saunders in jeopardy and clear Jacobs and a colleague, Doctor Michel LeBlanc, also from Montreal, from the charge.

In a brief statement from Jacobs when he was acquitted of the charge by Judge Cripps on September 29th he stated "Any first-year law student would have seen that the charge was bogus. Judge Cripps saw it immediately and agreed with me to play it all the way through in order to teach Miller a lesson.

"Unfortunately, Counselor Miller never learned anything in the way of ethics since our previous meeting in 1947. His need for favorable media attention will be his downfall, I am afraid."

Once again, Crown Prosecutor Miller was not available for comment, and it is not clear what his future plans for employment are at this time.

Martin finished reading both articles in the Gazette and tossed the paper on the couch.

The rest of the evening Jake and his mother looked after the last of the young ghosts and goblins as they came to the door. By the end of the night most of her fudge had been exhausted. Duncan Dickson had made a visit and left the England house a changed man with a bagful of homemade fudge and an offer to start work on Monday with England's House Painting Ltd.

Martin went back to his workshop and made sure he had an adequate supply of clean brushes for the new project his company had recently been granted.

Right after the terrible incident with Colonel Saunders two years ago, he had quit his job at the Renous Ammunition Depot and decided to return to his father's business. By good fortune, a series of jobs quickly fell into his lap and word suddenly spread in the community that Martin was back in business.

Things were finally looking good for Martin.

~ * ~

11 years later
Sunday, 8:00 pm
February 9th, 1964

Jake was lounging on the den sofa, every now and then glancing at his textbook titled *Principles of Mathematics.* It lay opened in his lap to Chapter 3, Calculus. He hated the subject and wondered for the umpteenth time why he had chosen this as an elective over biology. Frankly, he could never see where either of the Grade Twelve courses would ever be of use to him. Maybe if his school had been offering Music, he would have taken that. At the moment, his attention was drawn to the television where he saw his favorite rock group of all-time appear on the stage of The Ed Sullivan Show: *The Beatles!*

So much for Calculus, he said to himself as he turned up the volume on the TV and settled back on the couch to watch the show. Then his little brother came running in, all excited about something. He was followed by his dad, trying to get the six-year-old upstairs for his bath. Now Jake's sister Rebecca, a five-year old, entered the den and she started whining to his mom about *absolutely* having to get new shoes for the upcoming Valentine's Day party at the Community Hall. God, he wasn't able to hear the show, so he decided he may as well go upstairs to finish his homework. His father met him on the way up the stairs as he was coming back after getting his brother Josh settled in the tub.

"Hey Jake, finished your homework?"

"Just going up to do it, dad,"

"Before you do that, I have something I want to show you. It'll just take a minute son, come on," and he led Jake back downstairs. Martin went to a small corner desk where he kept various papers. He opened a drawer and pulled out an envelope that he gave to his son. "Have a look," he said.

Jake looked at the beige envelope and the familiar handwriting of his namesake and his dad's closest war-time friend. The return address read:

Jacobs, Hogan, Young, LLP

Attorneys

1500 Place Ville Marie,

Montreal, PQ

Jake was usually included in any correspondence the family received from Reg, and he quickly noticed his name appeared on the front of the envelope as well as in the opening salutation of the letter. The same light blue ink that Reg always used outlined his bold, business-like phrases.

Jake held the open letter and gestured toward the stairs. "Okay if I read this upstairs?" he asked, putting the letter back into its envelope.

"You sure can. I meant to show that to you yesterday, but I forgot. Sorry, Jake. Since you're familiar with the subject of the letter, I think it's important that you see what Reg has written..."

Jake took the packet up to his bedroom and eagerly got into the letter.

Dear Martin, Meg, and Jake

It's been a while since I last got to sending you a note and something happened last week that has prompted me to do so now. You will remember our old friend, Col Frank Saunders. Well, he passed away quietly in his cell on the night of Jan 10/64 after a lengthy illness battling cancer.

It seems Frank found religion in his last days. As you may also remember, he never did tell the authorities about any ill-gotten gains he might have made surrounding his involvement in the extortion business

with his partners in Veragno Italy back in 1944. Now here's the rub.

I was contacted by the Chaplin at Kingston Penitentiary right after his death; to tell me I had been named as the Executor of his Estate! It turns out, old Frank had purchased Canadian bearer bonds back then to the extent of almost $700. And with the interest of 5% accruing since then, these bonds are now worth the staggering sum of close to Two Million dollars!! Martin, the Colonel has asked that an educational scholarship trust fund be established for the existing families of the former Police Chief of Veragno, Capo Alphonzo Vitelli, along with any applicable children or grandchildren of his former partner and victim, Col James Fraser. He has further requested that the fund be named 'The Jacob England Memorial Scholarship' !

I am going to arrange for a proper ceremony to present this at the appropriate time and will advise in due course. It will no doubt be held over the March break to facilitate a trip for you, Meg, and Jake to the sunny Tuscany Region of Italy!

Ciao Folks!

Love,

Reg

Jake couldn't believe what he was reading. He ran down to see his parents watching *The Beatles* on TV, half-way through their latest hit titled 'I Want to Hold Your Hand'.

"Dad! Mom! This is amaz___." But his father sternly cut him off.

"Hey, quiet down, Jake! Your siblings have finally gone to bed and we're trying to watch something here!"

Jake started to apologize, then he realized both of his parents were only teasing him. Of course they had already read the letter from Uncle Reg and now they were chuckling. Jake then joined in, all of them laughing loudly.

The night continued in a happy vein. In fact, even the cold winds of February could not dampen the joy in the England household that night as the three of them cuddled on their old couch and continued watching television.

Author's Notes

Martin's War is my attempt to bring my father's story to people who suffer from PTSD or alcoholism. It is a novel loosely based on his time overseas during WWII, specifically the Italian Campaign. I relate some of the atrocities he experienced, and how those incidents impacted his return to a loving wife and everyday normality in his small Canadian hometown.

Man of the characters in the book are real, as are the dates and places of events, including a number of military battles depicted. I should add that the main characters, Martin England and Reg Jacobs, are respectively my father, Bombardier Leslie M Jardine and his very close friend Captain Thomas H Montgomery, Q.C., my namesake and Godfather. Both are now deceased.

For one of their actions in the novel (reference the capture of the Observation Tower near the city of San Fortunato, my father was 'Mentioned in Despatch' in the London Gazette on March 9, 1946 and Captain Montgomery was awarded the Canadian Military Cross.

One further note: Montgomery returned to his law practice in Montreal after the war and took a young law student under his wing whom he would tutor successfully through to the Canadian bar. The student would later describe some of his time with Montgomery favorably in his memoirs. This young man was Brian Mulroney, Canada's 18th Prime Minister.

Thomas Montgomery Jardine

Also, by the author
at
Rogue Phoenix Press

Iggy & Jake

It is 1969. Iggy and Jake are two rock musicians who decide to leave their mundane jobs and travel west in search of finding that elusive record label. Their journey takes them to Calgary where they plan to hook up with an old-time buddy, only to discover he has been the victim of foul play. Two jaded Calgary PD detectives utilize the talents of the streetwise musicians and they are soon involved in an international drug bust in which their lives and those of their friends are at great risk.

Ogopogo

A former GI vet from the Vietnam war, suffering from PTSD, has made his way to the peaceful Okanagan area of B.C. Here he chooses to target young Asian female victims who will serve his purpose as he assumes the persona of Ogopogo, a Canadian folk lore lake serpent who was said to inhabit Okanagan Lake.

Ignatius (Iggy) Myles and Jacob (Jake) England, two Kelowna streetwise detectives are nearing retirement, but their plans are put on hold as the killer's prey becomes personal and they are forced to pursue the monster through the mountainous wilds of British Columbia.

About the Author

Thomas Jardine is a late bloomer as crime novelists go. He is retired from the Canadian financial services industry, and a part-time musician. He lives with his wife Alexandra and Biewer Yorky Clancy in the Annapolis Valley of Nova Scotia.